Future P

A time travel comedy-dran
soundtrack. The songs ca
Collective Charm Records   or by
accessing all the usual st   platforms by
searching for *Future Proof the ..oum* by Memerine.

Future Proof, winner of the Page Turner Genre Award.

First published in the United Kingdom on 16th January 2023.

David Atkinson is an Edinburgh-based author. His previous books have been published by Joffe Books & Harper Collins and have been nominated for numerous awards.

If you want to contact him you can email direct to collectivecharmbooks@gmail.com or via his Amazon page or his Harper Collins author page.

Chapter 1
Running Rings

Like most afternoons, I'm slumped on the couch watching TV, the floor around me littered with empty crisp packets and scrunched-up Coke cans. The girl on TV is singing a track called Running Rings and I turn up the volume to try and drown out the yells and thumps on my front door. From where I'm sat I can see it vibrating in its frame.

I return my attention to the TV and notice the singer strobing in and out of focus. This might be an intended special effect or the result of me dropping the TV last week. Probably the latter.

The door frame and surrounding wood groaned, splintered, and collapsed onto the floor, along with the door itself, and in they charged. Four huge, human Rottweilers wearing identical jeans and trainers. The uniform of bailiffs. They paused wide-eyed, surveying the battleground, adrenaline pumping, ready for action.

The scene reminded me of an American cop show. However, instead of brandishing guns and pepper spray, these guys were armed with more sinister weapons; repossession paperwork, a court summons and an eviction order. They dropped the documentation onto my lap and set about ransacking my home, accompanied by the TV soundtrack. They opened drawers, pulled up carpets, and generally dismantled the place.

My appointed social worker, Sally Henderson, crept through the carnage behind them. I'm unsure who appointed her, but she said she'd been appointed, and I didn't dispute it. I watched the forty-inch TV being transported out of my flat and down the stairs. It wouldn't go very far towards repaying what I owed everyone. It wasn't worth much, to begin with. Less since I'd dropped it.

I felt curiously remote, detached, viewing everything from a distance, semi-invisible to the bailiffs, semi-invisible to the world, semi-invisible to myself. I wondered why televisions were still measured in inches. Televisions and penises seemed to be still subject to the imperial measurement scale; I couldn't think of anything else—one inch of TV screen for each year of my life.

Sally sat down on the couch, as far away from me as she could, pushing against the armrest. I should have mentioned that it was only being held in place by the fabric.

A second later, Sally disappeared. She'd plunged to the floor and landed on her ample bottom amongst the empty crisp packets and Coke cans. Her dark brown hair fell forward over her face. The situation seemed comic, but I had no urge to laugh. Extracting any humour from my predicament seemed inappropriate. Plus, laughing took effort; I lacked the energy.

Sally righted herself and perched on the edge of the now armless sofa. She is dark-haired and serious with a soft South London accent and nice teeth. She sighed and began to speak.

'Sam, I'm sorry it's eventually come to this, but I can't help you if you won't help yourself.'
I'd become used to her tone of voice, pitched somewhere between nursery and year one level with a

healthy dose of exasperation. However, her heart must have been in the right place for her to be spending time with the utterly useless like me.

I nodded, which seemed to encourage her to continue. 'You've got twenty-four hours to get out of here; the landlord's been more than reasonable, Sam; he's not had a rent payment from you in six months.'

I nodded again. It felt like the right thing to do as I couldn't disagree with a word she'd said.

She stared at a piece of paper for a moment, then looked up and made eye contact with me, 'If you remember, I got you to provide a sample of your DNA a week or so back?'

I had wondered about that, but other more critical issues had been at the forefront of my mind: eviction letters and a perpetually empty fridge.

'Well,' she continued, 'based on the DNA test results, I have managed to secure a care-assisted place for you in a residential facility. There are some conditions.'

There are always conditions. With everything in life, I'd discovered. I couldn't say I'd miss the little flat. I'd been here just over a year, lured to Birmingham with the promise of a call-centre job that lasted less than three months.

Sally elaborated. 'It's a mental-health unit. Technically you don't meet the criteria because you are more than capable of looking after yourself if you want to, but it seems your DNA sample means you are a perfect fit for a study they are conducting. You'll get to stay there only if you agree to participate in the project. It's scheduled to last for six to eight weeks, and during that time, they'll try to improve your self-esteem and overall mental health. The unit, called Perry Flowers, is in the north of the city. It might be just what you need.'

I wondered why a mental health unit would be named after something that sounded more like a florist; perhaps that *was* the reason, to make it sound less like its actual purpose and to make you think it smelled nice. Maybe it did.

I think that had been the longest I'd heard my social worker speak in the two months I'd known her. I nodded. I didn't have much to say about anything anymore. Had I given up? Maybe. I remained self-aware enough to know I'd been on a slippery slope for some time but discovered I lacked the motivation to do much about it. I'd accepted my situation—a consequence of making bad decisions.

The weird thing I'd found is that one wrong decision tended to lead me to the next one. I liken it to an addicted gambler who thinks the next big bet will pay off and return them to parity. It never does, of course, and another lousy decision inevitably leads to a similar outcome.

Perhaps I'd become addicted to bad decisions. It would explain a lot. I considered trying to explain this to Sally but decided it would take too much effort.

I watched as she assessed the increasingly stark room. 'Where will you sit?'

I didn't know, the floor maybe.

The bulky men removed the bed. It had been part of the furniture when I'd moved in. They were zealous these bailiffs, devoted to their craft. I'm not so sure the landlord would agree.

Sally watched as they squeezed the bed through the broken door frame, plaster dislodged and drizzled to the floor. We both stared at the little powdery waterfall until it ceased. 'Where will you sleep?' she asked as the bed disappeared down the stairs.

I had no idea. Sitting alone in my flat for the last few days, dreading this moment, had rendered me temporarily mute. I hadn't had anyone to speak to except Monty, my life-sized, fluffy Shetland Pony replica. He didn't answer back, his best feature.

They took him next. His glassy-eyed stare regarded me accusingly as they manoeuvred him through the broken doorway. I'd won him at a works raffle during my first week at the call centre. My supervisor Katy wanted him for her two young kids, but I'd taken him home. I'd never won anything else in my entire life.

We'd enjoyed some interesting conversations over the preceding months, usually after I'd had a few beers. Monty wasn't much of a drinker. A good listener, though, non-judgemental and patient.

I considered asking Sally if she wanted him but decided that trying to wrestle him back from the burly bailiff would end up in physical pain, so I didn't bother.

My social worker made a note and announced, 'This place is no longer secure; burglars could waltz straight in.'

I sighed, thinking they'd probably waltz straight back out again seconds later.

'Get your things together, Sam. We need to find somewhere for you to sleep until tomorrow.'

I duly obeyed, which took all of five seconds. I had a rucksack ready to go. My life in a twenty by fourteen-inch bag. Half the width of the TV.

Sally walked with me downstairs and plinked her car key. The boot to her old Mazda 3 flipped open. She regarded me momentarily, then said, 'OK, put your stuff in the boot and get in, but no funny business.'

I nodded, not a hundred per cent sure what she meant by *funny business*. I assumed she didn't expect me to make jokes. I'd long ago lost my jolly disposition. I dumped the rucksack that represented the remains of my life in the boot and sat in the passenger seat. I noted the empty crisp packets and Coke cans on the floor, a half-eaten doughnut, and the coffee mug with lipstick around the rim. We had something in common, after all. I felt quite at home as my trainers shuffled amongst the detritus.

Outside, Sally talked on her phone to someone, perhaps telling them she'd be taking me in her car in case I decided to try my best Peter Kay Car-Share impersonation whilst she drove.

She terminated the call, clambered in, started the engine, and pulled away from the kerb. I glanced back at the entrance to my building and noted the Rottweilers coming out of the door with rolled-up carpets over their shoulders. They were there when I moved in too. Zealous.

Chapter 2
November Rain

We drove across Britain's second city. Much of it remained a mystery to me. A year doesn't allow you to know a place, especially when you've spent most of it hiding from creditors in a small flat. I guess I could've taken a trip on one of the tour buses that introduced you to the landmarks and history, but I hadn't.

Sally informed me that she'd persuaded Perry Flowers Mental Health Unit to take me a day early. That explained the phone call.

Eventually, we turned off the main road into a small car park. The unit consisted of low-rise buildings arranged in a series of rectangular blocks. Small flower beds were placed underneath every second window. It being November, only the memory of summer remained as brown stalks and dead leaves rustled and shivered in the cold breeze.

Sally selected a parking space near the entrance and turned off the engine. She lifted a large leather bag onto her lap. I noticed a dark oily stain on the bottom right-hand corner. Something was leaking. She extracted a fistful of paperwork and handed me the top sheet to read. 'This is a summary of the placement. Much of the detail is unimportant, you need to participate fully, or they will find someone else.'

I scanned the page, which consisted of a list of provisions and rules. I would be provided with a single room and three meals a day. I had to keep the room tidy, and whilst there were no specified restrictions on my freedom, in terms of where I could go, I would be required to sign in and out and overnight absences needed to be sanctioned beforehand by the project leader. It felt a little oppressive, but I guess I'd run out of alternatives.

We exited the car and pushed our way through the heavy glass doors. Inside, seemed light and pleasant. My view of such establishments had been formed from movies like *One Flew Over the Cuckoo's Nest* and *Terminator 2*. I wondered why the project was interested in me. I wasn't an unusual case, I didn't think, plus I doubted that a few weeks of therapy would undo what a lifetime of poor decisions and recklessness had accumulated. Still, I'd run out of options—my next stop after this would be homelessness or death. The former scared me more than the latter.

There had been moments in the last few years when I'd have welcomed oblivion. I had contemplated ending it all on several occasions. One cold, wet evening last March, I'd sat on the precipice of a railway bridge, legs dangling in thin air, waiting for an express train to come along. Of course, it turned out to be the evening that all train services had been cancelled due to industrial action. You couldn't depend on anything anymore.

Looking back, it wouldn't have been fair on the poor driver, but I hadn't been thinking too clearly at the time. I realised that contemplating suicide might be considered a valid reason for seeking mental health assistance. Even more so than talking to a stuffed pony, perhaps.

After Sally had completed the paperwork for me, she said, 'I'll stop by every so often to see how things are going.' She picked up her bag, walked a few feet, then stopped and turned, 'Sam, this is probably your last chance. I think you realise that, but just in case, please don't blow it.'

She stared at me for a moment, like she was about to say something else, but then decided against it and left.

The pretty girl behind the reception desk led me to a small room reminiscent of a budget hotel. TV on the wall, a small shower room, and a bedside table with a drawer. I opened it, but no Bible. Fine by me. I wasn't seeking divine intervention.

The unit certainly didn't have the feel of the Jack Nicholson film. Nor, did it appear that I would be tied to a bed like Linda Hamilton, waiting for an orderly to lick her face, but I remained wary. The door had no lock that I could see, and the other people wandering around seemed relatively lucid and normal.

I showered, shaved, and generally tried to make myself presentable. The problem with being presentable is that it reminded me of a life where I once functioned normally, holding down a job, socialising and even being married. Being stinky and dirty presented a barrier to the world, a barrier against conversation and expectation.

When you're scruffy and unwashed, people don't ask you to do anything. Being scrubbed up might mean whoever's dealing with me may have high ideals of what I might achieve. They'd almost certainly end up disappointed.

The unit, or perhaps clinic was a better description, had been arranged as a series of interconnected low-rise buildings with corridors between them. Most were single storey, but the furthest away two blocks had a lower level. The single-glazed glass in the corridor windows failed to insulate the space properly, and I noticed a distinct chill when crossing from reception to the accommodation block. The buildings were set out in a large rectangle, which, in theory, should have made it difficult to lose your bearings, as you'd keep walking and eventually end up back where you started, but knowing me, I'd get lost.

As instructed, I returned to the reception after half an hour to find Nurse Paton (name badge) waiting for me. She sat me in a chair and took some vials of blood, which I assumed was a backup to the DNA samples already provided, but she might be testing for rabies, Covid, Green Monkey Disease or Ebola, for all I knew.

Later that evening, Dr Lynda Jaeger, the chief psychiatrist in charge of the 'project' as she called it, joined us all for dinner. She nibbled on a salad, no doubt making mental notes about our behaviour and social interactions. There were eight women and four men, including me, the full extent of the Perry Flowers' patients. I seemed to have been the last one to arrive.

We'd all been given name badges, first names only, with instructions that they had to be *worn at all times*. Molly was sitting opposite me. She had dirty blonde hair, green eyes, and a welcoming smile. When she smiled, she kept her head lowered most of the time, picked at her nails and avoided eye contact. Apart from her tendency to drift, she seemed perfectly normal. Unlike poor Ted, who sat two chairs down from me. He shook his head constantly and muttered, 'Charles Darwin.' Occasionally he'd get annoyed with himself about something and slap the side of his head with the palm of his hand. As he shook or smacked his head, a cloud of dandruff blizzarded down, coating his tomato soup in crispy flakes. His scalp storm contaminated a fellow patient, Amanda's soup too.

She pushed it away and berated Ted. Ted paid her no heed, so she turned to Dr Jaeger. 'Why is it my turn to sit beside Flaky Head again? I sat here yesterday; it's disgusting.'

Amanda, I estimated to be in her early forties with dark hair, grey roots, and sad eyes. Her life hadn't gone to plan either. Glancing around the table, that might apply to all of us; otherwise, why would we be here?

Angus, the youngest, late teens, maybe early twenties, had his eye on Molly and stared at her constantly. Molly didn't seem to notice, or perhaps pretty women, over time, just became immune to being stared at.

Despite being the last to arrive, I couldn't see that any meaningful friendships had developed aside from Angus's obvious crush on Molly. However, with the Doc (as I'd decided to call her) watching, maybe they were nervous.

It had been a long time since I'd shared a dinner table with anyone: let alone twelve strangers. I felt self-conscious eating soup, being careful not to slurp or drip. Of course, I failed miserably at both and managed to drip tomato soup all over the crotch area of my clean joggers. Later, I added some gravy to the mess, from the main course of roast beef, potatoes and veg.

After dinner, everyone dispersed either to their rooms or the recreation area. This consisted of a large room at the back. It housed a full-size snooker table, two table tennis tables, a pool table, pinball machines and a massive HD TV. A door opened onto the gardens, but no one would venture out there tonight, it being dark, cold and raining.

I'd decided to retire early to my room, partly due to not being comfortable with people and partly down to the red/brown mess all over my joggers. Dr Jaeger, however, had other ideas and intercepted me at reception. She invited me into her office for a chat. Not something you turned down, I assumed, regardless of the mess of one's trousers.

She sat on a chair at the side of her desk, a ploy, I imagined, to prevent the desk from becoming a barrier between us. She flipped through a thick folder, which probably contained details about me and my history. The Doc was attractive; she reminded me of Suzanna Reid from *Good Morning Britain*—a more serious version.

I placed my hands on my lap to try and conceal the mess.

After a moment or two of reading, she looked up and smiled, 'You never said a word during dinner.'

I pondered her statement momentarily before answering, 'I'm not a great conversationalist.'

She smiled again, 'You can speak then? That's a relief; I had begun to suspect you might be mute.'

Her idea of a joke. I smiled as I suspected that was what she wanted me to do. 'I don't have much to say for myself these days.'

'But, once upon a time, you did?'

I shrugged.

She put my file down on her desk. 'We'll start properly tomorrow, but I just wanted to check you're

OK. It must feel strange coming here, not something you thought would ever happen to you.'

'Thanks.'

She regarded me, trying to suss me out, I assumed. I noticed her wedding ring. I wondered what it must be like being married to a psychiatrist. Did she constantly analyse her husband's behaviour? Hoping to spot the tell-tale signs in case he went psycho on her or had been unfaithful. Of course, I'd made assumptions here. She might be married to another woman for all I knew.

Dismissed, I retired to my room and flipped on the TV. I channel-surfed for a while and settled on an episode of *Friends* until I felt my eyes closing. I cleaned my teeth, clambered into bed, and slipped away.

Early the following morning, a blaring alarm woke me, the rest of the residents and probably any dead people in graves within a two-mile radius. I had been warned about it, but the loud shrillness seemed unnecessary. I checked my watch, 7.15 am. Early, but not stupidly early.

I showered, dressed and joined my colleagues for breakfast. Would *colleagues* be an appropriate term? Prisoners seemed severe, patients too clinical, and victims a little dramatic. Colleagues would do.

Breakfast consisted of a buffet of cereals and either toast or croissants. I skipped the healthy options, spread a croissant with butter and jam, and washed it down with coffee. Nurse Paton appeared and instructed everyone to check the roster at reception. I'd been sitting beside Angus. It had been the only chair left. He didn't seem very talkative, which suited me.

I finished my breakfast and pottered through to reception, where a large whiteboard had been placed in front of the reception desk. I found my name second from the top—Sam Harris, Room 12, 8.30 am, Dr Janice Ramos.

The clock on the reception wall stated 8.25 am. I searched for room 12, deciding I shouldn't be late on my first morning. I found it tucked away at the end of a corridor. I knocked quietly, and a warm female voice said, 'Come in.'

I pushed open the door and discovered a vision in a white coat.

Chapter 3
Another Brick in the Wall

Even in my current reduced state. I could tell she was exceptional. She flashed me a smile, probably trying to put me at ease, but it had the opposite effect. I perched on the only other chair in the room, positioned on the opposite side of the small table that separated us and fidgeted nervously. Dark hair, caramel skin and impossibly exotic, she must be used to having this effect on men and some women, I imagined. She went about her business as if my nervous reaction to her hadn't occurred.

'Sam, as you will have gathered from the noticeboard, I'm Dr Ramos, but for our session today, I'd prefer if you would just call me Janice. Can you manage that?'

I nodded.

'Good.' Another smile. 'I also need you to relax. Will you be able to do that?'

I smiled and shook my head. 'Probably not.'

She nodded and said, 'I can understand why you're nervous; this is your first time receiving any kind of therapy, isn't it?'

'Yes.'

'Today, we'll not be doing anything taxing. I just need to ask you questions. All I ask is that you answer them as honestly as you can. OK?'

I nodded.

'Right, let's get started.' She flipped open a folder with many printed pages and, from what I could read upside down, a list of questions. 'We'll stop frequently for breaks, don't worry. I'll start with some general questions. What do you understand by the term mental health?'

This would be a long morning. 'I don't know, really,' I muttered, examining my fingernails. 'I suppose for me, it's about being happy. I've never really been happy.'

She made a note, 'When was the last time you felt content?'

Good question. 'Maybe as a kid, I'm not sure.'

She nodded and chewed on the end of her pen for a moment before saying, 'There are many incidents in life that can affect our mental development: childhood trauma, bereavement, redundancy, relationship breakdowns. Nearly everyone will experience at least some of these in their lives. Many develop coping mechanisms and muddle through, some of us don't, and this is partly what gives rise to anxiety and stress, not the situations we find ourselves in, but our inability to cope with them. Does this sound like you?'

'I guess I also make bad decisions.'

'Why?'

'I wish I knew.'

She paused, made a few notes, and then asked, 'How would you describe your relationship with your parents?'

'OK.'

'Was there much conflict?'

'No more than any other kid, I suppose. My dad worked away a lot on the oil rigs. My mum kept me around for company.'

'When do you first remember being unhappy?'

I sighed, would dragging up old memories do me any good? I supposed, given my predicament, it couldn't make things any worse. 'I got bullied.'

'When?'

'Constantly, well, that's how it feels.' Suddenly conscious that I'd used present tense, I checked if Little Miss Gorgeous had observed the change.

'Tell me about it.'

I groaned. 'Before I went to school, I didn't have much contact with other kids. I didn't go to nursery or playgroups or anything. I don't remember that, but my mum told me. As I said, she liked having me around. When I started school, I didn't know what kids were like; I felt I was playing catch up. Everyone else had learned to play, stick up for themselves, react or whatever. I stuck out, awkward, uncomfortable, different.'

Janice made notes, and I talked—more than I'd talked for years.

'I suppose that made me a target, one kid; Joseph Kennedy picked on me.' I stopped; I felt a stab of pain, a physical ache inside at remembering the little shit, what I wouldn't give to go back and clout the little bugger a few times. I felt angry now, angry at myself for being weak, mad at my mum for making me stand out and angry with the school for not intervening.

Janice sensed my reticence. 'Please continue, Sam, I can see this is painful, but ultimately this will help us to help you.'

What did I have to lose? 'Every morning at break time and occasionally at lunchtime, he came looking for me. I'd been in year one, and he was in year two. I know that doesn't sound much of a difference, but it is when you're that young. Plus, I'd been small for my age, and he'd been huge, or at least he felt huge to me. He used to kick me, mainly on the shins. Occasionally, he'd slap me, but nobody ever intervened. His focus was this dark-haired girl in my class, Luci Lawrence, whose mum had become friendly with my mum at the school gates. Luci's mum was Spanish and had been abandoned by her husband when Luci was small. She didn't know many people, and my mum took her under her wing for a while. In any event, we used to be around each other's houses playing. I'm not sure Joseph had, at that age, any idea about girls and boys and stuff. He just needed an excuse to hit me, but it felt like being punished for something my mum had done. It just wasn't fair. I couldn't have avoided Luci even if I'd wanted to.'

I paused and gathered my thoughts. 'He probably knew that. It gave him the excuse he needed if he needed one. He'd approach me and say, "You've been playing with Luci again. I've told you about that." Then I'd get kicked, punched, or pushed to the ground. Other kids just stood and watched. I was their entertainment. They'd stop what they were doing, football, running or whatever, and they'd all gather around for *bash Sam time.*'

Janice looked up from her papers, 'Is that what they called it?'

I nodded. 'The physical thing hurt, but the mental torture if anything, felt worse. He turned people against me. I'm not sure how he did it, manipulative little sod, but I never got picked by the other kids to play football or any of the other stuff, which is so important at that age. It always felt like being on the outside looking in. Maybe he threatened them; I don't know.'

'You felt excluded?' Janice clarified.

'I was excluded,' I replied.

'How long did it continue?'

I tried to remember. 'Six months or maybe a little more. I used to come home and tell my pet dog, Benji, all about it; he'd sit on my bed and listen to me as the tears streamed down my face. I loved that dog.'

'What about your parents? Did you tell them?'

I shook my head. 'They found out eventually. Luci told her mum, who told my mum, who told my dad. He just said, "Toughen up you stupid sod." It was like a personal insult to him that his son had become a victim. You need to remember my dad was a tough-skinned oil rigger, a man's man. I'd never had that kind of protective shell.'

'What about your mum?'

'She went along with my dad and encouraged me to come home at lunchtime, but it didn't help. It stopped eventually, but not for months.'

'How did it end?'

I winced, but no point in stopping now. 'After lunch one day, Joseph and two of his sidekicks, Derek and Freddie, cornered me in the boys' toilets. Occasionally, Joseph drafted them in to help pummel me or hold me while he did it. Anyway, this one afternoon, they all thought it would be hilarious to pull out their cocks and piss all over me.'

I could feel the tears pricking at the corner of my eyes as I told my story, the first time I'd even thought about it in any detail for, what must be, thirty-five years.

Janice stopped scribbling and peered at me. Pity in her eyes. A look I'd seen directed towards me a lot over the years. 'How old were these children again?'

I sighed, 'Six, maybe seven.'

'At that age, it's unlikely they'd developed sociopathic tendencies; perhaps they were acting out what they saw at home.'

I snorted. 'You really think Joseph Kennedy went home and watched his parents pee on each other?'

She smiled. 'I'd hope not, but I'm assuming his home life must have been far from nurturing. To exhibit that kind of behaviour at such an early age, is unusual.'

I tried to process that. I remembered returning to class, soaked in, and stinking of, urine and bawling my eyes out. The school had to take some action, and the ineffectual headmistress, Arlene Broch, invited all the parents involved in the 'incident', as she labelled it, to a meeting after school. Only my mum attended, as my dad was offshore. He always seemed to be offshore when something important happened.

Kennedy and his cohorts were forced to apologise, but they didn't mean it or care, I remember thinking, as they shuffled their feet and kept their eyes on the floor. Kennedy's dad tried to play the whole thing down, claiming his son and the others had been trying to see who could pee up the wall the highest, and I'd just got in the way.

Arlene Broch grabbed onto this explanation and held on for dear life, as any other option would have meant she'd have had to take some action.

Schools today are more switched on, but I'm sure there are still plenty of evil little ghouls inflicting misery and pain on other kids. I imagined much of it had moved online now, hidden, insidious.

Deprived of his immediate object of gratifying abuse, Kennedy redirected his attention elsewhere.

'Did the bullying stop after that horrible incident?' Janice asked, pulling me from my dark thoughts.

I nodded. 'Kind of, I still felt excluded from things by his manipulation, but I learned to live with that. In terms of direct bullying, he just moved onto someone else.'

Janice closed her folder. 'I think that's enough for this morning, Sam. Thank you.' She smiled again, another pity smile. What else should I expect? I stood and left, returned to my room, made coffee, and cried a little. I hadn't fully realised how much Kennedy had hurt me all those years ago. I hated myself, a fat, blubbering coward whose life had spiralled downwards in an unending whirlpool of excrement.

Chapter 4
Bad Medicine

After lunch, the whiteboard had been updated and I'd been scheduled for a session with the project leader, Dr Jaeger herself, in Cholis Lab 4. I had no idea what that meant, but Molly told me to go through the games room, as she called it, along the corridor, down a flight of stairs and the Cholis labs were at the bottom, in the lower level. I didn't know what Cholis meant but no doubt I'd find out at some point.

I found Dr Jaeger waiting for me when I arrived and took in the surroundings. Cholis Lab 4 didn't resemble any lab I'd been in at school or any that I'd seen on TV. There were no test tubes brewing mysterious green concoctions. No huge banks of fridges to keep cool whatever labs needed to keep cool and no huge, coiled springs connected to cables waiting for a lightning strike. (I'd probably watched too many old horror films for my own good.)

The only difference I could see from the room in which I'd met with Janice was that this one contained a hospital bed with white sheets, two pillows and an extra staff member.

The Doc said, 'Relax, Sam, there's nothing to fear. Before we start, can you step on the scales for me, as we need to make a few calculations.'

I cringed; I hated weighing myself. I'd piled on so much fat over the years that I never bothered any more. What's the point if you had no intention of doing anything about it?

I stepped on the scales. The digital readout said 118.7 kilos. Kilos were fine, I had no idea what that translated to in stones and pounds. The Doc made some notes but remained quiet. No fat shaming here. 'Can you lie on the bed for me now,' she asked. I complied and watched as she scanned her notes. From my higher vantage point, I could see the notes were Janice's from the morning session. She hadn't mentioned that they'd be shared, but I suppose I should have known that would happen.

'Did you attend university, Sam?'

'No, my mum died just after I'd turned eighteen, and I, well, I just didn't.'

Dr Jaeger considered my statement. 'We'll probably spot that later.'

'Spot what later?'

'Good question.' Dr Jaeger closed the folder and asked, 'Have you ever heard of Epigenetic Regression?'

I searched my memory. 'Nope, sounds like something they might try to do on *Star Trek*.'

The Doc laughed, a raucous deep laugh, not what I'd expected.

She nodded. 'You're not far off the mark there, Sam. It's certainly experimental. Let me explain as best I can. If I drift into jargon or lose you, please stop me.'

She shuffled her chair closer to the bed and began. 'Epigenetics are first mentioned scientifically in the 1940s, but it's only been since the millennium with technological advances that any serious progress has been made. The basic idea of epigenetics is that an environmental factor such as smoking, diet or trauma can fundamentally alter how your genes express themselves in your daily life.'

'Express themselves?' I asked

'Sorry, yes, well, gene expression is the process by which the instructions contained within our DNA are converted into a functional product such as a protein. For example, a poor diet can result in epigenetic ageing, meaning your genome doesn't perform as well as it should. This can lead to ill health and an earlier-than-expected death. It's like a switch, for lack of a better description, which gets blown by the trauma, in this case, lots of fast food. This stops a particular protein from being released which, in turn, affects the overall health of the individual.

'During an epigenetic episode, the body reads the DNA instructions differently than if it had not happened. Unlike genetic changes, epigenetic changes, we think, are reversible.'

'This is all very fascinating, Dr Jaeger, I'm well aware that I'm overweight and intelligent enough to realise eating badly is a personal choice. I'm fat because I eat too much junk food. Is that why I'm here, due to my weight?' I'd realised already that none of the other patients/colleagues were overweight.

She shook her head. 'No, your weight gain, I suspect in your case, is due to other traumatic aspects of your life. I'm assuming you weren't always obese?'

'No, I piled weight on after my divorce.'

'I thought there'd be a trigger. Another branch of epigenetics is the supposition that any traumatic event a person suffers throughout their lives lays down a biological marker on their genome that affects how the genes express themselves. We are particularly interested in how these markers, or switches if you prefer, can be applied to modern psychiatry. We now suspect that many modern and historical mental illnesses can be traced to certain crucial markers on a person's genome. Switches that were blown by a traumatic event.

'This is a huge over-simplification, but I'll use plain language to allow you to stay with me. For example, a person suffering from bipolar disorder or other cognitive issues or even having the propensity to become addicted to drugs or fast food will have a trigger. This trigger can often be traced back to one or a series of emotional trauma suffered at an early age and/or throughout life. Each of those emotional markers will have left a trace on the genome. Now, there's nothing new in the supposition that a person's life can be adversely affected by trauma. You only need to look at the survivors of atrocities like 9/11 or the Manchester bombing or soldiers returning from war zones to see that. However, the treatment has always been by traditional therapy, which is time-consuming and often ineffective, or by administering drugs that, long term, are even less effective.

'This method, we think, can give almost instant results. If we can target the broken switches on a person's genetic record and switch them back on, for want of a better analogy, it will free up gene expression and thus heal the patient.

'We focus on the earliest markers first, as the earlier the trauma, the greater effect on a person's personal development. As we get older, we tend to be able to cope with trauma better, due to experience and perspective. It's not always the case and obviously depends on the scale of the trauma and the resilience of the individual.'

'Doctor… Janice said something about that this morning.'

'Good, I expect you've had problems coping with what life has thrown at you.'

An understatement if ever there were one. I tried to understand all of what I'd just been told. I'm not a stupid man, but some of it sounded like science fiction mumbo jumbo, but mentioning that to the Doc probably wasn't a good idea if I wanted to stay on the programme. I'd had more lucid conversations with Monty.

'So, how does this apply to me?'

The Doc smiled. 'Ah, that's the big question, isn't it.'

Chapter 5
What I go to School For

The Doc and Nurse Paton faffed about in the corner, preparing two syringes. Faff, being a well-known medical term. The Doc eventually approached me with one of the syringes filled with amber fluid.

'What's this?' I asked the Doc.

She swabbed my arm. 'This is our special Genomic Plasma Compound, GPC for short, which will tag and mark the epigenetic episodes that have affected your genome, your gene expression, and, possibly, your psychological development. It also contains a mild sedative, which will help you drift off; we need you unconscious to measure the results.'

'What happens then?'

'We will target the earliest epigenetic episodes with our special protein compound and see if we can switch any of them back on and measure its effect on your mental well-being.'

'Two injections then?'

The Doc smiled. 'Yep.'

'And you're going to do this for all my blown switches?'

'If we can, yes.'

'How many blown switches do I have?'

The Doc paused before answering. 'Your DNA sample shows somewhere in the region of thirty-two.'

'Thirty-two times two, so, potentially sixty-four injections?'

The Doc nodded.

I pushed my head back into the pillow. 'So, you're saying I'll leave here with more holes in me than a forty-year-old dartboard.'

Nurse Paton eased the amber liquid into my vein, and I slipped into warm darkness with the sound of the Doc's laugh echoing in my ears.

From the fogginess surrounding my brain, I heard my name being called. I opened my eyes and looked up. 'Sam Harris. I can see you're here. Were you sleeping?'

I blinked a few times and shook my head, trying to clear my thoughts.

'Oh, so you weren't sleeping.'

Kids' laughter rang in my ears. What happened to the Doc? Where the hell was I? A stupid question, it being obvious as I looked around, my primary one class with Miss McFarlane staring at me.

'How did I get here?' I asked, bewildered.

'I assume you walked, Sam, like you do every day.'

Gales of laughter from my classmates.

'This isn't right,' I told Miss McFarlane, who looked twenty-four years old. She should be retiring soon, not standing there looking pretty. I'd forgotten how beautiful she'd been, or perhaps my five-year-old brain hadn't appreciated it back then.

'What's not, right?' Miss McFarlane asked. The smile had left her face, replaced with concern. She walked over to my desk. I looked down and realised how tiny my hands were. My body, too, I'd shrunk. I looked up into Miss McFarlane's soft brown eyes.

'I'm tiny,' I mewled.

She smiled at me. I remember her being a kind teacher. 'Of course, you're tiny. You're five.'

'I'm not; I'm forty, nearly forty-one.'

Everybody roared with laughter again; even the teacher giggled. 'Can I just say, Sam, I hope that when I'm forty, I have skin as smooth as yours.'

Then I realised with a jolt that I must be dreaming. It came as a complete relief, and whilst everything felt so real and solid, I postulated that it might be down to the amber junk that had been pumped into me. It must have some hallucinogenic properties; the Doc never mentioned that, but maybe she'd thought it would put me off.

I smiled up at Miss McFarlane. This might be fun, a five-year-old kid with a forty-year-old brain.

A bemused expression drifted across the teacher's face. She reached down and put her hand on my forehead. 'You don't feel hot, Sam. Maybe you should go along to the school nurse, just in case.'

I shook my head. 'No, I'm fine, honestly. I'm probably just tired. A coffee might perk me up.'

My teacher scoffed. 'I'm sure it would, Sam, but all you'll be getting in here is your milk at eleven. If you don't need to go to the nurse then, if you don't mind, I'll get back to teaching the class.'

'Be my guest.' I smiled.

She shook her head at me and walked back to the front of the classroom, glancing back at me a few times. Whilst she finished reading through the register, I took some time to check out the rest of the classroom. It certainly felt very authentic. My subconscious mind had reconstructed the room in an incredible amount of detail. The blue dragon mural on the wall near the door to the corridor, every kid in the class had contributed a little bit to it; my effort near the rear consisted of some blue scales with the names of my family on them.

On the back wall were some poorly drawn pictures of houses, except the one by Beth Graham, her cosy cottage collage seemed extraordinarily good for a five-year-old. I remembered Beth now, with brown hair and mousy features but brilliant at drawing. She moved away to London at the end of primary three. I wonder what happened to her.

Just to the left of me sat Danny McAdam, who habitually peed himself in class. I wondered if he'd do it today. I looked under his desk; no tell-tale puddles yet.

Then I spotted her, Luci Lawrence. She sat two rows in front, her back to me, but I'd know that dark mane of hair cascading over her shoulders anywhere. I remembered her face so well, too, with a little button nose and lovely red lips that always appeared as if they'd been enhanced with lipstick. But her eyes were her most memorable feature. Eyes of amber, glowing like some other-worldly ethereal creature, not of this earth. I'd never seen eyes that colour before and never would again. I suppose she'd been my first crush, but I wouldn't have known what those feelings were back then, but strangely, I could feel it now, a vague longing within my tiny immature body. I wondered when she and I last had a playdate.

Miss McFarlane finished her registration and handed out photocopied pages from a book called *Ben the Badger*. I don't remember things being so bad that we didn't get real books back then, but I needed to remember this was a dream, and my subconscious wouldn't get everything right.

'Now, class,' Miss McFarlane announced, 'I'm going to read the first few pages; try and keep up if you can, then I'll work with you on the tricky words.'

This seemed a bit much for a primary one class to cope with; I wondered about the date. I put my hand in my pocket to pull out my mobile, but of course, these were different times before mobiles took over the world. Anyone who owned a mobile phone would be pulling it about on a trolley.

No watch on my wrist either. Thankfully, the teacher had written the date on Tuesday, 17th of March, on the whiteboard.

That meant I'd been in school for nearly six months.

I smiled as the usual suspects raised their arms; Beth, of course, and another girl from the posh estate whose name escaped me. I never understood why her parents didn't send her to private school; they were loaded, and of course, Susan, with the un-ironed uniform way too small for her. Always untidy, dirty-looking and a little smelly. Her mum had mental health issues, not that I knew that then but with my forty-year-old brain engaged, I could see the reality now. Poor lamb, the stick she got from the other kids, me included, I remembered with shame. Given the treatment I'd been subjected to, you'd have thought I'd have known better, but I didn't; kids didn't/don't realise.

Miss McFarlane ignored the raised hands and said, 'Sam, how about you?'

I glanced up from my musings. 'About me what?'

Laughter from the kids and a smile from the teacher. At least I was amusing everyone today.

'How about you read page three to everyone.'

I shrugged. 'Yeah, OK.'

Miss McFarlane cocked her head to the left, puzzled. Benji, my dog, used to do that.

I hated reading aloud to the class back in the day, as I wasn't a very good reader, which is why I used to get picked, of course. I shouldn't have any problems today.

I pulled the photocopied sheets of grainy paper towards me, selected page three and began to read.

Ben likes his bed. His bed is soft, like him. Ben likes his bed.

Miss McFarlane stared at me with her eyebrows raised. 'Well done, Sam, you made that sound easy.'

It had been easy for a forty-year-old who'd been reading for a long time. I didn't say that, though, as that would spoil the rest of the dream.

'Now, can anyone tell me any interesting facts about badgers?' the teacher asked. The usual hands shot up. 'Beth,' Miss McFarlane said.

Beth beamed. 'Badgers only come out at night.'

'That's right,' said the teacher. 'Badgers are nocturnal.'

Miss McFarlane gazed around the classroom. 'Who else can tell me something interesting about badgers? Sam,' she said, fixing her eyes on me. 'What do you know about badgers?'

I paused for a moment, but in the end, I couldn't resist. 'They've got very smelly arses, miss.'

Chapter 6
Shock to the System

I spent the rest of the morning waiting outside the head teacher's office. Arlene Broch must either have been, very busy, or hoping to contact my parents before speaking to me. My dad would have been somewhere off the coast of Norway, in a force ten gale, trying to extract black gold from the seabed, and my mum would be shopping, shopping being her specialist subject.

Eventually, the door opened. Mrs Broch ushered me in and closed it behind her. She pointed to a chair in front of her desk, and I sat in it. My feet dangled in mid-air. I still hadn't gotten used to how small I was, plus how light I felt. Fantastic stuff, that amber concoction.

Miss Broch read from a file on her desk blotter, my file, I assumed. It's amazing all these files that people have on you. Health files, school files, work files, tax files, and so on. Most of the time, you never see what's written about you or how accurate it is. Most files would be digitised by my fortieth year, but a file's a file.

'Sam Harris. Miss McFarlane has reported you for using offensive and abusive language.'

How was a five-year-old supposed to understand that I had no idea? Maybe that was the point.

I looked up and replied, 'I said arse, it's hardly the crime of the century. I bet you swear more than that in your staff meetings every Friday.'

Mrs Broch stared at me open-mouthed. She flustered and blustered and eventually said, 'I'm surprised at you, Sam. What's got into you today?'

A forty-year-old brain, I wanted to say, but I just shrugged.

'It's not like you.'

How she knew that, I don't know; she'd barely said two words to me in the six months I'd been there. I knew that much.

She continued. 'Miss McFarlane said you were perhaps a little unwell earlier and wanted coffee. Not the sort of thing five-year-old boys normally say.'

Fair point.

She sighed, staring at the file on her desk, looking for answers she wouldn't find. 'Right, well, I'll type a letter for you to take home to your mother, seeing as I've been unable to contact her by telephone.'

She *had* gone shopping, another benefit of not having a mobile, when you were out, you were out.

'Now, before I let you go back to your class, Sam, have you anything else you'd like to say?'

I smiled; what the hell? 'Yeah, don't let Mrs Carter collect the year five London trip funds, as she'll spend it all on gin, and the trip will be cancelled.'

Mrs Broch stared at me open-mouthed. 'What?' I said, 'You know she's got a drink problem.'

The headteacher stared at me for ages before shaking her head and asking, 'How do you know all this?'

I shrugged, 'The older kids talk about it.' I lied.

The bell rang, signifying lunch. Mrs Broch dismissed me, gladly I reckoned, and I headed for the dinner hall.

School dinners were as dismal as I remembered, or rather my dream remembered.

Incredibly vivid, that's for sure, as I chewed on rubbery carrots and overcooked ham. I sat beside one of the cool kids, the only seat left; he ignored me. I drank the rancid diluted juice we were doled out. No chocolate milk or fizzy drinks back then.

After lunch, I headed to the boys' toilets, probably the disgusting orange juice going straight through me. I finished peeing into the trough that passed for urinals in the stinking block that we called *the bogs*. I fastened up my fly and turned to be faced by Joseph Kennedy, flanked by Derek Wilson and Freddie Charles. All three had their cocks out and immediately started spraying me with urine.

So, this was the day the amber liquid decided I should re-live in my dream. Fair enough. As the first drops of stinking pee landed on my clothes, I stared at them. Kennedy had positioned himself in the middle, aiming at my face, the other two directing their streams towards my clothes on either side. This time I wasn't a five-year-old kid with no life experience or defence mechanism; well, I was, but at the same time, I wasn't. I looked down at my feet as some pee sloshed into my hair.

I noted I had on my black leather school shoes, solid and reassuring. Perfect for kicking footballs about the playground and climbing trees if the occasion demanded. Also, useful for something else, perhaps.

I decided to test out my theory. Based on previous experience, Kennedy expected me to wilt and start bawling. Why wouldn't he? That's what always happened. Why would he expect me to run up and boot him so hard in the goolies that I wouldn't have been surprised to see them pop out of his mouth as he opened it to scream? He crumpled to the floor, and his mate Derek, who stood gaping, got the same treatment.

Sensing he'd be next, Freddie bolted out the toilet door, his little penis still hanging out of his trousers.

This caused some commotion in the corridor, and Mr Blake, the janitor, came charging into the toilets to witness the carnage.

Two hard kicks had been enough. Solutions can be so simple sometimes.

Back in Mrs Broch's office again, this time with parents or, in my case, parent present, my mum having returned from her shopping trip, I listened in silence as the pathetic threesome tried to justify their actions.

The two I'd kicked had red eyes from crying, and I noticed Joseph Kennedy kept wriggling his hips, still in some discomfort.

Kennedy's dad, a rough-looking bruiser of a man, tried the old excuse again that they'd been trying to see who could pee the highest against the wall. As I remembered, Mrs Broch wanted to believe him, but this time, I had a ready response. I raised my hand. 'Yes, Sam?' Mrs Broch said.

'That's not true, miss. If they were trying to see who could pee the highest up the wall, why were they standing in the middle of the room? What really happened is that I turned around from finishing a pee, and they were standing there with their cocks out, waiting to piss on me.'

A few gasps at my language. The headteacher said, 'Language, please, there's no need for that. I've already warned you today.'

'I'm sorry, miss, but the fact is I've been covered in urine by three-low-life....' I wanted to swear but had to remember that everyone saw a five-year-old kid, not an adult. I wouldn't be taken seriously if I lost it now. I had to remain calm and lucid, more lucid than any five-year-old coated in three boys' sticky, stinky piss had any right to be. I selected my words carefully. 'Little dicks.' (It seemed appropriate to me.) 'One of them, Joseph Kennedy, has been bullying me incessantly for six months.'

Everyone, including the three little dicks stared at me open-mouthed. Using the word incessantly, considering I'd barely been able to read Ben the Badger a day or so ago, might not have been the best idea, but I'd said it now.

Joseph's dad objected. 'My son is not a bully; if anything, it's *my* son that's been bullied. This little bugger kicked him so hard in the nuts that he might never be able to have children.' That started a whole barrage of objections and arguments between the adults, partly due to Mr Kennedy saying bugger and partly because his son being twice my size made it hard to believe he'd be bullied by a lightweight like me. It also occurred to me that if I'd affected Joseph Kennedy's future ability to reproduce, I might have done the world a favour.

I remained silent, watching the chaos that ensued. Sometimes lighting the blue touch paper and standing back is the best thing you can do. Eventually, Mrs Broch cleared her office, and with the deputy head's help, she invited only the children back in. She felt more comfortable dealing with children. I could understand that. I could still hear the parents arguing outside in the corridor.

I kept a straight face.

The head teacher yielded to the deputy head, Sharon Maxwell, who was much more down-to-earth and unlikely to be goaded by kids. Plus, as it were, she was closer to the coalface, as she still taught a class; year four this term.

She addressed Joseph, 'Is it true that you have been bullying Sam?'

He shook his head.

'Why would he say that then?'

'He's a lying little toad, that's why.'

Mrs Broch went to object, but Sharon spoke before she could, first turning her attention to the other two; 'What about you, Derek? Have you been bullying Sam too?'

He shook his head.

She turned to me. 'Has he, Sam?'

I nodded. 'Sometimes. I think he and Freddie only do it as they're scared of Joseph.' I could see from the corner of my eye the two boys nodding.

Sharon regarded me quizzically. 'That's very perceptive of you, Sam.'

I recognised this as a test. 'What does perceptive mean?' I asked innocently.

She smiled at me. 'Somehow, I believe you know fine well what that means, Sam Harris. You're not yourself today.'

'No, I stink of pee.'

She suppressed a giggle, not wanting to lighten the atmosphere. 'Quite.' she said eventually. Then she stared at me. I could almost see the cogs whirring around. 'Why today?'

'Why today what?'

'Why fight back today? Usually, someone who has been bullied a lot, like you claim to have been, doesn't fight back. That's what gives them their power.' She gave Kennedy a side-way glance as she spoke.

I sighed theatrically; great dream this. 'I think I'd just had enough, the last straw, the greatest humiliation. Everyone has their breaking point. It was probably overdue.' Thirty-five years overdue. I didn't say.

Everyone stared at me, wondering why a five-year-old kid had suddenly developed the vocabulary of an adult.

Mrs Broch said, 'You're very grown-up today, Sam.'

'I know, I think it's the shock of everything, to be honest, standing here stinking of... well, you know what, it's not exactly my finest hour.'

This time Sharon couldn't help but laugh. Kennedy relaxed and went to sit down.

The deputy head rounded on him. 'Stand still, Joseph. If I get my way, you will be suspended from school, and if you are ever allowed to return, I will be watching you very closely, do you understand?'

I think he understood.

At that point, I felt a little light-headed and promptly sat down on the nearest chair, my head in my hands. Sharon Maxwell said, 'Sam, are you OK, Sam?'

My eyes fluttered open, and I was back on the bed in Cholis Lab 4. The Doc lifted my left eyelid and shone a torch into my eye. 'Ouch!' I exclaimed.

'Sorry,' she replied. 'I just wanted to check your pupil reaction. You've been out for a little longer than expected, but everything seems normal. How are you feeling?'

I considered her question. How did I feel? Refreshed certainly and better. I felt better. How weird. 'Better?' I said aloud.

The Doc nodded thoughtfully. 'Good, that's good.'

'Did you flip my switch back on?'

'It's not as straightforward as that, but perhaps we'll know in a day or two. We'll continue your therapy tomorrow, but it's worth noting that you might have a problem sleeping tonight because you've slept during the day and might suffer from stomach cramps and possibly diarrhoea.'

'How long have I been out?'

'Four hours.'

Wow, I thought. I considered asking about the hallucinogenic effects of the serum but decided I'd leave that for later.

As I went to stand up, I noticed something alarming. I'd come in here wearing my comfy baggy joggers, and now I seemed to be in blue jeans. Why had the Doc changed my trousers? Had I peed myself? I plopped down onto the floor and realised that, as well as the change of clothing, somehow, in the last four hours, I'd shed at least seven stones in weight.

Chapter 7
Land of Confusion

'What's wrong?' asked the Doc.

'Where's my… I mean, I came in here fat. Now I'm not. Does that serum dissolve body fat? I mean, it could be worth a fortune. Where've my joggers gone? Did I pee myself…?' I asked, cringing the words rushing out of my mouth all at once.

Doctor Jaeger frowned. 'I'm not sure I follow you, Sam. Maybe you should sit back down for a moment. It's unusual for the serum to have this kind of side effect. Let's check you over.' She nodded to nurse Paton, who donned a stethoscope, listened to my heart, and took my blood pressure and respiration—a mini-medical.

The Doc waited until she'd finished and confirmed that everything seemed fine. The Doc nodded at her assistant, who turned and left the room. I felt utterly bewildered. Dr Jaeger asked, 'Did you have any sensations or memories when you were under?'

'Vivid dreams about my school days, specifically the bullying and the boys that peed on me in primary one.'

The Doc rubbed her chin. 'Interesting, as the first anomaly we worked on seemed to be very early in your genetic history. I suppose it's possible that the switch, to use the terminology we used earlier we tried to fix, may have been related to those events. Still, having vivid dreams about them, I suspect, is coincidental and more likely related to the trauma of revisiting those memories earlier with Dr Ramos.'

'Fair enough, but what about my trousers and the weight loss.'

The Doc shook her head. 'I don't know what you mean, Sam; you're the same weight as when you came in here and you were wearing jeans. I've not seen you in joggers.'

'I came in here wearing grey joggers as that's all that would fit me, plus this morning I must have weighed over eighteen stone: now I'm what? Eleven, eleven and a half.' I glanced around the room. 'You weighed me remember?'

The Doc nodded. 'I did, and I recorded your weight here, look.'

I scrutinised her notes and written in a box marked *weight; I* read the figure 73.65 kilos. 'That's not right; I weighed over one hundred and eighteen kilos earlier, I clearly

remember. We also talked about my divorce causing me to start eating crap.'

The Doc appeared worried. 'For some reason, Sam, you've woken up very confused. I'm not sure why.'

Me neither. Nor could I forget I weighed as much as a small car earlier in the day, and now I didn't. Could I have dreamt everything since arriving here? No, that wouldn't work anyway. When I'd been evicted, I'd been huge and stinky, I remembered Sally shying away from me on the couch without me realising why. Also, I remembered meeting Lisa, my ex-wife, in Tesco few weeks before I moved to Birmingham. I'd tried to avoid her by skulking behind a huge pile of toilet rolls, but she'd come to speak to me anyway. I can't remember exactly what she'd said, but I could see her looking at me, at the size of me, and I knew she'd have been thinking, 'Thank God I got out of that when I did.'

She'd testify that I'd been the size of a house, as would my social worker. This wasn't right. Something felt way off here, out of kilter. I regarded the Doc warily as she tried to convince me everything was normal.

After a few more minutes of me asking where my trousers were, the Doc said, 'Sam, I think we'll suspend your involvement in the project for a day or two until we can understand why you're reacting this way.' The words *suspended from the project* hit home. I remembered Sally's plea, please don't blow it, and it reminded me that I might only be a small step from sleeping behind the bins. I started to object but decided a night's rest might sort things. I might still be dreaming, all of this may be an illusion, and I could still be snoozing, fat inside my joggers. I agreed to go to my room and relax. The Doc reminded me that Sally would visit me after dinner. 'It might be helpful for you to speak to an outsider, just to put your mind at rest.'

I nodded and headed back to my room. I stood in front of the mirror and stared at my trim frame. Even my hair had changed. When I'd arrived, my hair had been of the salt and pepper variety; now, I had to look carefully to spot any grey at all. Perhaps they'd dyed my hair whilst I'd been asleep too. I shook my head at the craziness of it all and lay down on the bed. I let a ubiquitous antiques show murmur in the background, soothing and familiar. All I had were the dream shards, the memory of Miss McFarlane's face when I said badger's arse out loud.

Also, the incident in the toilet and my revenge, none of it real, just a dream. Then I realised that if I was still dreaming just now, would I be able to remember a previous dream?

A dream within a dream.

What on earth had been in that amber liquid? I took a deep breath; I had to calm down. I *had* to be still dreaming. How the hell else could I suddenly be seven-stone lighter and have had my hair dyed?

It all made my head hurt.

I lay still, trying not to think as my head filled with thoughts that didn't feel like mine. I tuned into the antique show, which helped.

I watched three episodes back-to-back by flipping through the various channels, then went for dinner. Sitting eating roast beef, Yorkshire pudding, roast potatoes, carrots and green beans, I observed everyone else around the table. Molly still didn't make eye contact with anyone; Ted still muttered about our most prominent evolutionist, coated his dinner in dandruff, and occasionally smacked himself. Thankfully he now sat at a small side table on his own. He didn't seem to notice or care. Angus still peered at Molly from under his floppy fringe. In fact, everybody appeared precisely as they had been earlier in the day and yesterday. Only I had changed.

I ate a mouthful, and the meat tasted tender and delicious. Would I be able to appreciate the flavour and texture of food in a dream? Plus, we'd had the same dinner last night as well. Perhaps that's all they served. I said to Angus, 'It's nicer than last night's roast beef.'

He replied with a mouthful of peas, some spilling and bouncing back onto his plate, 'We had lasagne last night, man, not this shit.'

I stared at him as he shovelled more food into his mouth. Lasagne? We didn't have lasagne, did we? I occasionally had trouble remembering what I'd eaten for lunch, usually crisps. Still, last night had been the first time I'd sat at a table with other people for as long as I could remember, and I'm pretty sure I'd had soup followed by roast beef and spilt gravy on my non-existent joggers. Despite the warmth of the room, I shivered. Something strange was happening.

After dinner, Sally appeared, and the Doc guided us into a small room with a couch and a couple of burnt-orange coloured hospital chairs. Functional and comfortable, if not aesthetically pleasing.

The Doc summarised what had happened earlier, my confusion and my 'dream'.

I asked my social worker, 'Don't you remember me being fat and smelly when you visited me in the flat?'

Sally frowned. 'You needed a bath certainly, Sam, but fat; no, you were the weight you are now; if anything, I was a little worried that you hadn't been eating properly.'

'I must be still dreaming,' I said quietly.

The Doc and the social worker shared a look, 'Sam,' the Doc said gently. 'This isn't a dream. This is real?'

'How can you be so sure?' I argued.

'You told us about the dream you'd experienced while asleep with the sedative. That was your dream. This is real.'

I shook my head. 'This might be a dream within a dream.'

Sally asked the Doc, 'Have you come across this before?'

'There's a condition called maladaptive daydreaming where the patient can experience intense daydreams that feel like real life, but from what I've read, it's not a condition that comes on suddenly. It usually manifests itself from adolescence onwards and can be debilitating, but the patient can usually distinguish between daydream and reality. Sam may be experiencing a psychotic episode, possibly brought on by the trauma of re-visiting the events of his childhood earlier today—'

'It wasn't traumatic,' I interrupted. 'In my dream, my first dream, I got revenge on the little dicks,' I smiled at my terminology, 'so I feel much better about life as a result, well, my dreamlife anyway.'

The Doc stared at me for a moment. 'What can you remember about the day Sally came to your flat?'

'I remember the bailiffs kicking the door in, throwing some paperwork at me, and then you came in behind them,' I recalled.

Sally nodded.

'Then you sat on the couch with the dodgy arm, and when you leaned on it, it gave way, and you fell to the floor amongst all the empty Coke cans and crips packets.'

Sally said, 'Yes, I fell on the floor, but it wasn't covered in rubbish. It perhaps needed cleaning, but that's about it. I think you might be thinking about the passenger side of my car.' She visibly blushed.

'That's when you phoned to try and get me in here a day earlier.'

She nodded. 'One hundred per cent.'

The Doc pondered for a moment. 'OK, then his short-term memory seems to be more or less fine; it's just that for some reason, whatever we did today, has had the effect of inserting certain events that didn't happen into his memory. False memories. It's unusual but not unheard of. Sometimes a patient can believe something to be true when it isn't. Old memories can interfere with or alter our new memories; in other instances, new information can make it difficult to remember previously stored information. As a patient then starts piecing old memories back together, there are sometimes holes or spaces in the memory, and the brain fills in the gaps.'

I tried to take this in. It sounded like a conversation I might have had with Monty after a bottle of wine, but it seemed more plausible than me still being asleep and dreaming, but I wasn't one hundred per cent convinced. 'Would this make me think I used to be fat when I wasn't?'

The Doc nodded. 'Possibly, especially if you thought you were fat when you weren't, which I'm sure you're aware is a huge issue for anorexia patients.'

This all started to make a confused sense, though the joggers to jeans thing still puzzled me. I decided not to mention the lasagne and roast beef conundrum.

Chapter 8
Bad Romance

I lay awake for a long time that evening, my brain racing, trying to process the conflicting information. I'd banged my knee on the bed and the sharp pain, and subsequent bruising, convinced me more than anything else, that I was no longer asleep and dreaming. Plus, my tummy grumbled and mumbled – the effects of the amber concoction the Doc had warned me about.

That meant the false memory mumbo jumbo the Doc had wittered on about must be the logical explanation of why my memory had dual timelines running through it.

I now had two versions of my life, similar but with subtle differences.

In both versions, I met up with Luci Lawrence on my last day of high school. Equally as painful. Her mum had found out my mum had terminal cancer, and Luci had come to see me. I'm unsure why; to offer support and hold my hand? A brave decision as I still had the vestiges of flour and eggs on me, making me resemble a half-baked cake.

A bunch of kids had ambushed me on my way out of the building, tied me to a chair and pelted me with flour and eggs.

She didn't care about my appearance and said it was shocking that I'd had to endure that.

Looking back, I can see that I had huge issues with my mum's diagnosis, and my way of coping was lashing out at anyone and everyone—even Luci.

We sat outside the school on an old stone wall surrounding the football pitches. A warm July day, with a light breeze, that ruffled her hair and carried over exhaust fumes from the nearby dual carriageway. Luci talked. I listened. The London Guildhall had accepted her to study Music and Drama, but she wouldn't go if I could give her a good reason not to.

I had no idea why she'd even made that offer to me. Our history was, well, history by then. Lost in time and space. Besides, I hated myself and everything and everyone at that point.

Why would she do something like that for me? I wasn't worthy. I didn't know that her mum and my mum had been chatting online for months and that Luci had been reading the correspondence. My mother never mentioned it.

She seemed to know about my trials and tribulations, my problems fitting into the school, and my issues with some teachers in the last year or two, coinciding with my mum's treatments and decline. Luci had matured enough to see how this had contributed. I hadn't and didn't. It felt like she'd been spying on me, and my mum had betrayed my confidence.

'I don't need your sympathy, Luci, I don't. Just go and enjoy your life in London and shag your way through the orchestra.'

She'd locked eyes with me, her mouth forming a perfect 'O' shape. Her lips now bore lipstick though she still didn't need it.

'Sam, I know you're hurting and….'

'What I am is of no concern of yours, I've not seen you for years, and you turn up here on my last day of school and... why are you here? Did my mum send you?'

'Of course not I...'

'She did, didn't she? I don't need you, Luci. I don't need anybody.' I really did, but in any event, I'd stood up and walked away, leaving her sitting with tears slipping down her cheeks.

In both versions of my memory, I'd married Lisa MacDonald. The weddings were identical, taking place three days after my twenty-eighth birthday—a hot August afternoon, standing in a sweltering registrar's office with no air con. A smattering of friends witnessed the formalities, mainly Lisa's and my dad, what remained of him. He hadn't taken my mother's death well, and a decade after that event, it showed.

Somewhere, deep down, I knew marrying Lisa would be a bad idea. Marrying anyone would be a bad idea. With long luxurious red hair, freckles across the bridge of her nose and beautiful blue eyes, I had no idea why she found me attractive, but she did. We met at an eighties-night in the local pub near my work.

I remember thinking as I said, 'I do,' that I should be saying, 'I don't.' I had the image of Luci Lawrence on our last day at high school, staring at me with tears in her eyes. What an arse I'd been that day, what a waste. That ship had indeed sailed early on in my life.

Lisa and I had gone on holiday to Crete six months after meeting. We found a beautiful little restaurant, perched on a cliff, overlooking the crystalline blue water. Two bottles of wine later, I asked her to marry me. I'm not sure why, and even less certain why she accepted. We were just at that stage where it seemed like a good idea: that and the wine, I suppose.

We stuck it out for the best part of three years, which is the best description I can offer.

Kids were out of the question; Lisa wanted them, and we discussed it, but I wanted to wait until we were more financially secure, like that would *ever* happen.

I'd been in the same job for nearly four years (a record for me), working in a small betting shop just off Wigan high street. Lisa moved into my two up two down terraced house, a five-minute walk from my work. She transformed it from a crummy bachelor mess to something you could call home. She'd been nesting. I hadn't realised at the time, preparing for the children, I wouldn't give her. She tried, she did. I can never fault her for that.

She left me on a bleak January morning. I'm surprised she'd lasted that long. I'd lost my job a few weeks before Christmas and hadn't expended much energy in trying to find another one. She took her clothes and Bo, our cocker spaniel, and said, 'Sam, I'm leaving. You know I have to, don't you?'

I did know. I'd always known.

The only difference between the two marriages was that in the second version, I'd left *her*. For her sake, not mine. Something I should have done before I did.

From that point forward, the two versions of my history converged, leading me to Perry Flowers. Except now I'm thin instead of fat and couldn't be sure what I'd eaten for dinner.

Weirdly, I'd once assumed that my fat frame had deterred people from hiring me, but of course, I'd never been overweight, or had I? I hadn't quite reconciled myself to the false memory thing. I didn't know what to make of it all. I didn't think I'd become insane, but if you are mad, you probably don't think you are. One of the symptoms, perhaps.

I awoke the following day feeling refreshed and calm. I still had the memories of two lives in my head, but the former version, where I'd been humongous, had begun to fade.

Therefore, I assumed the second version must be accurate, but what did I know? Just in case, I wrote down what I could remember of my first life, which sounded decidedly odd inside my head.

The Doc had suspended me from any further therapy until she decided I was fit to continue. I told her that my head had cleared and that the version she believed to be the truth, I now also believed to be the truth. She seemed relieved but still thought it worthwhile to wait a few days.

I didn't seem to be in danger of being kicked out, so I could live with that.

On Friday, my name appeared once more on the whiteboard. Another digging session with Little Miss Gorgeous. It occurred to me that I might be being both sexist and disingenuous; she'd spent God knows how many years at medical school and then a good few more training as a psychiatrist. More than I could ever have achieved. More than most people had achieved, all to try and help total losers like me. She deserved more respect than that.

Seated in her office again, trying not to let her beautiful face distract me, we ran over what had happened with Dr Jaeger. I'd bought into the false memory syndrome now. I had no choice, and we discussed it for a while. Janice eventually said, 'Dredging up childhood trauma can be very unsettling and distressing. I don't think I emphasised how strongly our session had affected you in my notes.'

I nodded. 'You're right, but just for the record, and for the last time, you are absolutely certain that I wasn't humungous when I came into the room with you earlier in the week?'

Janice smiled. 'Definitely not, plus if we could take seven stones off someone in one afternoon, we wouldn't be practising psychiatry, I can promise you that.'

I liked the fact that she'd made a joke out of it.

'Right, let's continue,' she announced, flipping through her pad and finding a fresh page. 'Last time we'd got to the stage where you were bullied in primary school. How did the rest of your time there pan out?'

'Better, I still got excluded from many things. Joe and his crew never dared touch me again, but they made sure I didn't get picked for things like football, cricket, anything really.'

'How did that make you feel?'

'Like an outsider.'

'Did you have any friends?'

'Thomas Carter, a small quiet kid who didn't fit in either and of course, Luci Lawrence, we were good friends. We used to walk about holding each other's hands. My mum and her mum were friends, so we had many play dates and trips.' I couldn't help but smile at the memories.

'She made you happy?' Dr Ramos asked.

'She did.'

'What happened to her?'

'She went to a different high school. We lost touch.'

I watched as she made more notes. 'How did you fare in high school?'

'OK.'

'Define OK.'

I had two different versions in my head. One was downright disastrous, the other slightly less so. I went with the second version. 'I had a rough time, but most kids do, right? High school's a tough gig. I didn't fit in there either, but I had nobody to blame but myself this time. I didn't need a bully to make my life miserable.'

'Can you give me some examples?'

I had so many to choose from. I sighed, 'OK, here's a few, and as they say on TV talent shows, in no particular order. In year eight, we had a beautiful teacher for French, Miss Baxter. I mean, model gorgeous. There wasn't a boy in that school that didn't fantasise about her. Probably a few girls, too, thinking about it.

'Anyway, in this one class, she had written a bunch of sentences on the blackboard, leaving a blank where the verb should be. She got kids to come out to fill in the gaps. I'd been daydreaming about her, staring at her, and… well, you can imagine. Suddenly she says, *Sam, can you complete the fifth sentence, please*? She's holding out the chalk, and I had to stand up, walk towards her and take it from her fingers. Of course, my fantasy had got me all hot and bothered, and as I walked towards her, she looked down at my school trousers…well, put it this way, school trousers don't hide erections. She could see it sticking out, and so could most of the class.

'She smiled sympathetically at me, but the place just erupted.' I cringed. 'It got brought up whenever willies were mentioned for the rest of my school life. You'd be surprised at how often adolescent boys and girls talk about willies.'

I waited for a comment from Janice but no genital shaming here, either. 'Then there's the time I got locked in the supplies cupboard.'

The doctor looked up from her notes. 'How did that happen?'

'A smart-arse kid, Jimmy Hall, did it. He'd told me that the janitor had hidden his stash of porn in there. He had a porn mag in his bag that he offered as evidence. Remember, this was just at the beginning of the internet. Most kids then didn't have access to it. Anyway, I'd been stupid enough to believe him, and as I scrabbled about amongst the mops and buckets, Jimmy slammed the door and locked it. I was stuck in there for an hour until someone found the janitor to get me out. I got detention for missing PE, whilst Jimmy Hall didn't even get pulled up. If I hadn't realised already, I knew from that day that life wasn't fair. Jimmy's dad was a school governor.'

I poured myself a glass of water from the jug on the table. Janice reviewed my confessions. 'These are embarrassing, I suppose, but not the sort of thing that would scar you like the primary one experience.'

I nodded. 'There are a few other things that happened, one of which, looking back on it, has a kind of symmetry. On my first day at high school, some of the sixth form kids tied me to a chair in the middle of the playground, poured water over me and pelted me with bags of flour and eggs.'

Janice looked up from her notes. 'Why did they do that?'

I shrugged. 'Because they could, I guess.'

'That's awful; what happened?'

'I had to go home and change.'

'No, I meant, what did the school do?'

'Not much. It seems it happened to some poor bugger every year. I was the poor bugger.'

Janice shook her head and made some notes. 'You mentioned a symmetry to it?'

'Yeah, well, the same thing happened on my last day after I'd finished my A levels. Some kids from the year below me tied me to a chair in the playground, poured flour and water over me and broke eggs over my head.'

'Why?'

'Because they could. They were leaving school; there were no repercussions for them.'

Dr Ramos threw me another sympathetic look. 'You didn't have much luck, did you?'

I shrugged. 'I've always been an easy target, plus I seem to have a knack for being in the wrong place at the wrong time.'

'Anything else?'

'Loads. I just stood out as being a victim. Plus, being painfully shy and scared of making an arse of myself meant I made an arse of myself all the time; I've always made bad choices.'

'Can you give me a few examples?'

'My dad suggested I join the debating society to help overcome my shyness.'

'Did it work?'

'No. At the first meeting, we were all given three minutes to deliver a talk on anything we wanted or felt we could talk about for that length of time. I decided to talk about the ankylosaurus.'

'What?'

'It's a dinosaur from the Cretaceous period, just before the asteroid hit. It resembled a giant hedgehog with a huge club on its tail. Anyway, I managed to stutter through about forty seconds and then ran out of things to say. I never went back to the debating society.'

'At least you tried.'

'I know, but it's another example of a bad choice. I had no chance of becoming a confident public speaker, so why put myself through that? The same thing happened every week at cricket, compulsory from April to July. I couldn't bowl, couldn't bat and wasn't much use in the field either. A few other kids were hopeless too, but as I'd already been marked out as victim choice number one, it would be my fault if anything went wrong.'

Janice looked over her notepad. 'Anything else?'

What the hell? I might as well be honest; otherwise, I wouldn't be able to help myself. 'My mum started to get sick during year ten. Breast cancer. She had a double mastectomy, but it had spread. It took another three years to finish her off.'

'How did that make you feel.'

I sighed. 'Angry mostly.'

Janice nodded. 'Understandable, you are an only child too, aren't you?'

'Yeah, and my dad wasn't there much. He worked on the rigs.'

'Did he not take time out for your mother?'

I shook my head. 'Nah, he pissed off to work for six weeks at a time. He didn't want to deal with it.'

'He was in denial.'

I scoffed. 'Probably, but that's how he dealt with most stuff. He'd head out to work, and by the time he got back, any problems had been resolved, usually by my mum. There aren't many things in life that will remain a problem for longer than six weeks.'

'Except cancer,' Janice said flatly

'Yeah, except cancer,' I agreed.

Chapter 9
Can U C Me

I also outlined the Luci Lawrence incident. More as an example of how I'd dealt with things at the time, maybe how I still dealt with things.

She closed her pad and said, 'That's enough for this morning; I'll tidy up my notes and thoughts and pass them to Dr Jaeger for her session with you this afternoon. Are you sure you're OK to try again?'

I nodded. I had no choice; I either complied or I'd end up bedding down behind the bins.

I wasn't very hungry at lunch and picked at a chicken salad. Not all the patients/colleagues were there. I assumed they were still being treated/counselled/consoled.

Molly had been unusually chatty, telling everyone about her dad, who worked as a croupier on a cruise ship. His ship would be docking in Southampton Harbour on Saturday morning, and she'd planned to spend the weekend with him. I didn't know we could leave at weekends, not that I had anywhere to go.

My afternoon session with the Doc started with a thorough check over by Nurse Paton. It seemed I was in A1 physical condition. Shame about my brain, then.

The Doc confirmed the details about my high school life and seemed particularly interested in my reaction to my mother's illness and rejection of Luci. Perhaps that sort of thing made more of a dent in my genome than being covered in flour and eggs, being locked in cupboards or tented trousers in French classes.

As I slipped into unconsciousness, I remembered I'd forgotten to ask the Doc if the amber liquid contained hallucinogenic properties. Oh well, too late now.

This time when I opened my eyes, I found myself leaning over my high school balcony as some burly rugby types carried Sweaty Betty's old Fiat 500 into the school playground. I'd forgotten about that. Sweaty Betty (real name Elizabeth Hargreaves) was a quiet and gentle English teacher. I used to like her classes, but a medical condition made her sweat profusely. Hence the name, kids can be pretty unoriginal as well as cruel.

I watched as she came running out of the staff room, her hands covering her mouth and close to tears. The deputy head Mr Thomson followed close behind her. Thomson WITHOUT A P, BOY, WITHOUT A P, as he used to shout at anyone in his history class who misspelt his name.

He remonstrated with the carjackers, and they eventually lifted the car and returned it to the car park. I suddenly realised with a shudder that once they'd completed that task, they'd start searching for something else to occupy the schoolyard and that I'd be the target. I never discovered who suggested me to them. I needed to hide.

I disappeared from the landing and headed across to the other school building, sneaked into the theatre and sat and watched years eleven and twelve present the end-of-term review. Most of it seemed to constitute rehashed scenes from *Blackadder*, but at least I felt safe.

I dared to leave the theatre at three pm and cautiously approached the front door. As I did so, I noticed an empty chair covered in flour and eggs in the middle of the playground. It seemed the prank had gone ahead, except with a different victim. I wondered which poor sod had taken my place.

It hadn't occurred to me until then that I must have been dreaming again. I stopped and took a good look around. My subconscious had once again done a splendid job of recreating my old school's sights, sounds and smells. Some younger kids rushed past me, and the whiff of stale cigarettes drifted into my nostrils. They must have been outside somewhere having illicit fags. Kids must think teachers were stupid. I also took stock of my seventeen-year-old body. So young and strong. I could feel the muscles in my arms flex, and I reached down and felt the tight tummy muscles against my school shirt. Whoever said youth is wasted on the young had been spot on. I felt like I would live forever, physically invincible, but mentally? Well, I had my forty-year-old head on.

I made my way towards the exit. Back then, at my school, at any rate, you left to very little fanfare. On my last day, I walked out the door and never looked back. There was no end-of-school prom, party, or formal acknowledgement that my school days were over. No watershed moment, no right-of-passage events.

Instead, waiting for me in the doorway looking beautiful, Luci Lawrence. My brain, over the years, had wiped that image, probably more pain than it could handle. Despite not seeing her for six years, she hadn't changed at all and, yet, had changed completely.

I inhaled deeply. I had perspective this time. My mum, in my head, had died nearly twenty-two years ago, though, in this dream, she'd still be at home, painfully thin and wasting away.

I forced a smile to my lips. 'Luci. This is a surprise.'

She hugged me. Her scent, as well as her arms, enveloped me. Peaches and maybe a hint of sweat. An intoxicating mix.

We sat on the wall, and like last time, I listened, but unlike last time, patiently, drinking in every word, every expression, every movement of her body. So lovely, so young, so full of potential. I knew what I'd become. I never knew what she became.

I smiled when she offered not to go to The Guildhall if I wanted her to stay.

I shook my head. 'Luci, you have a wonderful life ahead of you.' Of course, I didn't know if that was true. She might get hit by a bus when she's twenty-five or marry a loser like me. She certainly never appeared on any social media searches I'd run over the years, but I had to play the odds.

'I'm so honoured that you'd do that for me, even though we've not seen each other for years. I'm also happy that my mum has had your mum for support, me and dad, well…' I paused. 'We're not women, so we don't understand what she's going through.'

Luci stared at me. 'My mum said you've been having real problems at school and that your mum thinks it's because she's been ill.'

I had my forty-year-old brain fully engaged, possessing that wonderful thing called perspective, one of the few gifts ageing gives you. 'All kids have problems at school. I don't think mine were any worse than yours or anyone else's, my mum's very focused on the short term, living in the moment, as you do when you've not got long left.'

'My mum says she's starting some new treatment next week that….' She paused as I shook my head.

'It won't work. She knows that but won't admit it, and to be honest, why should she? She's trying her best to hold us all together, but my dad's away working, which is his way of dealing. And me? I suppose I get angry at things, it's unfair and horrible, and it does feel like I'm on my own.'

I paused and gazed into those incredible eyes. 'I watch her sometimes, my mum, I mean, when she's asleep. She always falls asleep, usually on the couch watching the news. Every day a little piece of her slips away, never to return, and I can do nothing about it.'

It all came rushing back to me, and as I stopped speaking, tears slipped from my eyes, and Luci hugged me. We sat like that for a long time. A few kids passed by, commenting or jeering, but Luci gave them the finger.

After a while, I felt better. We discussed the past, our shared history, the trips to soft-play, beaches, swimming pools, and the holiday Luci, our mothers, and I took to Ibiza for one Easter holiday. The days at the zoo, safari parks, and various playparks, all before the age of twelve. If only she'd gone to my high school, my life might have been different. Whilst our mothers had stayed in touch, we hadn't.

We tried to fill in the pieces of the last six years but found it difficult as we'd had so few shared experiences. She told me about her first few boyfriends and their clumsy fumbles at teenage parties. Then her first serious boyfriend. A controlling, nasty bully of a man/boy, eighteen going on three, according to Luci, who freaked out whenever she dared to speak to another male. She'd been fifteen then.

She recalled the night he eventually got what he wanted. 'We were out in his dad's car. He'd only passed his test three weeks before. I'm not even sure his dad knew he had it. Anyway, we drove out into the countryside and found a spot overlooking a lake, reservoir, or something like that.' She paused. 'I knew what was going to happen.' She searched my face for what? Judgement, jealousy, an opinion? I had no idea. I had no right to feel anything.

'Anyway,' she said smiling, 'it was quick, painful and forgettable. He dumped me two days later. I was a mess for ages afterwards. God knows why; he'd been a complete moron, a controlling, mean-spirited bully, but I guess I'd been too young to know any better. When I'd been with him, I'd become invisible, you know? Like I'd lost my identity, he controlled everything, and when he moved on, I didn't know how to be me anymore. It took time. I used to think, in school, when I walked along the corridor – *hey, look at me, can you see me? I'm here – please tell me you can see me.*'

I felt anger and sorrow, but, even with a forty-year-old brain engaged, I still felt impotent and useless, she might have only been six months older than me, but she'd become a woman in the intervening years. I'd remained a stupid immature kid.

Whilst emotionally, I could now relate, at the time sitting there in a seventeen-year-old body, I'd still been a virgin. I would remain so for another three years until a suffocatingly hot night in a Corfu hotel room where Aileen Reid from Inverness removed that particular burden, as it had become by then.

Eventually, we ran out of things to say. Luci pulled out a little Dictaphone and played me a song she'd written on her piano. Called, *Can U C Me*, she said it reflected her experience with Alex. 'It helped you know... writing it down, getting the emotion out, in a way I could relate to. It made me feel better anyway.'

I listened. Heartfelt *and naïve* was how she described the song, but it sounded pretty good to me. 'It should have been you, not him,' she told me, her amber eyes flashing in the summer sunlight.

I wanted to believe her, but she'd only said it to make me feel better.

After a moment or two of comfortable silence, she started asking questions, the answers to half of which I knew, but wished perhaps I didn't.

'Where do you think we'll both be in ten years?'

In a relationship that will ultimately lead to a miserable marriage. Instead, I said, 'I don't know about me, but you'll be a famous actress, singer or musician.' She wouldn't, or I'd have heard of her, but she deserved to be.

'Will you go to university?'

'Probably not. Mum needs me.'

'But what about after, well, you know?'

I shook my head. 'I doubt it, Luci. I'm not the academic type.'

She took my hand and stared into my eyes, her irises glowing like mini suns. I could feel her body heat, smell her scent, sense her compassion. 'Look at me, Sam.'

I couldn't have avoided those deep pools of love even if I'd wanted to. She was breath-taking. I could see that now. My angry, lost, younger self had been too consumed with self-hatred and injustice to appreciate this wonderful girl. My heart ached as her breath washed over me in an erotically charged out-pouring of emotion. She leaned her forehead against mine and spoke in a whisper. 'Promise me, Sam. Promise me this, whatever happens after your mum dies; you must go to university, OK? For me and especially for your mum. You have to make something of your life for her memory and me. *Please*.'

The 'please', a pleading entreaty that came straight from her heart, from some deep well of concern and emotion I had no right to tap into or receive. But there she sat, breathing into my face, an appeal made from the shared experience and shared love that I'd lost, misplaced, didn't deserve – maybe all three. I didn't know. With my old head in control, I now recognised that I'd just experienced the most passionate, charged and memorable moment of my life to date - maybe forever.

We held each other as if the world was ending, and we were the last people alive, the last people to experience a sunset, a sunrise, the waning and waxing of the moon, the call of a bird, the cry of a child. It felt like the whole human experience was tied up in that moment. I closed my eyes, breathed her in, and it felt like the world had tilted from its axis and plunged into the sun.

Chapter 10
Don't Say It

I opened my eyes to find the Doc and Nurse Paton standing over me, looks of concern etched onto their faces. 'We were getting a little worried about you there. None of the other volunteers ever take quite so long to wake up as you do.'

Disappointment didn't do justice to how I felt— bereft, lost, longing for Luci, an eighteen-year-old Luci who no longer existed, well, not in that form. I shook my head and quickly checked to ensure I hadn't piled on seven stones of fat or changed my trousers. All seemed to be as it had before, yet inside, I'd changed. I felt different but the same.

'How are you feeling?' the Doc asked.

'OK.' I lied. I didn't want a debate this time; I wanted to return to my room, stick the TV on and wait to see what happened. The nurse checked me over as the Doc asked me questions.

'Any dreams or hallucinations?'

'Not that I can remember clearly, something vague about high school, but that's what I'd been talking about earlier to Dr Ramos.'

The Doc made some notes. 'Interesting, as the marker we targeted today seemed to coincide with your late adolescent years. It doesn't seem possible that targeting a marker would invoke a psychological reaction, but we are in unchartered territory.'

I didn't take in much of what she said. I just wanted out of there to think. Eventually, I headed to my room, flipped on the TV, lay down on the bed and tried to gather my thoughts. I now had the threads of three lives running through my head. The first time I'd been fat; the second time, I'd been thin and stood up to the bullies in primary school but had been mean to Luci and now a new third thread where I'd experienced that intense interaction with her seemed to be forming in my mind.

The first thread seemed to be fading fast. I could feel it dissipating into fragments. I didn't know if that was a good thing or not. What if that was the real reality and the others only illusions born from dreams? Wouldn't that mean I'd leave here more messed up than when I'd arrived?

The most alarming thing about my latest adventure was that I had a head filled with stuff I didn't recognise. That freaked me out more than anything. Literature. My head was full to bursting with it. As I wracked my memory, I could suddenly remember many poems and the themes of many great literary works. For example, *Catcher in the Rye;* protecting innocence, especially of children, and *The Crucible;* examining reputations, mass hysteria, lies, power, envy and guilt. Charlotte Bronte's *Jane Eyre:* depicting a poor orphaned girl's rise to become a successful and independent woman when it had not been fashionable or permissible to be such a person. Originally, Bronte even had to publish the novel under a male pseudonym. I knew all about Emily and Anne, the sibling rivalry, the death of their younger sisters and mother, and the amount they managed to pack into their tragically short lives.

I grabbed a hold of my head. Why had all this stuff taken over my brain? I didn't know any of this earlier today. The deeper I thought, the more I learned. I had a whole dissertation about Edgar Allan Poe, entitled 'The Original Goth'. What the hell?

What on earth had been in that amber liquid? I took a deep breath. The literary knowledge was a puzzle. You can't suddenly start knowing stuff you didn't know before from a dream, can you?

It all made my head hurt.

I lay on the bed, trying not to think as my brain filled with thoughts and experiences that didn't feel like mine. I watched another random show about antiques, which helped me not to think. It felt like I had received more therapeutic value from antique programmes on TV than Dr Jaeger. Who'd have thunk it? I lay still as more information dripped into my brain like raindrops into a puddle.

Then the connection arrived. I had fulfilled my promise to Luci. I went to Edinburgh University six months after my mother died and studied English Literature. That explained the stuff dropping into my mind. Well, not explain it exactly. I must be going mad.

With Luci's letters of encouragement (we'd written to each other, lots. Letters, not emails), I'd decided the best way to deal with the grief following my mother's death had been to throw myself into the coursework. I could understand why I'd chosen English. As an only child with few friends and an introverted outlook, reading books had been my way of escaping reality. I must have read a book a week growing up. I remember the secret delight I felt when the class were given Dickens to read for GCSE English and *The Great Gatsby* for A level.

During that intensive first-year period at university, I discovered the macabre delights of Poe, probably reflecting my melancholic mood for a time.

I remembered my notebook from the other day and pulled it from my drawer. All the notes I'd made about being fat and living in joggers were still in my scrawled untidy handwriting. Reading them felt more like reading a diary account from a stranger rather than something personal to me.

I updated the pages with the second set of memories and my new shiny university-educated version. Comparing the three, the latest version felt accurate, alive, and relevant. The second version, where I'd lost all the weight, read like someone else's diary entry, and the first version felt like poor fiction.

In my most recent life, for want of a better description, the letters Luci and I had written to each other were filled with passion, longing, and sadness at being apart. We'd been an item for a while, a long-distance relationship. She was in London studying drama and music, and I in Edinburgh, my head buried in books. We met up during the holidays and the occasional stolen weekend. I lost my virginity to her and my heart, though I suspect she'd always had that. We split up during my second year (her third year), but we kept in touch. She'd told me during a tear-filled weekend in London, 'Sam, you know I love you, don't you?'

I nodded, dreading the next bit. She'd been acting weird all weekend, and I knew something had been brewing.

'We're still so young, so inexperienced. I think we should take a break for a while.'

'There's someone else, isn't there?'

She didn't meet my eye. Tears trickled down her cheeks. 'Liam's his name. We've been talking—a lot. And I like him. Not in the way I like you. You and I have this deep connection, but I need to....' She paused, searching for the right words or perhaps words to make it hurt less. There weren't any. 'I need to experiment, I suppose.'

She stared at me for a long time, waiting for me to speak. Luci was gorgeous, far too gorgeous for me. I'd always known that. She must get hit on constantly, but her heart had always been true. She'd never cheat on me. I respected her honesty but hated her now in a way that made me hate myself more. My feelings for her were so intense, so raw, and always had been.

I'd spent most of my waking hours wondering what she was doing, where she was. It wasn't healthy and probably verged on obsession. I had no self-confidence or self-love, and it showed in a situation like this when all I could do was clam up and bury my feelings.

I didn't speak. I just picked up my bag, walked out of the flat she shared with two other girls, and got on a train back to Edinburgh. She phoned me and left messages, but I blanked her. Three days later, I wrote her a letter, then another letter. The first letter I filled with my pain and anguish. I think I may even have threatened to kill myself. In the second letter, I begged her not to leave me, disgusting, passionate, pathetic, loving, obsequious, clever, horrible and beautiful. It didn't work. She didn't reply to either of them. Instead, she recorded and sent me a song, ***Don't Say It***. The words reflected some phrases I'd written in my letters to her. Very clever. I hated it, and I loved it. I'd known by then that she used music to collate, filter and process her emotions. Sending me the song also sent me a mixed message. Did she still like me? I didn't know. Eventually, I just accepted it as her way of summing up her feelings and left it at that.

I lost myself in Poe, Horace Walpole, Daphne Du Maurier, Emily Bronte, and Sheridan Le Fanu. The darker, the better.

Towards the end of my third year, she sent me a letter out of the blue. It didn't promise anything, just a 'how are you getting on' note. I replied cautiously, not wanting to scare her away with anything crazy. I hadn't gotten over her, but my jealous possessiveness had lessened with time and distance. Plus, I'd met and dated a few girls, students mainly and a nurse called Brandy, during the last year, which had helped me with some perspective. It also made me acutely aware that there had only ever been one girl for me.

We started talking on the phone, and she surprised me one weekend by appearing at my flat door with a holdall. 'Can I come in?' she asked with a cheeky smile.

We spent most of the weekend in bed. It wasn't as it had been before; something had changed. Maybe we'd just grown up a little. The passion and love remained, but Luci felt reserved, like she was holding something back. I asked, but she just laughed it off. I knew her too well, though, she knew that too, but I didn't push it.

I asked about Liam, and she just scoffed and said it hadn't lasted long, and she didn't want to talk about other people. She only wanted to talk about us. Again, I didn't push it. She mentioned the song she'd sent me.

There had been a clue in there, after all, that we weren't over forever. My dense brain had missed it. I thought she'd been playing me, but perhaps I deserved that after my petulant outbursts. Love was complicated.

The weekend after my finals, in early June, she came to Edinburgh again for the last time. I'd been down to London only once since we'd got back together, if we were back together, exclusively. Not something we'd discussed. Anyway, final exams were all-consuming.

'Sam,' she'd said as we sat in a small, cliched Italian restaurant, eating pasta and slurping cheap red wine.

I gazed into her eyes, amber pools of infinity that appeared to be flashing and flickering, reflecting the candle stuck on the top of an empty Chianti bottle. I did mention it was cliched. 'Yeah?'

'What are your plans?' she asked, not meeting my gaze and picking at the melted wax on the bottle.

'You know my plans. I'm off to the Northeast to work in a car factory, graduate trainee scheme.'

'Yes, I know, but don't you want to do something exciting before that?'

'I've only got two weeks.'

She stared at me, probably wondering if I was being deliberately obtuse. I wasn't.

'Can you maybe not take the job and come travelling with me? I want to see the world, and I know if we both get jobs, we'll never do it. We've both finished our finals, are young and free, and will never be like this again. It's a once-in-a-lifetime opportunity.'

Luci had completed her honours year. I'd had enough of studying and wanted out into the big bad world of work. I wanted to earn some money. That, perhaps more than anything, clouded my judgement.

Her entreaty, like most things with Luci, was sincere and heartfelt; her enthusiasm and, I don't know, her 'VA VA Voom' as I'd always thought of her sudden ability to make the most mundane situation exciting, infused her now, lighting up her face, her whole body animated like a toddler overdosing on sugar.

I smiled and laughed and loved her but refused. I'm not sure why. I suppose it's one of those moments in life that you regret later, even though it felt like the right decision. I likened it to her dumping me just over a year ago so she could go and shag around, though I never said that to her in those terms. It felt, to me, like she'd needed to prove something to herself.

She painted a wonderful tapestry of exotic places Thailand, Vietnam, and Australia. I almost caved into her addictive enthusiasm. The fact that she'd dumped me held me back. I understood why she'd done it. She could have seen other people without me knowing and, at the same time, kept our relationship smouldering in the distance, but she wasn't that sort of person.

I guess I'd lost a little bit of trust, and deep down, even though she denied it later that evening, I couldn't help feeling that I'd been a convenient fallback for her travelling idea. Maybe what she'd been holding back was that Liam or Bob or Jimmy, or whoever else she'd been sleeping with, had turned her down, and I'd been her last choice, her dependable fall-back option.

Perspective, that wonderful thing, as I've said earlier, that age and distance give you, means I now recognise that she came to me because I'd been *the one,* she *wanted* to travel with, not as a last resort, but as a first choice. Someone she could trust with her life and her heart, or so she thought. I threw that back in her face. I have a self-destructive streak that niggles away at the back of my mind, constantly pouring negativity on anything positive.

As a fat loser, I hated myself so much that I abused my body and mind. As a skinny loser, same result and now, as a university-educated man, I remain a loser, making bad choices.

She spent an evening begging me. How the hell I resisted; I don't know. Or why.

I still remember her tear-stained beautiful face as she boarded the train from Waverley station. I'd let her down. I'd let myself down. I never saw her again.

I still went on to marry Lisa McDonald. This time, our marriage ended after only eighteen months. She'd found the stash of letters from Luci. She took a sickie and read through them one day when I'd been at work. She couldn't relate the level of passion and angst in the letters to the way I reacted towards her.

'Why did you marry me when you felt like that about someone else?'

I couldn't really answer that. 'Lisa, I was young and….'

'You were twenty-one when the last letter arrived. Why didn't you go with her?'

'I don't know.'

'Do you regret it now?'

'Regret what?'

'Not going with her to see the world.'

A real Catch-22 question if I said no, she'd not believe me. If I said yes, well, I did say yes. Two months later, she left me, and from then on, my life spiralled downward like before.

Since the latest trip with the amber elixir, I'd gained a degree in English and lost the love of my life that I never even knew I'd had. Tennyson had said *tis better to have loved and lost than never to have loved at all.* I wasn't so sure. I felt worse now than I had before, which kind of put paid to that theory.

I now began to suspect that my 'dreams' weren't dreams at all, but the alternative explanation seemed so outlandish and crazy that it further made me doubt my sanity. It did, however, seem to be all I had left to explain the complete craziness now infecting my persona (assuming I hadn't slipped into insanity). Sir Arthur Conan Doyle's Sherlock Holmes often quoted meme from *The Sign of Four* came to mind *when you have eliminated the impossible; whatever remains, however improbable, must be the truth.*

However, I wasn't quite prepared to go there at this point, or the Doc might think I'd lost my marbles completely. Then I *would* end up in a strait jacket having my face licked by a perverted intern.

Chapter 11
Let Her Go

I didn't own a mobile at this stage in my life, well I did, but as I couldn't afford the monthly contract, I had been cut off, so to speak. It languished in my bag with its charger, unused and unloved. However, I didn't need a contract to use the Internet. Over the weekend, I charged it up, logged onto the free Wi-Fi and did some digging.

I had a Facebook account with thirty-two friends, most of whom seemed to be Filipino women looking for a husband. I didn't remember *Friending* them, but given my current personality flux, that didn't surprise me. In any event, I wouldn't wish me upon any of them, and I doubted they'd hang around long once they got their UK citizenship and found out what a misery I'd become.

I searched for Luci Lawrence but found nothing. Luci was bouncy, bubbly and beautiful; it was inconceivable that she didn't have a social media presence. I had looked before, but not with the motivation I had now.

She may have married and changed her name, which might explain her absence. I spent most of Saturday afternoon searching for her. The weekends had been designated therapy-free days for the project, so I did not need to be anywhere or do anything except mealtimes.

Angus had asked me to play pool after breakfast, and my initial reaction had been to tell him where to stick his pool cue, but my new, smarter, trained brain said to me that being involved in some social interaction might be good for me and him, given his dark outlook.

I discovered to my consternation, that I had developed some skills at pool and snooker. I had no memory of playing this at university or any other time, but I must have acquired it at some point as I won four pool games in a row and concocted a break of fifty-nine in the one game of snooker we played.

Angus expressed his admiration. 'You're shit-hot at this shit.'

I'm unsure when shit had become such a universally useful word, but it seemed to be Angus's go-to phrase.

He said, 'You've changed in the last few days. You seem to have got your shit together, where I'm still stuck in the shit trying to work out *my* shit.'

He'd lost me by then, but I nodded. Agreeing with him seemed to be the easiest option. It had crept around to lunchtime by then. He sat beside me complaining about the shit he'd had to put up with as a teenager and the shit sandwich his parents and he had formed and how when they'd eventually split up, he'd expected things to get better, but the shit just got deeper.

I wasn't sure if he meant the shit had become psychologically more complex to understand or deep, as in up to his neck in it. I left him in a morose mood, contemplating his shit, I guess, and returned to my room to continue my internet search.

I googled all kinds of musicians called Luci. Who'd have guessed there'd be so many? None of the searches or pictures resembled her at all. I searched actresses in case she'd gone down that route, but nothing. She hadn't become even a tiny bit famous, which I had known, but I'd developed a vague hope that her last interaction with me had somehow spurred her on to use her talent. I had no idea why that might be the case, but now working with the assumption that my dreams weren't dreams, I thought something I'd said or done might have skewed her development in a positive direction.

I then tried a different tack and searched for Luci's mother, Beth. Almost immediately, I discovered her Facebook profile but couldn't see any mention of her daughter in recent posts. I did note she'd found herself a partner, Peter Robinson. Luci's father had disappeared shortly after she'd been born and had no input into her life. Maybe that's why her mum and my mum got on so well; their husbands had deserted both of them. Luci's permanently, mine regularly.

A feeling of doom settled in my stomach when scanning Beth's sixty-fifth birthday photos from four years ago—no sign of her daughter. Surely Luci would attend her own mother's special birthday?

I delved deeper into Beth's timeline and found a photo and a few notes at the bottom of the history, taken well before Facebook existed—a sad little footnote. A picture of Luci, gorgeous and glowing, standing on the busy main street of some exotic country, palm trees and old-fashioned cars in the background, Cuba, I reckoned. The note said.

The last photo ever taken of my beautiful, kind and loving daughter Luci. She died in a car crash in Miami two weeks after this was taken. RIP, my graceful girl.

I sat for ages staring at the photograph. Stunned didn't do my feelings justice. That's why I never heard from her again. She never came home, never made music, never fulfilled her potential, never married, never had children, never did anything.

An aching sadness settled into my soul, and tears flowed freely from my eyes. I should have gone. I could have saved her, or maybe I could have persuaded her not to go at all. What a waste. My self-loathing plumbed new depths for making another terrible choice.

I did an internet search to find more details about what happened, but the crash took place a few years before the digital age exploded, and I found nothing. I supposed that it would have been just another car wreck to the rest of the world, but to me, it meant so much more.

I had to assume that this had happened in all the threads of my life that I'd experienced. I sat contemplating everything that had befallen me. My brain was sharper than it had been when I'd arrived here, no doubt about that. University had trained it to think differently and to encompass different perspectives. I contemplated and cogitated and decided it came down to three distinct possibilities:

> 1.   I had slipped into a kind of mania, an insanity born from either the treatments being administered to me, the trauma of my life, or a combination of the two. I didn't accept this as my mind had never felt so clear, and my understanding of things had never been so comprehensive.
>
> 2.   I'd been and continued to be dreaming everything, like in *The Wizard of Oz* and at some point, I'd wake up, not in bed like Dorothy in

Kansas with my family staring at me, but back in my crummy flat waiting for the Rottweilers. I didn't believe this either, as too many things had happened, especially the dream within a dream sequence. Plus, I'd hurt myself a few times, banging my knee and stuff, and I could never recall a dream where I'd felt pain.

3. The third possibility I called my Sherlock Holmes postulation, which required a step, or more like a giant leap, into the *Twilight Zone*. Every time the Doc put me under with her amber concoction and attempted to erase the marker or switch on my epigenetic malfunction, I physically ended up back in that part of my life where the tag lay. A kind of time travel, as crazy as that sounded in my head.

Therefore, the different threads in my head weren't threads of memory but threads of timelines that had altered. The first one had almost faded now; all I could recall were the notes I'd made of being fat and very unhappy. The latter being the cause of the former.

I pondered on this for hours, arguing with myself about how it could be real. How did it happen? Did it occur to others on the programme? The last question I'd try and find an answer to at dinner, but the rest just gave me a sore head.

I'd become Angus's new best friend, and he plonked himself beside me at the table. He didn't have Molly to stare at and I probably made a poor substitute. A few of the other patients had vanished during the afternoon.

They'd gone home, I assumed, or to meet with boyfriends, girlfriends or significant others. Even Ted had found somewhere better to be than here, leaving only six of us for dinner.

The evening meal had been set up as a buffet, and I chose a well-done steak in a mint-gravy sauce. Angus went with chicken and roasted peppers. I let him eat most of the main course before asking, 'Angus, can I ask you, when they inject that amber stuff into your vein, do you have intense dreams?'

'What?'

I decided to use Angus speak. 'Amber shit. Do they inject you with amber shit?'

Angus smiled at me. 'You're shitting me, man, aren't you?'

'I don't think so,' I replied, not understanding his response.

He shook his head. 'I don't know what you're on about. Have you been smoking some shit?'

I didn't know shit could be smoked. I wouldn't imagine it would be a pleasant experience. 'I haven't been smoking any shit, Angus. What you're saying is that they don't try and fix your damaged genome?'

'Hey Sam, you know we're not supposed to discuss our treatments, or they'll kick us out, but I don't get injected with any shit. I just sit and chew the shit with the docs, that's it.'

I wondered if only I had been receiving the amber liquid treatment or just Angus *not* getting it.

After dinner, I managed to corner Stephanie, and she didn't know anything about any amber shit either.

Maybe I was the only one getting it, maybe not. I didn't feel I could challenge the Doc without exposing that I'd been asking around. Something of a dilemma. Plus, if I was the only one being injected with this experimental gunk, did I want them to continue?

Chapter 12
Someone Like You

Monday followed the usual routine. Dr Ramos focused on my university days, making notes about my descent into Gothic literature and, ultimately, my disastrous decision not to go travelling with Luci.

Of course, I didn't mention the other two versions of my life where I didn't attend university. I had to check something, just for my sanity or perhaps my insanity.

'Have you got anything in your notes about me thinking I'd been fat when I came here?'

'Fat?'

'Yep, a huge, humongous, flabby flab face?'

She frowned. 'There's nothing about that, Sam. Are you feeling OK?'

'I'm fine. I just had a notion that I might have been overweight.'

'Underweight, maybe.' She made a few notes. It didn't matter to me; I'd got my answer.

The first version now felt like a ghost of a life, slowly fading out of existence, and the second version vague and unsettling, like the remnants of a nightmare that quietly fizzles away as the morning wanes.

'Do you blame yourself for her death?' Dr Ramos asked, returning to our original conversation.

I scoffed. 'Of course I do. I could have prevented it.'

'Even if you'd gone with her, she might still have died.'

'Maybe, but perhaps I could have talked her out of going in the first place.'

'The way you've described her, passionate, headstrong, intelligent and determined, I doubt that.' She stared at me for a moment, nibbling on her pencil with her perfect teeth and perfect mouth, distracting me.

'Why does her death feel so fresh for you?'

Probably because I'd only found out about it a few days ago. I shrugged. 'I'm not sure, maybe because I've not thought about it for a long time.' Since Saturday and all day yesterday.

'So far, Sam, we've discussed your early childhood, your high school experience and now your university career. Has this brought you any peace or resolution?'

She had no idea. 'Yes, I think so.'

That must have been the correct response, as our session terminated soon after, and I had a good chunk of the morning left to hang around my room, reading and watching mindless TV.

Reading is something I'd never have done in my previous timelines unless it was a magazine or some trashy redtop.

After lunch, I made my way to the lab and found Dr Jaeger, alone this time, waiting for me.

'Take a seat, Sam. Before we go any further, we need to have a chat and restate some ground rules.'

Uh oh.

'Stephanie Fredericks let it slip in our discussion this morning that you've been asking her about her treatment.'

'I only asked her if she'd been getting the amber shi… amber liquid.'

'The rules are we do not discuss each other's treatments.' I liked how she said that as if she was *also* being experimented on.

'How many of the twelve are being given the amber liquid treatment?'

Dr Jaeger stared at me for a moment before answering. 'One.'

'Just me then.' The answer didn't surprise me.

'Just you.'

'Why?'

'The simple answer is that you had the most corrupted DNA sample. As you know, thirty-two pieces of damaged genome that can be targeted.'

I hadn't realised what a mess I was/had been compared to everyone else, but then I should have.

The Doc set her notes aside, leaned forward and asked me. 'So far, we've undertaken what we hope are repairs to two faulty switches and, in theory, your brain should now be receiving improved chemical messages as a result. How are you feeling?'

'Better, I suppose. I might have felt better anyway just being away from the stressful situation I'd gotten myself into. It's hard to know, really.' It sounded like a very non-committal response as it emerged from my mouth, but being honest would bring on the straight-jacket scenario. 'Can I ask? Before me, how many have received this treatment?'

'You are the sixth.'

Now the big question. How to phrase it. 'Did any of the others display… or exhibit any strange behaviour as I did initially?'

The Doc considered the question.

'They manifested some unusual reactions. One woman, Rebecca, had convinced herself that she'd become a time traveller. We had to discontinue her treatment as continuing might have led her towards a dissociative identity disorder. She may have been harbouring the condition before we began her treatment, but we had no record of it. She had been certain that before her first session, she'd had red hair and that we'd dyed it blonde whilst she'd been sleeping.'

She paused, and I watched her as she smiled. 'Do I look like a hairdresser to you?'

I shook my head, though the same had happened to me, as my grey hair had vanished along with the excess body weight.

Exactly.' She continued, 'She'd convinced herself that she'd returned to her childhood and prevented her younger sister from drowning in a lake. Strangely enough, her natural hair colour *was* red, but when she'd arrived here, her hair had already been blonde. As for her sister, she turned out to be alive and well and living in France.'

I tried to hide my excitement at this revelation and nodded thoughtfully as the Doc continued.

'Some of the others were a little bewildered and confused after their treatment, but that is to be expected, and as we went on, it seemed to lessen, and the confusion reduced as we progressed.'

The Doc admonished me about speaking to the other patients then Nurse Paton appeared and undertook her usual health check.

Later, as the syringe slipped into my arm and the dark warm blanket of unconsciousness slid over me, I felt confident that my version of reality was, in fact, the only version of reality that mattered. To me, anyway.

I woke up in the tiny room of my old-shared student flat in Edinburgh. I'd lived in the residence halls near Haymarket for the first year of my university course. Then, I rented a room in a shared flat in an old tenement block for the next two years. The apartment, situated just off London Road near the Omni Centre, was within walking distance of at least fifteen bars.

Thinking about it. Almost anywhere you live in Edinburgh is within walking distance of at least fifteen bars.

If this had happened previously, I would have believed I'd been experiencing a very vivid dream, but I realised something I should have realised sooner.

Smells. I could smell. I'd never been able to smell in a dream before.

In my first timeline, I remembered my primary school teacher's perfume, and in the second one, the stink of cigarettes from the kids as they rushed past me and Luci's intoxicating scent as she leaned close to me. Now, the pungent stench of my university bedroom assailed my nostrils. It was overlaid with something else that I couldn't quite place.

I checked the date on my watch Sat Jun 5. I didn't know the year. Was it my second or third at university? Beside my bed, splayed on the floor where I must have tossed it earlier, I spotted a manual from the car manufacturer I went to work for after graduating. I picked it up, and the page I'd given up reading had been all about health and safety. I assumed then that this must have been/be my final year. I realised with something approaching elation that Luci had not yet died or travelled to Miami. Judging by the pile of female clothes and paraphernalia lying around the room, she'd gone either to find food or to the bathroom. The latter, never a pleasant experience for visitors to a flat shared by four blokes.

It wasn't an enjoyable experience for any of us either, but we'd got used to it. Then I recognised the overlying scent that pervaded my room, the smell of sex.

Luci came bursting back through the door, wearing one of my shirts and her knickers. 'Jeez, Sam, that bathroom stinks. It's a rancid health hazard. I'm sure someone has died, and you've hidden them under the floorboards.'

I stared at the loveliest face I'd ever seen, ever would see. All the emotions of the last few days rose to the surface, tears formed in my eyes, and I started wailing. A shocked Luci immediately sat on the bed. I grabbed onto her, never wanting to let go, ever.

'What's wrong, Sam?' I couldn't speak. 'OK, I'm sorry I won't mention the bathroom again.'

'I've missed you so much,' I squeaked from under her breasts.

'I've only been gone a few minutes.'

'It felt like forever,' I mewled.

'Are you OK?'

'I'm emotional.'

'Now that, I could have guessed.'

I took a deep breath and lifted my head. She kissed my tears away, and I smiled, drinking her in, her face, eyes, body, scent, everything. 'You're freaking me out, Sam.'

I shook my head. 'Sorry, I don't mean to. I just want to stay like this forever.'

'You'll probably get hungry.'

'I'll eat you.'

'So, you'll become a cannibal.'

'If that's what it takes never to leave your side, yes.'

She pushed me away playfully. 'What's got into you?'

'You?'

She cocked her head to one side. 'Actually, it's probably the other way round, isn't it? And now I've been to the toilet; we can do it again.'

'Yes, please.'

Making love to Luci is/was the nearest thing to heaven I'll ever experience. Yes, for the then me, it had probably only been a few hours, but for forty-year-old me, it felt like the first time. I literally never wanted to be apart from her, holding that body, kissing that mouth, touching that face. I felt myself welling up again but managed to sniff down the tears. Lying entwined together afterwards, Luci asked me what I knew she'd come here to ask me. The last time she'd waited until we'd gone out to eat, but my emotional outburst must have made her decide this would be a good time.

'How set are you on starting this new job?'

'Why?'

'I'm thinking of going travelling.' She rolled over, leaned on my chest, rested her chin on her hand, and stared at me. Those eyes, God, I loved those eyes.

'Travelling where?'

She shrugged. 'The Far East, Thailand, Vietnam, Australia, maybe the Caribbean and Florida too.'

I, of course, knew the outcome of that, but I couldn't exactly blurt out, '*Don't go to Miami or you'll die*'.

'Why are you telling me?'

She gently punched my arm. 'Because I want you to come with me, silly.'

I smiled. How could I have ever resisted that face? I still felt that she was holding something back. That intuition from years ago persisted in the here and now, or was it there and then? The timeline thing confused me.

'There's something you're not telling me?'

She frowned. 'Is there?'

'I think so.'

'Well, if there is, I can't think what. Well, what do you think?'

And here it was, the chance to change history. Rebecca had saved her sister. Could I save Luci? What repercussions would that have for my life, for her life, for the world? If she lived, what effect would that have on her mother, the people she'd meet and interact with? Changing something like this could have huge repercussions, but would anyone realise? Probably not. I used to be fat, but now nobody but me seemed to remember. Even I only remembered because I wrote it down. I wondered why my notes didn't vanish, a puzzle to puzzle over later.

It wasn't like Luci would go on to be a mass murderer. All she could bring to the world would be happiness and light.

'If I say no, will you go anyway?'

She stared at me. 'Probably, but I'd rather go with you.'

'What about the other guys you dated over the last few years? Why not one of them?'

She smiled. 'And there it is, the little green-eyed monster. I'd been wondering when he'd show up.'

'That's a little sexist. Why should jealousy be a male?'

'If you're jealous, then it's a male. If I'm jealous, then it's a female.'

I considered her answer, 'OK, I'll let you have that.'

'Very generous of you. Now back to my question, are you coming with me or not?'

'I might.' Inside I was jumping up and down, screaming YES FOR CHRIST'S SAKE, YES, but I knew that's not how the twenty-one-year-old me, twenty-two in three weeks, would react.

'And what would it take to turn that might into a yes?' she asked, slipping her hand under the covers. God, I was horny *again*. When people say *I'd love to be twenty-one again,* they say that knowing it'll never happen, and yet here I was, living that statement, living that moment.

'That could work?' I said, pulling her on top of me and locking my lips to hers. What the hell did she see in me? I had to try and remember that back then, I hadn't spent another two decades simmering in misery, brewing up the self-hatred potion I chose to sip from for all that time. At this stage in my life, I had hope and ambition. Plus, I'd stopped the bullying in primary school and hadn't pushed this incredible girl out of my life on the last day of high school. I'd also lived up to the promise I'd made to her to make something of myself by going to university after my mother's death.

Now I had the opportunity to save Luci's life, not that she knew. She'd probably never know that, but it didn't matter.

Later, sitting in the Italian restaurant sipping wine we couldn't afford, she asked me again. This time I said yes, 'But there are a few conditions.'

She leaned over and kissed me. 'Wonderful, what conditions?'

I'd spent most of the afternoon thinking this through. I handed her a notebook and pen.

She looked at them. 'What, I'm your secretary now?'

I giggled, so happy, so high on life. Being with this girl after so long felt incredibly liberating; I felt like I could fly. I'd never been this optimistic, this joyous. How could life have ever been this good? Well, it never had for me. 'Just for a few minutes. I want you to write some stuff down and never forget it, even if I do, OK?'

'Why would you forget it?'

I laughed it off. 'Just in case my head's mush after all the exams.' I didn't know if, when the younger me got his head back, if that was the proper term, did any of what I'd said and done whilst I'd been in there, stick. Or did the younger me return to a few blank hours or days, depending on how long I got to hang about? This would be my insurance policy, Luci's insurance policy.

'First of all, we're not going near Florida.'

'Why not?'

I had an answer ready. 'I want to take my kids there one day. I want it all to be a huge, mysterious and exciting surprise for me and them.'

She peered at me for a moment. 'Kids, future, that's not like you, Mr Harris.'

'There's a lot you don't know about me, plus it's the US. It's not that exotic, is it?'

She chewed on her lip. I loved it when she did that, and then she grinned. 'Yeah, OK, no biggie.'

'Go on, then write it down.'

'OK, bossy. Next.'

'When we get back and get jobs, we need to buy as many shares in the following companies as we can, Amazon, Nike, Alphabet Inc, Apple, Microsoft, Domino's Pizza, any pharmaceutical group and pretty much any computer games manufacturer,, but to be safe just stick with The Games Workshop PLC, and I suppose we have to include JD Sports though the owners not everyone's cup of tea.'

'What is all this?'

'Have you written it all down?'

'Yeah, I think so, but I've not heard of half of these companies.'

'You will do.'

Luci put the pad and pen down, leaned over and searched my face. 'There's something different about you?'

She wasn't kidding. 'I've just grown up a bit.'

She shook her head. 'It's not that. I came here this weekend expecting to have to force you to come with me on this trip; in fact, I'd been preparing myself for you saying no. I'd thought you'd never walk away from the job you'd been offered, not even for me, especially not for me after what happened.'

I'd forgotten how bright Luci was. I might just have tickled her spider-sense. I needed to tread warily. I sighed and took a slug of wine. 'Luci, when you broke up with me, it shattered me. It really did. I'm not going to lie, I even briefly might have hated you for doing that to me, but my literary journey over the last few years has taught me that the line between love and hate is very slender.

'After I'd had some time to simmer in my own bitterness, I eventually understood why you did what you did. We were young, we're still young, and you needed to *be* young. I'd been too possessive, too suffocating, and too....' I searched for the right words. 'In your face, I guess, it's the best I can come up with. Now, I'm different. Yeah, I'll still make mistakes, mess up and no doubt piss you off, probably without even knowing I've done it or how, but one thing's remained constant, even when I've been dating other girls, you were the one for me. You always have been, always will be.'

I sat back and drank some more wine and watched her face as a frown became bemusement became a smile. 'You never told me you'd been out with other girls?'

'Ah, the green-eyed monster,' I smiled. 'I wondered when *she'd* show up.'

Chapter 13
Wherever You Will Go

I added a few more conditions to the notes, and as much as we wanted to order more wine, neither of us could afford it. Especially when we could nip into the local supermarket and buy three bottles for the price of one in the restaurant, and that's precisely what we did.

We drank wine and made love for hours, eventually falling into drunken slumbers. Our bargain concluded, well, almost concluded.

I feared that when I awoke next, I'd be back on the Doc's bed with her hovering nearby, waiting to interrogate me. But I didn't. I woke up with my beautiful girlfriend lying half in the bed, half on the floor. Not that there was too much difference between the two, my 'bed' being little more than a mattress on a shallow wooden frame. The floor wasn't that much dirtier either, well, not considering all the dried and drying bodily fluids on the sheets.

I stared at her sleeping face for a few minutes, enjoying watching her whilst she didn't know. Her dark hair had fallen half across her cheek. However, I could still see her perfect nose, slightly turned up at the end, her lips, still looking like they had lipstick perfectly applied, impossible given the amount she'd used them in the previous few hours, her long eyelashes and highlighted cheekbones. If you set out to design the perfect face, I was looking at it, but I was biased and in love.

Even though we'd ploughed through almost four bottles of wine, I only had a mild headache and a slight thirst. I forgot that the young me, the young everybody, seemed immune from hangovers. If I did that now, I'd probably not be able to move for three days and would need to drink the taps dry like the tiger from *The Tiger That Came to Tea*. Not all my literary subject matter had been Gothic.

I gently nudged Luci with my foot. She mumbled something and rolled over, now entirely on the floor. I stepped over her and relieved my aching bladder in our fragrant bathroom. When I returned, she'd woken up and had pulled some fresh clothes from her bag.

'Are you not having a shower before you put clean clothes on?'

She blinked at me. 'You sound like my mum, trust me, that's not good. When did you turn forty?'

I laughed. 'About ten months ago.'

'Yeah, don't do that, eh? Besides, I'm not having a shower in this place. I'll catch Ebola or something worse.'

'COVID.'

'What?'

'Nothing, just a virus nobody's heard of yet.'

That look again. 'Like those shares.'

'Yeah, listen, it's just something one of the economics students told me about. Who knows, eh?'

Her expression showed me she didn't buy into my explanation, but she looked too weary to care. Plus, she'd achieved her objective much easier than expected, but that's hindsight and perspective for you.

She pulled on her jeans and trainers. 'Let's get some breakfast. There's a cafe on the corner, isn't there?'

'Yep. Something fried and bad for you.' I smiled.

'We've all got to die of something.' She laughed, pulling me out of the flat.

Just not in a car wreck in Miami, I hoped.

We sat in comfortable silence and focused on eating. Luci mopped up some egg yolk with a piece of toast, finished chewing, then asked, a note or two of concern in her voice, 'You're sure you *are* OK about giving up this job?'

I nodded, my mouth full of sausage and fried egg. I gulped it down. 'Totally, I'd have hated it; doubt I'd have lasted two years.'

'Why apply for it then? Plus, the last time I spoke to you, you were so enthusiastic about it.'

Good question. Then I remembered the employee manual on the floor beside the bed.

'I read through all the HR shit they sent me, and it's far too rigid a regime. Like being in the army.'

Luci frowned, her spider sense tingling again, I expect. I had to remember that she knew me better than anyone in the world, yet despite that, she still loved me. (That old self-hate still survived inside my forty-year-old brain, trickling poison into my psyche).

'Anyway, if I did that, I'd always wonder, what if? Wouldn't I?'

'You really should use your degree properly. Are you sure you wouldn't like to try teaching?'

I shook my head vigorously. 'Trying to get high school kids to appreciate Shakespeare, Dickens and Hemmingway, no thanks.'

'Well, as long as you don't blame me for giving up this opportunity.'

I smiled. 'I won't, sweetie, I really won't. What are you going to do when we get back?'

'I haven't thought about it, I've made a showreel that I'm supposed to send to producers and things, but I've not done any of that because I'm now going away with you. I'll maybe do something with it when I get back. Loads of the folk from my course are attending auditions in the West End, but I'm still unsure what I want to do.'

Luci had played the piano from an early age. I remember watching her when I used to go to her house for a playdate—squished up beside her on the padded piano seat, mesmerised as she coaxed swirling melodic magic from the keys.

I hadn't seen her play for over a decade. She must be fantastic by now. 'That song you sent me was incredible. Why not become a songwriter.'

'Just like that.' She laughed. 'I wish. I can play OK, but songwriting is changing. It's become much more producer focused with the growth of DAWs.'

'Doors?' I asked, puzzled.

Luci smiled, 'D-A-W-S.' She spelt it out for me, 'Digital Audio Workstations, computerised musical software, it'll revolutionise music, and how it's written and produced, we did a lot of that in our final year.'

I didn't understand what she'd said, and it didn't seem to explain why she couldn't write songs, but it didn't seem important at that point.

She finished her coffee and announced, 'I need to go home today, and by home, I mean home to my mum, not London. My London days are behind me for a while, but no doubt I'll end up back there, seeing as it's the centre of the universe for the arts. I should spend a few days with her before we head off. Plus, we need to organise tickets and stuff. How much money do you have?'

I pretended to do a calculation in my head, counted some numbers out of my fingers and eventually said, 'Let me see if I include that and the money from there and the cash in the box, it'll all add up to about twelve pounds fifty.'

Luci giggled. 'I thought as much. What about your flat deposit?'

'Well. Assuming they give me anything back, considering the state the place is in, that's six hundred max, but I'll need that for the next place.'

'Worry about that later; that'll at least get your plane ticket. I've saved about three grand, mainly from money my mum gave me, but I didn't spend. If I add that to my flat deposit and throw your money in, that gives us about four and a half thousand pounds. Not a fortune, but it'll get us somewhere and pay for budget hotels, plus we can get bar jobs and stuff as we go along. It's enough.'

'I can't let you pay for me.'

'Course you can, you can pay it back when we get home as you're likely to get a proper job, and I'll end up waitressing and waiting for auditions. I'm under no illusions of how hard it will be, so I need to do this. Are you not going home too?'

'I suppose; grumpy pants works on shore now, but he's considering emigrating to Australia to live with his brother. He says I don't need him anymore.'

'You're all growed up,' she said in a baby voice, smiling.

'I am, but I never really needed him, did I?'

She sighed. 'I suppose not. I'll pack up my things and get out of your hair by lunchtime, OK?'

'It's not OK.' I could feel tears pricking the corners of my eyes. Her eyes were liquid too. 'I need you now,' she whispered. I became instantly hard, harder than I'd been in Miss Baxter's class all those years ago.

Later, before she slipped out of bed, and before this version of me slipped away forever, I asked the question I'd been waiting to ask all morning and most of last night until the wine pushed it towards the back of my mind.

'There's something you're holding back, Luci. Before you leave me again, even though it's only for a week or less, I need to know what it is?'

She lay back on the pillow, turned, faced me, and pushed her forehead onto mine like she'd done all those years ago on my last day of high school. 'I don't want to talk about it.'

'I know, but I need to know.'

'You don't need to know, you just want to know, and I want to tell you, but I don't know how.'

I could feel a circle of anxiety forming in my stomach, a whirlpool of acidic worry beginning to spin into a frenzy of unrest. It must be something terrible. 'What happened?' I whispered.

Tears formed in her eyes. They slowly spilt out and fell onto my cheek and the pillow. I shared her tears. How intimate was that? Her breath mingled with mine, and she said quietly, 'A few months after we split up, I did something stupid with someone I didn't like. I had unprotected sex and ended up pregnant.'

'Who, the Liam guy?'

'No, an older guy, a lecturer, I know, so stupid. He wasn't interested in anything long-term. Besides, he was married and… Oh, Sam, I had an abortion. It was so awful.'

I didn't move or say anything, trying to figure it out, but I couldn't. As a man, I didn't possess the emotional intelligence.

'How did they do it? I mean, is it painful?' I knew nothing about abortions.

She shook her head. 'No, you just take some tablets, and it's done if it's early enough, just like a bad period. It's just the mental side of it, you know.'

I didn't know. How could I? I just held her tight as she cried. I cried, too, for many reasons and for many people, most of them different versions of me and her that I'd known. 'I love you, Luci.'

She snuffled. 'I love you too.'

We drifted off to sleep. Our foreheads pressed together, skin to skin, erotic, comforting, natural and beautiful. We fitted so well together, physically and mentally.

I awoke bewildered and distraught to find myself back in Cholis Lab 4. The Doc and Nurse Paton were peering at me. They did the usual checks and asked me some banal questions.

I answered the best I could. 'Doc, I'm sorry,' I said eventually. 'I'm always a little confused after these sessions, and my mind usually needs a few hours to settle.'

I gave her a vague version of meeting up in a dream with Luci at university but didn't elaborate. After about half an hour of interrogation, she let me return to my room. I sat on my bed with my personal raincloud floating above my head. I should have returned from this timeline bouncing around the room with elation. I'd been with Luci, and I'd saved her from dying, I hoped. The memories from this version of my life had yet to drop into my head, so it remained a mystery, but something troubled and dug its nails into the soft, vulnerable tissue at the back of my mind. The feeling of lying naked, warm, and loved up lingered, and I tried to bask in its glory.

As I lay on the bed, I realised my body had morphed again. Not back to humongous but no longer skinny, I had muscles, six-pack abs and bulging biceps. I'd become a gym bunny.

The other timelines had faded further. The original version of fat me waiting in the grubby flat for the bailiffs had gone completely. Only the notes I'd taken remained.

On the table in front of the mirror sat a MacBook and a set of car keys. I picked them up. Ford. I owned a car, a step up from my previous timelines. Attached to the car keys were other keys, house keys? Flat keys?

I still didn't remember, then the missing jigsaw parts of my memory plink plonked into place like a crazy game of Connect Four. As they landed, I gasped, groaned and finally howled as my poor tortured soul once more screamed to the heavens for release.

Chapter 14
Summer Smile

Time, as a wise man once pointed out, is what stops everything from happening all at once. The problem with new memories is that you don't get the time and space that real memories accumulated over time afford. As they drop in, they produce surprise, unguarded pain and pleasure like a series of electric shocks. This time, more than any of the others, their effect on me felt greater. Raw and intense, probably because the changes I had wrought were more pronounced.

Bonus memory, Luci didn't die in Miami. We had a ball, cycling through jungle villages in Vietnam, the hedonistic cities of Phuket, Pattaya and the craziness of Bangkok. Then we enjoyed the peace and tranquillity of Southeast Cambodia, followed by the relatively civilised time we had in Melbourne working in a bar for four weeks to earn enough money to get back home. I waited tables, and Luci played the grand piano every evening, dressed in a ball gown with a ridiculous tiara perched on her head. One evening Luci sang one of her original songs that summed up her feelings about her time in Australia. Called *Summer Smile*, it went down a storm with the locals. She played it every evening after that.

We'd grown as people and as a couple. During our last evening in Melbourne, emotions were running high. Our time together with no responsibilities and no real cares apart from where to eat, sleep and make love was nearing an end. We sat in a small restaurant overlooking the St Kilda Sea baths. I didn't want to go home. I didn't want reality to interfere with our wonderful dream.

As we sipped ice-cold Chablis holding hands, I gazed at my beautiful girl's tanned face and said, 'Luci, I love you more than life itself, more than anything. Will you marry me?'

Tears slid down her face, happy tears, I hoped, as she stared deep into my eyes. She nodded. 'Of course, I'll marry you. Why wouldn't I?'

On that warm September evening, I'd become the happiest person in the universe: no doubts, no concerns, just pure, unsullied joy.

Back home a week later, reality set in.

I had to go back and live with my dad in his small flat and Luci with her mum. Both parents were happy for us, but at that point, we didn't have two beans to rub together and getting married seemed like a distant fantasy.

Another thing. Britain smelled terrible. I wish we'd stayed in Australia. So clean and organised compared to home. Plus, Oz had space, Britain didn't. Well, at least my part of Wigan didn't. Our street was filled with 1930s tiny, terraced houses bumped up against one another with dingy backyards and overflowing bins. The refuse collection strike being the main cause of the stink.

Every night of the last three months, I'd fallen asleep entwined in Luci's arms. Now I squirmed in a small single bed with a lumpy mattress.

I had to take a job, any job to be near Luci, to try and save some money to get a place. I answered a vacancy for a counter-staff role in a Manchester bookmaker, just a stop-gap. I told myself. I might have said that once before, but I couldn't be entirely sure. Bookmakers seemed to be another common thread too. Weird how things repeat themselves.

Luci found a job waitressing in a restaurant, long hours, exhausting work minimum wage.

I hardly saw her.

Talk about crashing down to reality.

We settled into our new restricted lives. Luci had a few auditions in London for West End roles, but they didn't turn into anything. 'I need to be there when stuff comes up.' She explained, 'Half the time, open auditions only get advertised on the day or the day before, and I can't get there on time.'

I could see the frustration building, four years at Guildhall to work in a restaurant seemed like such a waste of her gift. Not that I'd been using my degree either, checking betting slips and emptying bins.

My dad had sold the flat, and I'd soon be homeless. If we pooled our resources, we might just be able to rent a flat in London, nowhere nice but somewhere where we could be together again. Luci eventually found a place near Catford described as a studio flat consisting of one large room and a separate bathroom containing a full-size bath. Luxury indeed.

We moved in a month later. I transferred from the bookies in Manchester to a branch just off Lewisham High Street, and Luci found a job waiting tables in a bistro pub called Angelo's in Greenwich. We were all set. I could tell Luci wasn't happy being back in London, but what choice did she have? What choice did *we* have?

One rare evening when neither of us were working, we sat sharing a bottle of wine, taking stock of our lives. It's hard to be objective when you're both permanently knackered. My hours were stupid, Luci's were worse, but she also had to try and squeeze in auditions between her shifts.

The nights when we used to fall asleep entwined in each other's arms felt like a distant memory. Luci also objected that any spare money we had, I'd sunk into shares of companies that had yet to hit anyone's radar in a big way.

I pulled myself from the past for a moment to consider something. I'd been watching my memories play like a movie on Netflix. I stopped and went back in my head to the days before we went travelling. The younger me seemed to have no recollection of being invaded by the older me, which I couldn't quite compute. It felt like, in the previous times when I'd intervened in the shittiest bits of my life, the me of the time just accepted it and moved on.

Whilst I could remember the high school intervention and, obviously, the still fresh in my mind, and my loins, if I'm being honest, the day Luci came to my flat in Edinburgh, there remained no residual clue that the older me had ever been there. If I wasn't mad already, and I'd started having doubts, this would get me there, PDQ.

I remember reading a quote in my studies that said, *all we are is memories*. It felt very relevant.

I needed a break from thinking and pottered out of my room into the car park, bleeped my key fob, and watched as the lights and door locks on a white Ford Focus lit up and popped up, respectively.

I opened the driver's door and sat in the seat. It felt familiar and unfamiliar at the same time. I had some new memories of driving this car and also, of living in a flat in Solihull that by some miracle seemed to be mine, supported by a small mortgage. Exactly how I'd ended up living in Birmingham again escaped me at that point.

I felt like I'd drifted into the asylum or maybe I'd never left. A few days ago, according to my notebook, which I had no reason to disbelieve, I'd been evicted from a dirty rented flat, had been pushing twenty stone and didn't have a penny. My childhood sweetheart, for lack of a better description, had been killed in Miami, not that I knew that at the time, and a social worker had taken pity on me and got me into a programme to try and help with my depression.

My notes also said I'd once tried to kill myself, but I had no recollection of how. Oh, and I used to stink.

In this timeline, I'd ended up married to Lisa again. It felt like a failure, more for Lisa than for me. I could feel the disappointment in my soul, but it seemed that I ended up with her no matter what I did. I wondered what she'd done in a previous life to deserve me.

Luci and my fate made me want to scream, so I refused to go there yet. I wanted to know about the me of today first. Plus, I'd realised something. The time I spent in the past didn't marry up with the time in the present/future or whatever now was/is. I'd spent around thirty-six hours with Luci in my stinky student flat, but that only translated to three or four here. I couldn't quite get my head around that.

I returned to my room and powered up the MacBook. By osmosis, I assume, I knew the password and the password to dozens of other things I'd never owned or possessed before.

An online share portfolio icon blinked on the desktop, and beside it was an online bank account, I checked the bank account first, and it had a healthy balance.

I had to check the share account three times before I could understand them. The total value of shares spread across a portfolio of investments sat at a few pennies over one hundred thousand pounds. Well, shag me backwards with a hairbrush.

Chapter 15
All Messed Up

I joined the other residents for dinner, and none of them seemed to have changed or been changed by my experiences. I didn't know if I should be surprised at this or not. Angus still talked about shit, Ted still mumbled about Darwin and smacked himself on the head regularly, and Molly still didn't make eye contact. It was weird to think that none of them had changed, and yet my life had altered beyond all recognition since coming here, and none of them knew or noticed.

I'd also acquired a proper iPhone with a contract. I scrolled down my messages whilst munching on cheese and biscuits. Angus said, 'That's rude, man.'

I smiled. 'I suppose it would be if anyone had been trying to make conversation, but we're all sitting here like zombies, so I don't think it is.' I carried on scrolling, looking for something from Luci, not that I deserved any contact from her.

I read a few texts from Hannah, my girlfriend. She'd sent me a pic of her sitting on her couch in her underwear, pushing up her boobs and pouting. Hannah and I were intimate. That memory had dropped in just before dinner. She is a lovely woman. I liked her. I didn't love her. Despite being wealthy, healthy and, from what I could tell, living a decent life, I'd still ended up in Perry Flowers.

After eating, Angus and I played pool for a while. Neither of us said much. Angus didn't seem very happy. I wondered what 'shit' he'd been sharing today. I asked,

'Have you noticed anything different about me since I've been here?'

He peered at me from under his floppy fringe. 'Nope.'

'I mean physically or personality-wise?'

He stared at me. 'What are you on about?'

I smiled. 'Never mind.' We carried on playing pool.

I escaped to my room a few minutes after seven, opened the Mac and logged onto Facebook. I had hundreds of friends now, not that I considered any of that real in the sense that I'd become popular. Most seemed to be acquaintances from school and university. I still had a smattering of Filipino would-be brides and a few other dubious contacts. I scrolled down them all; Luci wasn't there, not that I should be surprised by that.

I found her easily enough. She wasn't married, but her status said 'in a relationship' with Sandy. Sandy, a muscled rugby type, appeared in a few of her pics, usually with his arms around her waist, looking like the cat who had got the cream. Why shouldn't he? He undoubtedly had.

I hoped he treated her better than I did. No kids that I could see. I wondered about that. Had she been too busy building her career to have any? Did she still harbour the guilt of the life she ended before it began all those years ago, or did it just not happen for her? Questions I'd never know the answers to.

I typed her name into Google and discovered her Wikipedia page. It listed all her major stage roles. She'd never crossed over to TV or films and had spent her whole career to date on the stage, not to be sniffed at but not the level of fame I might have expected given her talent. Still, she'd looked happy on her Facebook page, though I struggled to remember a Facebook photo when someone didn't look happy, so that might not tell me the whole story. Whatever she'd achieved, it had been better than dying in Miami. Despite the pain I'd caused her. I *had* saved her life. Not that she'd ever know that.

Now that all this time had elapsed, maybe I should find her and try and explain the truth of what had been happening to me. Then I realised that there would only ever been one timeline for her, and she'd never believe me. Nobody would. The straitjacket beckoned.

I also had to remember the version of me that had screwed up, didn't know *what* he'd screwed up, nor the number of chances he'd already had to get it right. He didn't understand any better. Could ignorance be an excuse? No, not really, but we all make mistakes and bad decisions; we're human. It's what we do.

I switched off the computer, lay back on my bed and let the painful memories wash over and through me.

The recollection of our parting stabbed at me. Time to fully remember and embrace it, I supposed.

I'd still been working in the betting shop, but Luci had been successful in a few West End auditions, building up her profile through roles in smaller productions. Her break came when the female lead in the musical version of *Fifty Shades of Grey* (don't ask) went down with tonsilitis. Luci had been her understudy and stepped up, proved better than the original and kept the part to the end of the run. Only three weeks, but I'd been surprised it ran *that* long.

It provided the springboard she needed, and after that, she began getting invited to auditions rather than fighting to get them.

I remember the night she came home bouncing off the walls after landing the lead role in *Oklahoma*.

I'd just got off work, and despite being exhausted, her enthusiasm and VA VA Voom perked me up. We'd gone out to celebrate, dinner at The Hobbit (an expensive themed restaurant in Lewisham) and then into town for drinks and a club in Soho. For us back then, that was really pushing the boat out, believe me.

Her days of waiting tables were over.

I'd been over the moon for her and proud, so proud. She'd worked incredibly hard and suffered much disappointment. Sitting in an alcohol-fuelled bubble in the club, she'd said, 'We can get married now, Sam, well soon anyway.' She glanced down at her crappy engagement ring. I know the tradition is to spend a month's wages on a ring, but if we'd done that, she might have got a nice ring, but we'd have ended up sleeping rough and dining out at some of London's finest soup kitchens.

She didn't care. It was symbolic, anyway. One day I'd buy her a beautiful ring when all the shares leapt in value, which didn't look like happening any time soon at that stage in our lives.

I wanted so much to be her husband. I'd have been so privileged that I'd have never looked at another woman ever again.

A few days later, on a rare evening at home together, Luci decided to ruin everything. Well, in reality, I did that, but she started the ball rolling.

'Sam, before we start planning our wedding properly, I need to tell you something. I don't want there to be any secrets between us.'

I sat up from my slouch on the couch. I didn't think we had any secrets, but her face had such a serious expression etched on it that it worried me. I started running through some possible scenarios. She'd been shagging the director of *Oklahoma*, but then I remembered the director's name, Brenda, and I don't think my fiancée had any lesbian tendencies. Maybe she'd started an affair with her stunningly handsome opposite number David Hopkirk, but then Luci had said he was so in love with himself that nobody had been good enough to bask in his aura, male, female or anyone in between.

It came from the past. Our past.

She took my hand and put her forehead against mine, as she'd done so many times before and said, 'Sam, I know you won't take this well, but before you react, I need you to try and think about where we were and what we were doing at the time OK? I should have told you then, but I didn't have the courage.'

'What is it?' I whispered, my stomach churning.

'Remember the abortion I had.' She gulped. I nodded.

'It wasn't a lecturer that got me pregnant. It was you.'

I pulled back from her like the polarity of two magnets suddenly reversed. I tried to think it through, but it didn't make sense. I should have figured out the answer myself, but I asked. 'Why?'

She stared at me. Tears formed and trickled down the face I loved, which I'd adored for as long as I could remember. 'We were so young, and I....'

She paused and tried to compose herself. I watched as she swallowed a few times, trying to stem the flow of tears. 'I didn't want to give up on my dream. I knew what you were like. You'd have wanted to keep it for us to be a family. I wasn't ready.'

The pieces fell into place one by one. 'So, you didn't want to go away and experiment at all? You hurt me so much when you did that.'

'I know, Sam and I spent so much time trying to think of another way of dealing with it, but I couldn't. I just needed some space. I felt guilty enough and seeing your face would have just made it worse. Please forgive me.'

I did forgive her, well at least I said I did, but it changed things between us. Looking back now, I know it shouldn't have. We loved each other, our love should have been stronger than that, but her success had begun to grate on me. Would that have happened if she'd never confessed? I don't know.

Even now, that sounds muddy, muddled, and selfish. I have the luxury of knowing how my life played out without her; back then, I didn't. I had changed my destiny and Luci's by letting her have a life, but I didn't know that then either. Confusing or what?

It took the wind out of my sails. I'd been ready to jack in the betting shop job and try to do something where I could use my degree. A recruitment company had lined up some interviews for me with financial firms in the City, and I also had a meeting with a digital magazine based in Canary Wharf. I didn't go to any of them.

Hindsight is wonderful for pointing out the mistakes you have made in your life. It's not so good at pointing out what you got right. It's a harsh judge, even with the benefit of time travel.

Basically, I blew it. On the second Friday of January, I'd gone out for a few beers after work. Luci had been on a run of twelve straight performances, including two matinees, and we'd been like ships in the night. It had been like that for a while.

None of that would have mattered without her confession. Now, for me, it did. Doug, the betting shop manager, had treated us all to cocktails and flaming sambucas on empty stomachs. One by one, everyone drifted away, leaving just Doug and me. We were the only two without someone waiting at home. Divorced Doug and a West End Widower, as the other cast members' other halves called themselves.

We went to a club and after a while, Doug disappeared with some ditzy blonde. I'd been on the verge of going home when Gina, the daughter of one of our regular customers, spotted me. I knew her quite well by then. She often came into the shop begging us not to let her dad squander any more of his money on the horses.

We eventually banned him from the shop, but I doubt it would have made any difference as there were about six other bookies within walking distance of ours.

Gina was easy on the eye, blonde hair, electric blue eyes and privately educated. She spoke with that kind of Keira Knightly accent that was just heaven to listen to.

Now, I could use the excuse that I'd been drunk, horny, stupid, tempted, all of them, but the real reason was that I was lonely and resentful. Resentful of Luci's success, as small and as petty as that sounds, especially after all I'd done to encourage it.

I slunk into our flat at 5 am, and Luci instantly knew I'd cheated. She could tell, I don't know how, probably just how I looked at her.

She screamed, bawled, hit me, and did everything I'd expected her to do. Yelling at me in Spanish, which she always did when she got furious. Of course, to the twenty-three-year-old me, this had been the first time I'd let her down, but to the forty-year-old me, it was at least the third and maybe more, as my memory of the previous timelines had become tenuous.

Eventually, she calmed down, packed a bag of essentials and said, 'I'm going to stay with Camilla for a few days, then I'll look for my own place. Don't contact me, Sam. I never want to see you again.'

Camilla? I didn't know Camilla unless she'd made a new friend in the Royal family, but that summed up how much I'd been involved in her life of late. Was that my fault for not making more of an effort, or both our faults – who knows, whoever knows in situations like that?

A few weeks later, she emailed me a song she'd written. Her way of coping with things, I guess. Titled *All Messed Up*, it was very apt. Later she probably wished she'd never sent it. It only encouraged me.

The anger and frustration built up—a catalyst to making many more poor decisions. Not attending my father's funeral, being broke was not a valid excuse in this timeline, marrying poor Lisa again, and then there was the stalking.

Encouraged by her sending me the song, I had this forlorn hope we could fix things. Perhaps there would have been had I not acted like a crazed loon.

One particular freezing February evening came to mind. There'd been a bitter wind blowing, biting and ripping at my jacket. I'd concealed myself in amongst the autograph hunters and the fame seekers at the stage door. All of whom, hoped that a fleeting meeting or a smile from a performer will either: 1. Rub off on them and allow them to climb their own escalator to fame and fortune, or 2. Impress the actor/actress/performer/singer so much that they will fall instantly in love with them on eye contact. Yeah, I know, about as likely as me winning Boyfriend of the Year.

The door opened, and a few of the cast emerged. I stood waiting for the autograph hunters to do their thing. Besides, Luci hadn't appeared yet. I watched the usual scramble of books, pads and occasionally, a bare arm being scrawled on with biros. Then she emerged, standing at the door, her head facing inwards, talking to someone, her dark hair fluttering in the breeze. She turned, spotted me and visibly wilted.

This had been the eighth successive night I'd stood here and been ignored. Just as she went to turn and disappear back inside, I pushed through the pack and yelled, 'Luci, please don't leave me here again. I only want to talk. You won't talk to me. You won't answer your phone. I love you, please I want you back.'

That was the first time I got duffed up by security and arrested for trying to force my way into the theatre. It wasn't the last.

A fist in the face from a huge security man, followed by police intervention, handcuffs and a trip to the local nick.

That bitter winter evening gave me my first experience of being on the wrong side of the law and my first taste of a police station at night—an alien landscape populated by drunks, working girls and a few other assorted nutters like me. The booking sergeant undid my cuffs to allow me to sign his sheet.

'A caution this time, son,' he said to me. Calling me son felt incongruous. He wasn't much older than me. I signed, and they booted me out into the cold darkness.

The next time I had to remove my belt and shoelaces and spent the night in the cells.

The desk sergeant and I became familiar, but not in a good way. I usually turned up with a black eye or busted nose courtesy of the theatre security staff. The last few times, I'd been picked up before the show ended and transported to my evening accommodation, a thin mattress on a cold metal bed and a cold metal toilet.

Solicitors became involved, and I was fitted with an electronic tag and warned. Eventually, common sense prevailed, and I gave up.

How we'd gone from leaning our foreheads together to a restraining order in under three months evaded me.

As I sat cogitating in my Perry Flowers room, I knew for sure that whenever Luci wasn't in my life, my life wasn't worth being in.

I could feel the resentment and injustice the twenty-three-year-old me still felt, shocked at how everything had fallen apart around him/me in such a short time.

I don't know if it boiled down to her denying me a child when, ironically, I had done that to poor Lisa multiple times now, which did give me a new angle on her feelings. Beyond that, however, I think it came down to the fact that Luci had *told* me.

She didn't need to. It felt unnecessary. Should couples tell each other everything? I don't know, but based on this example, probably not. Ignorance really can be bliss. I know her motivation had been true and beautiful, like her, but she'd also carried the burden of that truth for a long time alone. I'm pretty sure there had been an element of unburdening going on.

But who else could she have unburdened to? Plus, I truly loved her and should have been able to accept and share that burden. But I didn't.

I could understand it but tempered by my multiple trips down my own particular and personal rabbit hole, looking back, all I had to do was forgive her, and I didn't, couldn't.

Chapter 16
Two Out Of Three Ain't Bad

All the money had come from the shares, and even despite making some poor investment decisions like investing in a building project in Dubai that went bust, I had plenty.

I also had a rewarding job. I wrote technical copy for car makers, engineering firms and white goods manufacturers. For anyone who needed an idiot's guide put together for consumers to refer to, I'd become the go-to guy. I ran a limited company with myself as the sole employee/director and felt proud that I'd achieved something professionally that didn't involve hiding from creditors or working in a bookies.

Self-respect was a new emotion for me and combined with a healthy amount of Self-respect and self-discipline, big changes had certainly been wrought, despite my failures with Luci. I couldn't help but smile, despite losing Luci, undoubtedly all my own fault, I had at least learned from my mistakes and made myself a life, a good one by all accounts.

I'd met Hannah at a local book group I'd joined, mainly to get out of the house. Being self-employed and working from home turned out to be quite a lonely and isolating experience. My simple brain said, *you like books join a book club.*

Hannah wore her dark brown hair short, her face revealed two perfect dimples when she smiled, and her hazel eyes were flecked with green. She possessed a fit persona that she worked hard on maintaining with running and gym work. As a teenager, she'd been a gifted middle-distance runner who'd made the England reserve squad for the Commonwealth Games. A recurring calf injury eventually put paid to any chance of her being a professional athlete, but she remained svelte. Her motivation had been behind me in developing and maintaining my current fitness schedule.

Whilst Hannah didn't look like a bookworm, she managed to read her way through three novels a week. We sometimes didn't make love until she'd finished her latest book and I'd taken to arranging my conjugal visits (well that's how it felt) between novels. It gave *between the sheets* a whole new meaning. All this stuff had appeared in my head and felt real and unreal at the same time, like living inside some weird US science fiction series.

Hannah, sexy, funny and her book obsession apart, was brilliant company. So why didn't I love her? Well, the answer to that is easy. Luci. Even though in this timeline she's with someone else and I have no chance of ever being with her again, my stupid psyche won't accept this and hankers after what it can never have.

Recently, my spirit and personality had sagged, which is why Hannah encouraged me to send in a sample of my DNA to Perry Flowers for this project.

She'd read about it in a magazine. 'Sam,' she'd said, turning the page around for me to read. 'Look at this, it's a study of depression.'

'I'm not depressed,' I'd countered.

She'd tilted her head to one side and raised her eyebrows in the way she did when she wanted me to know she disagreed with me.

'Not yet, but you're on the way and they want to catch people before they fall down the slippery slope, at least that's what it says.'

I complied and duly sent off the sample and, yes, this time I wasn't wheeled in by a desperate social worker, I applied, got accepted probably due to my incredibly damaged DNA and walked in all by myself, well walked in from the car park at any rate.

I wondered what my poor put-upon social worker Sally would make of all this. The Doc did treat me differently this time, as a bona-fide volunteer not some sad sack at the end of his tether. The reason for that of course had been completely down to the Doc's treatments though she obviously didn't know that, and I couldn't tell her. It did give me an idea though.

I had a session the next day with Dr Ramos, but my follow-up with the Doc had to be postponed as she'd gone off sick with food poisoning. I kicked my heels for a few days before she felt well enough to return and requested a meeting with her before we undertook any more procedures. In the previous versions of myself, I doubt she'd have agreed to meet me like that.

I sat in her office, wondering how to frame my request. It would be awkward, but it felt to me like something I had to do.

'I hope you're feeling better,' I offered as an introduction.

'Much, thank you, but I'm guessing you didn't want to meet to discuss *my* health?'

'No, now I know this will sound off and it may not be allowed, but I've been wondering if it would be possible to meet up with any of the other people who have been undergoing this…' I paused to find the right word, 'experimental treatment. I'd just like to compare notes with them.'

The Doc sighed. 'Patient confidentiality is paramount in our programmes. What exactly do you want to compare notes about? I might be able to give you some details without breaking any ethical codes?'

I needed to tread carefully. She wouldn't remember our conversation about the girl who thought she'd saved her sister. 'It feels like things have changed a lot for me since I arrived in here and started the treatment, I feel so much better, and I wanted to… well I guess I wanted to see if it continued to provide long-term benefits. Talking to someone else who's been through it might help.'

The Doc peered at me. 'I haven't noticed any huge changes, Sam, you seem very similar to the day you walked in here?'

I remembered that her version of me and my multiple versions of me were a million miles apart.

'I know, but I really do feel a lot better, and do you think there comes a point where you feel as good as you're going to feel, and any further intervention becomes unnecessary? If I could compare notes with someone who had already completed the programme, then I might be able to judge when that would happen.'

A shaky excuse I felt but the best I'd been able to come up with.

The Doc tapped her pen on her pad. 'The questionnaire you completed prior to coming here stated that you suffered frequent mood swings.'

I had no recollection of completing a questionnaire. Maybe that memory had been lost or hadn't appeared yet. I wondered how long it took for my cognitive processes to fully embrace the new timeline. I also worried that my brain might run out of space like a computer's memory. Perhaps mine was nearing its capacity and I didn't think I'd be able to simply upgrade my storage limit or offload things to the cloud.

Mood swings. I suppose that might be true, especially after the mess I made of things with Luci sixteen or so years ago, but it didn't sound like something I'd put on a form. I shrugged. 'Well, I suppose they may be a reflection on how I hadn't been dealing with life particularly well.'

The Doc frowned. 'Sam, I'll be honest with you, your genome is one of the most damaged we've seen, so far, which is why we decided to invite you onto the programme. As you know the treatment is experimental and controversial, but, when we first met you, we thought we'd made a mistake with the genetic testing and ran it again.'

'Why?'

She puffed out her cheeks. 'Well to put it bluntly, we expected you to present as a complete basket case, with no social skills, almost unemployable and displaying a lack of self-worth and poor self-esteem. But you are a successful man with a partner, and a business and come across as intelligent and well-rounded. Given the trauma you've had in your past, this is something of a revelation.'

If only she knew. 'So far, I've had, what, three treatments with the GPC?'

'Yes,'

'Yeah, OK, but that's three treatments and as you know I'm always a little confused when I wake up. Each time have you noticed any subtle differences in my appearance or manner?'

The Doc pondered my question. 'Appearance?'

Jeez, this was complicated. 'Nothing major.' I lied. 'Just like maybe, I don't know increased muscle tone or fewer wrinkles around my eyes or something?'

Jaeger smiled. 'This isn't a cosmetic surgery facility if the GPC had properties like that, I'd be taking it myself.'

'Fair enough. OK, what about mental sharpness and an improved outlook on life?'

'Is that what you've experienced?'

Given I'd come in here an uneducated smelly fat lout and now had an English Lit degree and ran my own company I'd say that qualified. I nodded. 'Yeah, I think so.'

'Well, by removing the anomalies on your genetic record and freeing up those particular proteins to do their job, so to speak, I suppose this may have had some effect on your overall well-being. After all that's what we're hoping for, but you presented to us as reasonably well-adjusted, to begin with, so in your case, any changes will be subtle.'

If only she knew. 'Let's suppose, I'd been what you'd expected me to be, lacking in self-esteem, unable to look after myself, overweight with poor hygiene, etc. What changes would you expect in an individual like that?'

I could see the wheels in her head going around as she thought about my question. 'I suppose we'd expect more recordable improvements. Removing the anomalous emotional markers for such an individual would bring about changes in behaviour, self-worth, confidence and the ability to make decisions based on logic. We'd also expect them to be able to assess the consequences of their decisions with understanding and foresight.'

'So, what you're saying is that if I had been obese then by removing the switches that made that behaviour part of my psyche, I'd lose weight?'

She nodded. 'Probably, over time with proper diet and exercise and the right mindset.'

'Also, would you expect this person who has lost out in life to be able to go out into the world and live well, attract a partner and undertake a meaningful career?'

'That would be my hope yes, and much quicker than we'd expect that to happen using conventional treatments.'

'This GPC concoction, what's in it?'

'That I can't discuss.'

'OK. My dilemma here, Dr Jaeger, is that I can feel the subtle changes you have alluded to, but I have nothing to compare it with. You've got your notes from previous patients and therefore have some way of making a comparison, I don't. That's why I wanted to talk to someone who has already been through it.'

I didn't think my entreaty would be enough, but she surprised me.

'I can't promise anything, but I'll speak to a couple of our previous participants and see if they'd be willing to talk to you. I need to contact them every so often for a follow up anyway, but it will be entirely up to them if they say no then that's the end of it, I'm afraid.'

Better than I'd expected. 'Thank you.'

She nodded and as I got up to leave asked, 'There's something you're not telling me isn't there?'

Sharp cookie. There was so much I hadn't told her, couldn't tell her. I had to give her something. 'You're right. I have absolutely no memory of filling in that questionnaire.' I left quickly before she could respond.

Chapter 17
Complicated

The following day, I awoke and found that the latest memories had taken centre stage, and the other lives I'd lived had become mere whispers in the background. Perhaps my brain had uploaded the extraneous material to a cloud somewhere, after all.

I had a telephone conversation with Hannah, which felt normal and surreal at the same time. We'd been together for nearly two years, yet part of me had never met her. I wasn't sure how we got on, whether she'd be a confidant of all my secrets or if I kept a lot to myself.

Because I couldn't remember completing the questionnaire, I took it as a warning that not all my history of late with her would be complete. I probably came across as guarded and vague, but she didn't say anything. Perhaps that's how I always came across. It wouldn't surprise me. We still lived in separate homes, after all.

After she hung up, with a promise to call later, my mind felt muddled and confused. I took out my notebook, wrote down the latest saga in my life, and read back over the older notes to remind myself of my incredible journey. Journey. That sounded like a *Britain's Got Talent* contestant spiel. Trip might be better, tripping even—a better description.

I didn't for one second disbelieve all the various accounts. Even if, they did all feel like they'd happened to someone else. What resonated was the pain I'd caused Luci and, consequently, myself across multiple timelines. That all felt real, too real and poor Lisa, I'd inflicted myself upon her three times at least. She must be a glutton for punishment.

After breakfast, Dr Jaeger called me into her office. Today, for the first time, she hadn't donned her white coat but wore a short summer dress, entirely at odds with the freezing weather outside, but what did I know? It made her look younger and more feminine. Her dark hair had been pinned back with a clasp, and she seemed more approachable. The white coat put up barriers between her and her patients. Maybe that was the point. She smiled and beckoned me to take a seat.

'I have some news for you, Sam. One of the previous programme participants is happy to discuss her experiences with you. The only drawback is that she didn't complete her full treatment plan, but it's the best I can do. There were a few issues with her participation. She had a strange reaction.' She once again told me of the time travelling obsessive.

After a moment, the Doc paused and stared at me. 'Have we discussed this before? It feels like déjà vu?'

I shook my head. Interesting. Perhaps that's what déjà vu is, or what happened when someone else's timeline crossed yours and changed things. Worth thinking about later. In the meantime, I didn't want to interfere with my chances of speaking to this person.

'Anyway, Rebecca, whose real name is Elizabeth Auld, can only see you today as she's working the rest of the week, so you need to get a move on.'

'Why Rebecca?'

'On clinical trials like this, we publish the results periodically and therefore allocate pseudonyms to all the volunteers.

'OK.' What did I know? 'She'll talk to me in person?'

'Yes, she said it cannot be discussed on the phone.'

'Where does she live?'

'Dartford.'

The Doc handed me an A4 piece of paper. Printed in a small font was her address and phone number.

I stood to leave when a thought occurred to me. 'What's my pseudonym?'

'Bob Cratchit.'

'Oh, OK.' Being named after a literary character felt strangely appropriate.

I quickly returned to my room, picked up my jacket and notebook, and headed to my car. The car I'd never driven and yet had driven every day, probably. I put the address into the sat-nav, and it told me it would take around two and a half hours.

The traffic on the M1 turned out to be horrendous, and nearly three hours after I left, I pulled into a fashionable and new-looking block of apartments, amazed I'd arrived in one piece. I'm confident I'd never even passed a driving test in at least two previous timelines.

I found her name on a list of buzzers at the apartment building entrance and pressed the button. A tinny voice said, 'Who is it?'

'Sam Harris, Dr Jaeger spoke to—' I didn't get to finish as the door clicked open.

I entered the foyer, unsure of which flat she occupied, not the ground floor, I assumed, as her name appeared halfway up or halfway down the list, depending on how you looked at it. I started to climb the plush carpeted stairwell, and on the first landing, a door opened, and an attractive woman wearing a green top and jeans with red hair and pale skin appeared. She reminded me a little of Lisa, whom I kept marrying for unknown reasons. She said, 'Sam?'

I nodded.

'Have you got any ID?'

'Driver's licence?' I fished about in my wallet and stared at it like it was the first time I'd seen it, which it was really. I handed it to her. She read it, nodded, and said, 'Please come in. Sorry, you can't be too careful.'

I followed her through to a large sunny lounge overlooking a park across the main road. 'Nice view,' I observed.

'The reason I bought the flat,' she explained. 'Tea, coffee?'

'A coffee would be lovely, thanks.'

She disappeared through a door which I assumed led to the kitchen. I appraised the furniture, grey leather couch and matching chairs, wooden flooring and a smattering of photographs around the pale cream-painted walls. Two in particular, caught my eye.

The first one, set against an exotic backdrop, palm trees, and a sunset, showed Elizabeth and another striking looking girl, holding hands.

The second one depicted Elizabeth, a few years younger, her arms around another girl, who bore more than a passing resemblance despite the dark blonde hair. Her sister, I assumed. The one she'd told the Doc she'd saved. I don't think the Doc had ever told me her name, she might have, but if she had, it had got lost somewhere.

Elizabeth returned to the room carrying a tray and caught me staring at the picture. 'Me and Charlotte.'

She said smiling, 'The photo that never should have happened.'

'Dr Jaeger mentioned that you'd left the programme early because you insisted that you'd travelled through time. Can I ask, how many treatments did you have?'

Elizabeth sat in the chair, took a sip of coffee and appraised me. 'You look all right.'

'Thank you. I think.'

She smiled. 'Not what I meant. Things might have changed on how she picks people now, but before I attended the clinic, I'd been a complete mess.'

'Me too. Did you go to Perry Flowers?'

'Is that a florist or a holiday resort?'

I laughed. 'It does sound like it, doesn't it? No, it's a clinical set-up in Birmingham.'

'I went to the Derwent Facility in Margate, overlooking Dreamland.'

'The theme park? I went there a few times as a kid with my mum. Very run down from memory. It closed; I think.'

'Yeah, well, it's open again and seemed busy and noisy enough, that's for sure. Back to you? How many treatments have you been through?'

'Three so far.'

'Have you noticed any changes?'

'Before we talk about me, can I ask about your experiences?'

Elizabeth drained her mug, plonked it down onto the wooden coffee table stared into my eyes, searching for something. I'm not sure what.

'Sure.' She sighed. 'What the hell.' She reached over to a bookshelf near her chair, pulled a notebook from under a pile of magazines, opened it and quickly scanned the first few pages. She took a deep breath and began.

'I started with a kind of soul-searching session with a therapist called Virginia, then the chief of the project, Dr Jaeger, tried to explain what she had planned for me but to be honest, at the time, I probably wasn't in the best place, to take in much of what she said.'

I nodded. 'Same here.'

'I remember drifting off to sleep and waking up in my old house.' She paused and looked at me. 'I know how crazy the next bit will sound, but I found myself back inside my body as a little girl, a few days short of my seventh birthday.'

I smiled encouragement, 'Go on.'

'Well, it turned out to be the day we were due to head off to the lakes in Cumbria. My parents had rented this cottage on the edge of Lake Windermere. Initially, it felt like a dream, just watching events happen, but then I realised I could influence things and make changes. I sneaked out and deflated one of the tyres on the car. That held us up for an hour or two, but we still went.

'When we got there, I tried to explain to my dad that renting a canoe could be dangerous and risky.' She smiled. 'I remember him staring at me like I'd become possessed, you know? Here was I, this little girl using grown-up language and pleading with him like an adult with this full understanding of risk and consequence that I don't think even *he* had. I freaked him out.'

I watched her pause, and her face dropped. 'Charlie still drowned that day. My dad didn't listen and still rented that bloody canoe. Just as the ambulance arrived too late, I keeled over and woke up in the clinic, totally distraught. I convinced myself and the doctor that it had only been a bad dream. Dr Jaeger blamed it on the earlier discussions where I'd dragged up my sister's death.'

I interrupted. 'They did that to me as well. I suppose that's how psychiatrists think.' Something puzzled me. 'Dr Jaeger told me that your sister hadn't drowned and had been happily living in France all along.'

Elizabeth smiled. 'Yeah, she is now.'

'I don't understand.'

'A few days later, they put me under again, and I fixed things properly this time. I smashed a bloody great hole into the canoe with a hammer.' She giggled. 'My dad came out to find me wrecking the bloody thing. I think he genuinely did believe I'd become possessed. When he tried to take the hammer from me, I started snarling, screaming, and threatening him. Anyway, it worked. We never did go out in a canoe, and my sister never drowned. Happy days.'

I told her about my earlier experiences and waking up seven or eight stone lighter, and nobody believed me, then the whole saga with Luci. 'I genuinely thought I'd lost my mind.'

'I'm not surprised.' Elizabeth smiled at me. 'You're certainly not fat now.'

'One thing puzzles me about your sister, this epigenetic thing they do, targets the faulty switch or gene and fixes it. If they did that the first time you went back, how could you return to the same time and place again?'

She shrugged. 'I'm guessing it didn't get fixed because I didn't save her the first time.'

I had to think about that. The answer seemed obvious, of course, but I hadn't considered it. The epigenetic regression, or whatever it's called, only works if what is wrong with the timeline/genome is sorted. The actions I took to fix the things that went wrong reset the faulty switch, allowing the Doc to move on to the next one. The revelation made my head hurt.

Elizabeth then posed the question I suppose I'd come to ask myself. 'Are we time travellers?'

'Either that or we're both suffering the same psychosis; unlikely but not impossible, I suppose. If we are travelling through time, it's not in the way you read about in science fiction books or see in films but in a fashion that's very specific to us. Very personal. I wanted to hear your experience as I'm still unsure if I'm deluded, mad, or both.'

Elizabeth agreed. 'I'm sure Dr Jaeger has no idea at all about the incredible forces she's meddling with. She had all kinds of psychological explanations for what had happened, which I half believed at the time. The key is that stuff they injected into us. All her experience is counting against her.'

'How so?' I asked, keen to hear someone else's view of the whole thing.

'She's too educated and grounded in her profession. She'd never believe any explanation like ours, and why should she? From her point of view and all those around her, nothing has changed.'

Elizabeth reached out and touched my arm. 'We've had an incredible chance to put right what once went wrong in our lives. I got booted off the programme when I tried to explain it, plus my hair had changed colour. I'd dyed it blonde for some reason but didn't remember that until later. I accused them of colouring my hair whilst asleep.'

I smiled, 'The doc mentioned that.'

'The thing is.' Elizabeth continued. 'My main regret in life had been fixed at that point, so leaving didn't bother me.' She stared at me for a moment. 'Your life perhaps went a lot more wrong than mine?'

I nodded. 'Maybe.'

'So, I'm guessing you've still got unfinished business with this girl of yours.'

'I think so. I'm in much better shape than I used to be.' I focused on her notebook. 'One thing puzzles me, well…' I laughed. 'Lots of things puzzle me, but your notes, my notes, are the only link I've got to who I used to be. I assume yours are the same. Why does everything change when we return, yet the notebook remains unaltered?'

'Not just the notebook.'

'What do you mean?'

'I typed everything into my laptop, it's all still there, but it doesn't save to the cloud. If I try, it vanishes.'

'How weird is that?'

She smiled, and her eyes sparkled. 'I know because we wrote them, they are not tarnished by whatever changes when we go back. I don't know why that is yet. I've been reading a lot of stuff, theoretical science mainly, since this all happened to me. I have a few ideas. It might be because, for lack of a better word, we temporarily exist outside of the various timelines after each event. Only for a short while, until all the memories are fully established in our heads.'

She squeezed my hand. 'I'm so glad you reached out to me. I wish I'd taken the chance to do it earlier. Dealing with this, wondering if you're the only one or if you're completely barmy, isn't easy. I haven't encountered anything that explains or even partly explains what is happening to us. Maybe it's multiple universes, some quirk in quantum mechanics or perhaps a benevolent God. Who knows? Honestly, I don't care that much. I'm just glad it happened.'

We were silent for a moment pondering on everything, and I mean everything.

I asked, 'How is your sister now?'

Elizabeth scoffed. 'She's fine. She married her boring accountant boyfriend and moved to France. We don't see much of each other. We never really got along all that well.'

'After all, you did for her?'

Elizabeth laughed. 'Yeah, well, she doesn't know that does she? I tried to tell her once, but she just looked at me like Dr Jaeger did, and I never mentioned it again.'

'Still, it's a shame.'

'It's complicated.' She stopped speaking and studied me for a moment. She indicated the photograph I noticed earlier. 'That's Paula, my girlfriend. We split up recently. We'd been together for three years. I thought we were forever, but nothing's forever, I guess.' She dropped her eyes. 'My dad's always been cool with it. I think he knew early on, I'm not sure how, but neither my sister nor my mum were comfortable with my… life choices, I suppose.' She stared at me for a moment. 'Can I share an observation?'

I nodded.

'From what you've told me, it feels like every time you go back. It's like you're trying to future-proof your life.'

'Like you did?' I countered.

She considered that for a moment. 'Not really. I had a terrible childhood. Charlotte died, and then I told my mum how I felt about myself and the world a few years later. Back then, she genuinely thought it had been an illness, a mental aberration, which could be cured. But then, by that point, she'd already lost one daughter, and I guess the guilt weighed heavier on her than me, and my dad never forgave himself. Well, you wouldn't, would you?'

I shook my head, agreeing with her.

Elizabeth took a moment. 'At the time, I thought that perhaps her attitude towards me had been about losing a daughter, but her emotions never changed even when I'd returned and fixed that. It had nothing to do with my sister's death and everything to do with my mother.

'In the first version of my life, I left home at sixteen and shacked up in a hovel with a drug dealer called Mick. He abused his own body and mine.

In the second version, that never happened. By going back and saving Charlotte, I changed her life by *giving* her a life, but by doing so, it changed mine immeasurably for the better. You need to do the best you can. It's not an exact science.'

'If it makes you feel any better, I've married and left the same woman at least three times now.'

She gawked at me. 'Why?'

'I have no idea. Whenever I wake up and relive the latest timeline, poor Lisa's in there.'

'It's like fate. Elizabeth said quietly.

'Bad karma, more like we're not good for each other.'

'Weird.'

I rubbed my face. 'It's all beyond weird. I reckon I need therapy to help me deal with the therapy.'

Elizabeth guffawed a real belly laugh.

I didn't want to pass judgement but said, 'It's the twenty-first century. Nobody cares anymore about gender, sexuality and stuff.'

'My family does.' She sighed. 'It's OK. I've learned to live with it. No choice.'

We chatted for a while about Dr Jaeger and Elizabeth's plans. She'd applied for a new job in central London working in the operations department of an investment bank and joined an online dating site. As I got up to leave, she took a selfie of us. 'Just in case I ever doubt this meeting happened.' she smiled. I knew what she meant. I wished her all the best with everything.

On my way back to the clinic in my car, I felt sure I could now tick insanity off the list of possibilities.

Elizabeth might be right, of course, and we were sharing a joint psychosis, perhaps a side-effect of the amber concoction, but I didn't think so. I had Elizabeth's number and promised to phone her after my next session. If I shifted the timeline again, would she remember my visit? That would be an interesting exercise but one for the future, or maybe for the past. I'd begun to lose track.

Chapter 18
I'm Not In Love

Back in Perry Flowers, I phoned Hannah and had a strange conversation about people and places I didn't know and yet knew very well. She said she missed me. I agreed. A part of me missed her, both her nature and her warm body. A portion of me didn't know any of this at all and watched on from the sidelines, wondering what the hell was going on.

I fell into an uneasy sleep around eleven PM.

I awoke the next day feeling refreshed and updated my notes with the latest changes while I still could. I showered, admiring the hard, fit body I'd acquired, dressed and headed down for breakfast. I ignored the croissants and ate fruit and cereal. I still drank coffee.

It is very unsettling knowing that until recently, I had been a different person, mainly because that other person still lurked somewhere under the surface, waiting for his chance to eat crisps and cake, become miserable and drip poison into my brain.

I had my session with Janice and recalled my most recent failings. She told me I'd not be needed until two-thirty, so I arranged to meet Hannah for lunch. She had a half-day and wanted to see me. I was curious to meet her, too, to see if my thoughts and memories of her matched the reality.

At three minutes past twelve, I found myself sitting in the small Italian restaurant she said we loved just off Broad Street. I'd eaten here with Hannah many times and yet never at all.

We'd gone to see plenty of movies afterwards in Cineworld, including the various reboots of *Jumanji*. Hannah always teased me about getting the hots for Karen Gillan in her shorts. We also went to see any new blockbuster action movies that came out. Hannah loved them. I always pretended not to enjoy them, but I always did. A kind of game we played, sipping Diet Coke and sharing popcorn.

The restaurant menu seemed familiar and a mystery at the same time. I knew what tasted good and what I usually ate. I ordered Chicken Penne Arrabbiata for Hannah and a crispy-based pepperoni pizza for myself, along with two Diet Cokes.

She'd texted me telling me to order, which I'd already done, weird, whilst she parked her car. Two minutes later, she plonked herself down opposite me, leaned over, kissed me, and smiled.

Prettier in the flesh than in my memory or the photos in my phone, she had an animation about her that I remembered now as she sat opposite me. Her arms waved around as she talked, and her smile and dimples widened and waned as she told me all about her boss George, ticking off her friend and colleague Amber, for not wearing the company attire this morning.

Hannah worked for an online insurer. I couldn't for the life of me remember which one. I have said before. Not everything comes across intact. I did remember George being talked about as a stickler for rules. He wandered about the office with the procedures manual open, checking stuff. I had met him a few times, and he'd seemed OK, but I didn't have to work with him.

Eventually, Hannah wound down as our food arrived. She speared some pasta and asked, 'How's it going then?'

I nodded. 'OK. I feel better.'

She smiled. 'See, I told you, you would. Sometimes you need to listen to someone who loves you.'

I smiled. 'Yep, you were right. I hope I can go home soon. I know I could walk out anytime I want, but I suspect a few more treatments will ensure I don't relapse.'

'Treatments?' she asked.

I didn't want to mention being injected with experimental 'shit', as Angus would say. 'Yeah, you know, therapy sessions and stuff.'

She put her fork down. 'They're not doing weird stuff to you, like electric shock therapy, are they?'

I scoffed. 'Of course not. That's not even legal anymore, is it?'

'I don't know, is it?'

'I don't know.'

We both laughed, and Hannah picked up her fork and ate. 'I miss you,' she said from under her long eyelashes.

'I miss you too,' I replied. Most of me did. A chunk of me didn't know what I *might* be missing, and a small piece of me didn't even know who the hell she was.

I munched on pizza and wondered what Hannah saw in me. Thirty-two, nearly eight years younger than me and lovely. I knew her relationship history, the miscarriage she'd suffered with her ex-boyfriend Paul, the messy breakup where he emptied their bank account and re-mortgaged her flat without her knowledge. He used the money to pay off some gambling debts that Hannah knew nothing about. Then he'd posted some videos online of them having sex. It took her nearly six months to get them taken down. They still occasionally popped up on obscure porn sites, so she told me. I'd never gone looking for them.

I'd told her about Luci, but I don't think I ever explained the pain that parting had caused me. Another blip on the genome, I suppose. We all have them. I just seemed to have more than most.

I reckoned a bit of me, well, quite a lot of me, still viewed myself as the fat, miserable loser who messed everything up. I probably appeared attractive, fit and successful to Hannah, though she had spotted some hint of the darkness inside me. That's when she'd encouraged me to apply for Dr Jaeger's programme.

I didn't know what might change if I took another trip into the *Twilight Zone*. I might still be with Hannah, or perhaps I wouldn't. My life now felt like it had got into some decent shape, in fact, very decent shape. Would another course or two of the treatment make things worse or even better? I didn't know.

Should I stick or twist?

It would be so easy to go home now with Hannah, accept the status quo, which was undoubtedly a million times better than where I'd been a week ago and count my blessings. I could rip up the notebook, scatter the paper into the wind and accept what I had, by all accounts, a pretty good life.

A part of me however, would always wonder, what if? Could I live with that?

Again, I didn't know. That was my problem.

My relationship with Luci had been wrecked, but so what? Doesn't everyone have relationship regrets? Why should I be any different? Why couldn't I move on and accept the love of a wonderful woman and live my life from there?

The answer seemed very clear. I didn't love Hannah. As much as I knew I liked her, it wouldn't be fair to her as things stood. She'd suffered enough with her twat of an ex-boyfriend for me to '*Do A Lisa on Her*'. That wouldn't be fair to her or me in the long run.

The real problem, I reckoned, was that whilst a large part of me had parted with Luci many years ago, a piece of me had only suffered that fate a day or so ago and had not had time to process and heal. I felt conflicted, unsure and off-balance mentally with everything. If I waited and let the other memories completely fade and perhaps destroy my notebook, I'd eventually settle into this version of me and might grow to love Hannah as she deserved to be loved.

But what if I didn't? I knew I'd been lucky to land like this. Hannah was gorgeous, intelligent and funny and yet…I shook my head …enough of the self-indulgent introspection. I fully engaged with Hannah and focused on her for the remainder of lunch. We talked about her work, and thankfully, she mentioned the name of her employer, Parador Insurance, and as soon she said it, the missing bits plink plonked into my brain. Memories of some Hannah work nights out that I'd been invited to also dropped in. Jen, who shared a pod with Hannah, sang in a local band. We'd been to see them a few times. Jen liked to dress minimally out of work, and Hannah teased me about me staring at her thighs, trying to glimpse her knickers in the micro-dress she wore on stage. A task made even more intriguing when Hannah told me Jen generally didn't wear any.

After lunch, we walked in the park across the road. The afternoon, warm for late October, allowed us to saunter with our jackets undone, kicking through the piles of fallen leaves like kids. During moments like this, I saw Hannah as she was, viewing the world with child-like innocence, despite the dark times she'd endured. As well as her scummy ex-boyfriend's antics, her father had died just before Christmas last year following a stroke. Sudden and shocking, with no time to say goodbye. It deeply affected her for a while, which is why we'd not moved in together. We'd talked about it often, but after her dad passed, it hadn't been mentioned for a while until now.

'I've been looking at houses on the internet.'

'Have you now,' I said, smiling.

'Just curious, we'd have to sell our places first, but you know it's maybe time we moved on?'

I nodded. The part of me that had been with Hannah for ages knew this had been coming. The other bits of me just watched. 'Let me finish this therapy. Then I'll look with you, OK?'

'Really?' she said, grinning. 'I thought I'd have to use some of my charms to persuade you.'

I pretended to be disappointed. 'Aww, silly me. OK, then I'm not moving in with you, never.'

She giggled. 'Too late now, Mr Harris.'

'Damn.'

Interestingly, her gentle demand helped me make my decision. It made me feel uneasy, like I'd be giving up and saying goodbye to Luci forever. I knew I had lost Luci in this life, but perhaps I still had a chance in another life. Decision made, I'd finish the therapy with Dr Jaeger and see where it took me, que sera, sera.

Chapter 19
Misunderstanding

Later that afternoon, I lay down again on the bed in Cholis Lab 4 and discussed my feelings and perceptions of the world with Dr Jaeger as we worked through Janice's notes. She briefly asked me about my meeting with Elizabeth. 'She still believes she travelled back in time and saved her sister.'

The Doc narrowed her eyes and searched my face. 'Is that what you believe is happening to you?'

'Of course not,' I lied.

I'm not sure if psychiatrists are fitted with a better version of a bull-shit detector than ordinary folk, but she just nodded and said, 'We like to undertake follow-up sessions with all our patients. Elizabeth Auld is one of the few who, so far, has resisted such an approach. One of the reasons I had for asking her to meet you is that I hoped speaking with someone from the programme might change her mind. I want to talk to her again, help her perhaps.'

'I think you did help her,' I said, smiling. 'She saved her sister.'

The Doc shook her head and returned the grin. 'Yeah, OK. Back to the matter in hand.'

I drifted off to sleep as usual as the needle full of glowing amber liquid flowed into my veins.

This time I opened my eyes to complete darkness and silence. As my eyes grew accustomed, I could make out some shapes and heard a distant car horn.

In the warm bed beside me, I recognised the sensual scent of Luci Lawrence. It could be nobody else. The question was where and when.

I carefully slipped out from under the duvet and shivered in the cold. Winter then, I assumed. I carefully picked my way across the room as I recognised the restricted space and furniture of our London flat.

I emptied my aching bladder in the bathroom and checked my watch, 3.45 am. As elated as I felt to be back with Luci, and as much as I wanted to wake her up and make love, I knew she probably had rehearsals and a show tomorrow and wouldn't welcome the attention.

I didn't know the date. Was this before or after her confession?

I needed to gather some intel before I made any huge gaffs. I didn't fancy groping around trying to find Luci's phone. Also, putting on the TV at that time in the morning was a non-starter. What else had a date on it? Of course, sitting on the breakfast bar, which also doubled as our dining table, hot desk, coffee table, occasional sex platform (once, not to be repeated), and general dumping ground was yesterday's *Evening Standard*. I tried to view the date, but the light wasn't good enough, so I carried it through to the bathroom and closed the door before flipping the light on —Thursday, 12th January.

That meant today was Friday the 13th, which sounded ominous enough without working out the day's significance, which I hadn't yet.

Creeping back into the main room, I spotted Luci's mobile. A Motorola RAZR, in red, that flipped open. Bought to allow her to get advance notifications of auditions. She'd been so proud of it. I remembered the two of us sitting for ages waiting for a video to load on the 3G technology. How far we'd come since then.

Working in the bookies, ten minutes from home, I didn't need a mobile.

I slipped back into bed and snuggled, spooning against Luci's back. She mumbled something, and I slipped my arm around her. She held my hand but didn't wake up. I smiled in the darkness. I felt like I'd returned to where I was meant to be.

I awoke to an empty bed, well half-empty. I rolled over and saw Luci sitting at the breakfast bar, reading a magazine and drinking coffee. The clock at the side of the bed said 07:15. I needed to leave the flat in less than an hour. I felt like taking a day off, but that would bring forth many questions I probably wasn't equipped to answer.

'Hi,' I said.

'Sleeping beauty awakens.' She smiled at me.

God, she looked stunning, even just awake with no make-up and sleepy eyes. I stared at her. I couldn't help it. Whenever I spent time with her, I felt like the luckiest man alive. I compared it to the recent lunch with Hannah, and I'm sorry to say it didn't compare. The strength of feelings I had for this woman was simply incomparable.

'When's your first interview?'

What interview? 'What interview?'

She smiled. 'You told me last week that a recruitment agency had scheduled some interviews for you.'

Of course, they had. That meant today, or rather tonight, was the night. Another massive blot on my genome, I suspected. Friday the 13th should have been enough of a trigger to etch it into my memory.

'Next week, I think. I've got a note of the dates somewhere.'

'Good, you need to get a proper job. You're wasting your talents in that hovel.'

Only one talented person occupied this flat – the goddess sitting on a bar stool staring at pictures of shoes. I might have put her on a pedestal this morning, but my psyche felt super psyched as part of me hadn't seen her for years. I laughed at my insight.

Luci looked up from her magazine. 'Someone's chipper today.'

'It's Friday.'

'And that's good because?'

I knew what she meant. For her, it involved performing to a packed house. All her performances were in front of packed audiences, but Friday evenings sprinkled an extra magic ingredient into theatreland. It was the evening when most of the audience didn't have work the following day and tended to over-indulge both pre/during/post theatre, making them a little more restless and raucous.

Then, of course, hot on the tail of Friday, Saturday followed with a matinee and an evening show. Luci always came home exhausted on a Saturday night.

For me, Fridays were very busy. Those who still got paid weekly usually appeared between 3 pm and 7 pm to place their weekend bets, and then on a Saturday, a steady stream of punters pressed up against the counters with betting slips and cash.

Yep, Fridays for us weren't anything to celebrate, but today would be different. Today would be the day I fixed things, I hoped.

I accepted the coffee she offered, banished my morning dog breath, and replaced it with coffee breath to match hers. I kissed her, passionate and desperate, hungry for her taste and the feel of her tongue.

She laughed and eventually pushed me away.

'Stop it. You've got work.'

'I've missed you so much.'

'What are you on about? We've just got up.'

'Yeah, but last night and every night I miss you, you come home late and exhausted. I miss the way we were.'

'Australia and Thailand, you mean.'

I nodded, but I'd been missing her for nearly two decades.

'Dreamy days.' She moved to sit on the bed and beckoned me over. We kissed and lay back on the wrinkled sheets. We lay facing each other, foreheads touching like old times, very old times for me. 'I love you so much, Luci. I don't know what I'd do without you.'

She frowned. I could feel her forehead skin against mine as it moved. It was strangely erotic. 'You've been a little distant recently,' she observed.

'Life gets in the way.'

'It does,' she confirmed. 'The show's due to finish its run in four weeks. It might go provincial, but I don't know if I'll do that. I've got another offer.'

'You have?' I said, surprised. 'You never mentioned it.' Of course, she might have, but this version of me had no memory of it.

'I only found out yesterday, and we were so late last night I, well, I just didn't have the energy to think about it.'

'What is it?'

She sat up and looked down at me with wide eyes. 'I got the lead in Jacobites.'

Now this is where the time-travelling game really sucks. Her reaction meant this must be a huge deal, a mega part, and I hadn't the faintest idea what she was on about. She'd obviously been for the audition and discussed it with me, but at that moment, my brain offered nothing, zero, zilch.

'That's amazing,' I said enthusiastically, but she knew me too well.

'You don't even remember what Jacobite's is, do you?'

'Of course I do. You went for the audition.'

'When?'

'Oh, I don't know, a week or so ago.'

I must have got that bit right. Then she said, 'What's it about then?'

'Jacobites? It's about the Jacobites'

'Doing what?'

Now I was grasping, 'Jacobiting about.'

No smile. No smile wasn't good.

'What part did I go for?'

'I don't remember.'

'How can you not remember? I went on and on about it. That's the problem. You don't listen to me anymore.'

'I do listen. I just don't remember.' This was the truth, but not how she'd understand it.

'If you listened properly, then you'd know. You couldn't possibly forget.'

I wasn't so sure about that. I'd spent two years studying for a physics GCSE and listened very carefully but still failed. I decided this might not be a good time to use that as an example. 'Luci, I'm sorry there's so much going on. I…'

'You what? Need to focus on giving out betting slips, emptying the bins, and picking up fag ends? Such a mental strain that must put on you. The man with an English Lit degree is so caught up with his demanding job that he can't remember the most important role his girlfriend has ever landed.'

'Fiancée,' I corrected.

She scoffed. 'Yeah, for now.'

This was going well. 'Luci, I'm….'

She just waved me away. 'Go and get ready. You'll be late for work, and we still need the money.'

She snatched up her magazine, lay back on the bed and picked up where she'd left off, staring at shoes.

I watched her for a moment, so beautiful and talented, and I knew this morning's argument had been about much more than me forgetting the audition or, to be accurate, not yet remembering the audition. No, this went deeper. This was her reaction to the distance she'd mentioned earlier and about me not getting over her confession. Tonight, would be the disastrous conclusion to that lack of forgiveness.

I couldn't fix the argument, but I could fix the evening. As I walked to work, the Jacobian stuff dripped into my brain.

Luci had won the starring role of Flora MacDonald in the musical drama, which would be staged in the West End in May. Assuming Luci got the part, which she had, rehearsals would begin in February. I could march back to our tiny flat and recount all this to her now, but she'd think I'd phoned someone or read *Variety* or something. No, the damage with Jacobites had been done. I just needed to make sure I didn't make things any worse.

Chapter 20
The Power of Love

As I predicted, Friday afternoon was mega-busy. I usually got a half-hour break at 4 pm and phoned Luci to wish her good luck. She never needed it, but it had become a ritual between us. I didn't get away until after five; she'd be in make-up and dressing by then. My call went to voicemail. I left an apologetic message and returned to work. I rarely missed calling her; it would only add fuel to the fire of the morning's argument.

I needed to get a mobile phone, even if only to send her texts at times like these.

At 7 pm, we shut the doors, and I breathed a sigh of relief.

As I remembered, Doug took us out for drinks, and by 9 pm, only he and I were in the club from the group of six that had started out. Once more, I found myself talking to the captivating Gina, but three things were different this time. 1. I'd drunk much less, 2. I'd had some food, and 3. I had perspective. I kept glancing at my watch as we talked.

'Am I boring you?' Gina said with a smile, but I detected irritation in her voice.

'No, I'm sorry, I'm meeting my fiancée after she gets off work, and I need to be going in a minute.'

'Oh.' I didn't know you were seeing anyone.'

'Sorry, I should have said.'

'You should.' Her eyes left mine, and she scanned the club, looking for what? Someone else to take home now I was off limits. 'Is she a nurse?'

'Who?'

Her eyes met mine again, with a frown. 'Your fiancée.'

'No, why'd you think that?'

'Because it's nearly half past nine on a Friday night.'

I smiled. 'Right, I see. No, she's an actress and a singer. She's playing Laurey Williams in *Oklahoma* in The Ellipse Theatre.'

Gina's eyes widened, and she said, 'Oh.'

I went to the toilet and then sneaked out the exit without saying goodbye to Gina, which was not at the top of my priority list. As I walked back towards Leicester Square, it started to rain, and by the time I took my place at the stage door, amongst the crowd of well-wishers and autograph hunters, I'd got thoroughly soaked.

A middle-aged man who bore more than a passing resemblance to Rupert Giles (AKA Anthony Head) from *Buffy the Vampire Slayer* nudged me and said, 'Who are you hoping to see?'

'Luci Lawrence.'

That excited him, 'Oh me too, she's so talented and beautiful, and that voice, ooh.'

I'd seen Luci perform many times by now, I'd watched her in this show alone at least eight times, but I knew what he meant.

I nodded. 'She's terrific.'

'Rupert Scott,' he said, introducing himself.

I shook his hand, smiling. I'd been half right.

The crowd began to stir and surged forward as the rain got heavier. It took me back to my memories of standing there in the freezing weather, like now, but with no hope of forgiveness or redemption.

A few of the supporting cast appeared and quickly signed a few programmes, autograph books and the odd bare arm before hustling away into cabs or cars waiting to pick them up.

Then she emerged, tossing her dark hair behind her as she raised the hood of her thick coat to try and protect it from the rain. I hoped it got soaked. I loved the smell of her wet hair, the pheromones that poured from the top of her head into that tousled mane.

Lost in the moment, I watched her sign some autographs, including Rupert's. Then her eyes met mine, and she stood there staring. I stared back. My vision blurred slightly as tears formed in my eyes.

Eyes across a crowd, eyes across time, I'm not sure which had the greatest effect on me, but something shifted in my soul. She came to me. We held each other. I buried my soaking wet face in her hair and inhaled her scent, her essence, her life force, all of it contained in that single moment of affection. 'I have missed you so much,' I said into her hair.

This time she didn't challenge me about only being together a few hours ago. I don't know why. Maybe she sensed something of the real me had returned, the one that existed before her confession, the version of me who'd had nearly two decades to dwell and regret a mistake that took her away from me forever. At that moment, she sensed perhaps that I'd forgiven her. Forgiven her for something that wasn't her fault, something that didn't need forgiveness, just understanding and love. I now had plenty of both.

Rupert broke the moment. 'Hey,' he said, trying to barge in between us. 'Don't I get a hug?'

Luci broke from our embrace, still holding my hand. 'I'm sorry?' she smiled.

'Why are you hugging him?'

'He's my boyfriend.'

Rupert replied, 'He never said.' He turned to me. 'You never said you were her boyfriend.'

I laughed. 'No, I didn't because I'm not.'

'Oh,' said Rupert, thoroughly confused.

'I'm her fiancé.'

We shared a cab home; I dripped on the carpet and shivered. Luci put the heating up full, not that the ancient radiators would respond quickly, but I appreciated the gesture. 'Why were you standing in the rain like an idiot?' She asked, smiling.

'I needed to see you.'

'You'd see me when I got home.'

I shook my head. 'I couldn't wait. I had this… I don't know, longing. After being such an arse, this morning, then not being able to call you this afternoon—'

'I got your voicemail,' she interrupted. 'It's OK. I know how busy you get on a Friday.'

'That's not it. I've been brooding and unfocused, and you've… we've been so busy we don't get time to….' Time to what I wondered. 'Time to just be us.'

She nodded, drops of rain sprinkling from her hair onto the worn carpet. 'I know, it's been crazy, but another two weeks and I'll get some time off. Maybe we could go away somewhere?'

'I'd like that.'

'Me too.'

We stared at each other for a moment, and then we kissed. It felt like the first time for me. In a way, it was, the first time for a long time. Our snog this morning didn't count. It became sensual full-on pre-sex kissing, the kind that hurts and bruises lips, passion and adrenaline taking over. Outside somewhere distant, thunder rolled and roiled as I buried my face in her luxurious damp hair, revelling in her scents, her liquid exquisiteness and her touch, oh her touch. Across time, the feelings didn't abate or lessen; they increased, broiling and burning my mind, firing need and longing into my bloodstream. We pushed our foreheads together. We didn't speak. No words were necessary. Words were superfluous. We let our bodies talk, feeling rather than saying, sensing rather than describing. Love can be silent and deafening at the same time.

Later we talked. A lot. We took some time out of our lives to reconnect to build back up some of the connections we'd lost. The reasons were many and few, work, sharing the same tiny space day in day out, her confession, the stress of having no money, the day-to-day hassle of living in London and for Luci, the fear of the ever-changing profile of her *chosen* occupation and for me the never changing shape of my *enforced* occupation.

The latter I could do something about, to earn more money, be more fulfilled and take some of the pressure off her. Perhaps the reason she'd never evolved beyond the theatre had been her need to have a steady and regular income. With me contributing at last, she may be able to achieve more.

I'd finally forgiven her for something that required no forgiveness and avoided sleeping with Gina. Surely now we'd live our lives together. We talked about weddings, the future, children and how great life would be. We lay skin on skin, pressed together under the duvet listening to the rain hammer on the single-glazed window behind our bed. We kissed ourselves to sleep, warm, secure and deeply in love once again. We only needed to talk and kiss and love each other.

I awoke expecting Luci to be pressed up against me but discovered Nurse Paton holding my wrist instead. Checking my pulse, I assumed.

The shock of not being next to my beloved took a moment to register then another realisation seared into my brain. I had no memories of the time after we snuggled yet, they would take time to drip through. I knew that now, but what alarmed me, no, alarmed isn't severe enough, scared the living shit out of me, would be a better description, was what I saw when I looked down.

The blimp had returned, bigger and wobblier than ever. I struggled to sit up as I realised with shame and humiliation that I must be pushing the scales towards twenty stone.

Chapter 21
The Sweetest Gift

It took me a moment to realise the Doc had been talking to me. My hard muscular body had vanished under a tsunami of fat. I could live with the shock of piling all my old weight back on, but I knew that it signified something calamitous had probably occurred, but the what's, the why's and the how's eluded me for the present. I'd left my younger self and Luci in good shape. What the hell had I done this time?

I needed to return to my room and hide until I figured it out. I took a deep breath, composed myself and answered the Doc's questions.

Yes, I felt OK. No, I hadn't noticed any significant changes, apart from loading on over eight stones in the last few hours. I didn't bother mentioning it as I knew no one would notice any weight changes but me.

I felt slightly disoriented, as always, when I woke up and plodded back to my room. Unsurprisingly, the MacBook and car keys had vanished. I felt like I'd fallen back to square one. Although hazy, I remembered my thoughts when lunching with Hannah and the decision to *stick or twist*.

I'd twisted and bust, obviously.

Had it been worth spending a few hours in Luci's company and reverse being unfaithful to her? It didn't feel like it, but I had no memories yet. I noticed a letter on the table beside my bed. I scanned it and discovered it was from Sally Henderson, my erstwhile social worker, reminding me that she'd be coming to review my progress on the 19th at 6 pm. The date on my wristwatch informed me she'd be here in just over two hours. Joy.

I lay back on the bed, which creaked and complained under my immense weight, closed my eyes and waited for the inevitable.

The first memories that slid in were full of love and intimacy. Luci and I continued to enjoy each other with fondness and passion. She'd got lead role after lead role, I'd landed a job at a digital publishing company in Canary Wharf, and shortly afterwards, we'd moved to a two-bed rented flat in Covent Garden. It wasn't cheap, but we could afford it. We only took a six-month lease, the plan being to move out of London and buy somewhere. We spent our free time scouring estate agents for houses within commuting distance of London and occasionally shooting off to view one or two that caught our eye and were within budget.

We inevitably ended up disappointed. We'd postponed any idea of a big wedding. Our plan now was to jet off to Portugal and get married on a beach. It suited our personalities better than some big religious bash with remote family members we didn't know or like. We'd invite our nearest and dearest, and that'd be that.

A few months later, we spotted a two-bedroom cottage near St Albans, a 'fixer-upper' with a fixed, eye-watering price of £285,000, but cheap for that part of the world, even then.

We raced over to see it on a Monday morning, put in an offer at eleven and by three, we'd provisionally bought a house. Then the scary bit trying to raise enough money for a deposit and get a mortgage.

I reluctantly sold some of the many shares I'd accumulated, not knowing that most of them would quadruple in value over the next five years, and we managed to convince a building society to lend us the rest. Even with a large mortgage, it still worked out £200 per month less than we were forking out for our Covent Garden flat. It felt like a bargain.

On a rainy Monday in November, we rented a car (no sane person who lives in central London should own a car), drove out of the capital early and collected the keys as soon as the estate agent opened. Not the sour-faced estate agent receptionist, the persistent drizzle, nor the cold north wind could dampen our enthusiasm. I tried to carry Luci over the threshold through the old oak door but tripped on the uneven floor and dropped her on her bum. It remained bruised for a week. I inspected it every evening.

We had no furniture, bedding, or electricity at that point. The fireplace worked. We built a fire using broken pieces of furniture we'd found lying around the rooms. We bought some wine at the local shop and ordered a Chinese takeaway. We'd brought a double sleeping bag and a blow-up mattress which developed a slow puncture during the night.

We lay listening to the rain battering off the decrepit roof.

'Do you think we've done the right thing?' Luci asked as we snuggled up together.

'Definitely,' I replied. I'd have been happy living in a cave so long as we were together.

After the wine and the Chinese, we slept. We both agreed in the morning that it had been the best sleep we had ever enjoyed. The feeling of being in our own place, the security it gave us, and the general atmosphere of the cottage felt just right. I've never been a spiritual or superstitious person, but when Luci said, 'The cottage likes us. It wants us here. It will protect us from harm, shelter and welcome us.' I agreed one hundred per cent. It felt like home.

We had to return to London, and work kept us from returning for over a week, and when we did it was all business and planning. Luci's Uncle Jeremy is a builder, though you wouldn't know it to look at him. My image of a builder is a scruffy individual, wearing overalls, covered in dust with a pencil poking from behind his ear. Jeremy wears sharp suits, shiny shoes and carries a briefcase. He looks more like a financial adviser than a builder. His verdict? Just about doable on our budget.

We wanted to be in by Christmas, but that landmark came and went. Work began in earnest in January, and on 12th April, the cottage remained unfinished but liveable. We gave up the tenancy on our London flat and moved in. It took another three months of tradespeople turning up at odd hours of the day to get the place finished. Our savings were gone, including most of the shares, Luci was touring with Jacobite's, and I lived in the cottage alone for the first two months. She occasionally made it home on Monday for a night, but I usually had to work, so we were like the proverbial ships again.

The tour finished in July, and my fiancée returned to me. She'd already auditioned and been offered the female lead in a musical called Celebrate, roughly based on the life and times of Tom Petty. 'It's going to be a huge success,' she explained. 'We have a massive budget and it might even be made into a film. Imagine that.'

I loved it when Luci started a new project. The enthusiasm and drive she had, amazed me. I didn't know much about Tom Petty, but no doubt I'd be able to write his biography by the end of the run.

The best bit about this new show would be that she got most of July off. I took a few weeks' leave, and we settled into our cottage properly as a couple for the first time. Our lovemaking went off the scale. I came down one morning and caught her taking a tablet.

'What's that?' She showed me the bottle. 'Folic acid. What does that do?'

'Helps make healthy babies.'

'You're pregnant?'

She laughed. 'Hardly, I've still got my coil in, but I'm getting it removed tomorrow then, Mr Harris, we're going to be doing a lot of baby-making practice.'

I felt a delicious shiver slip down my spine. We were going to try and make another human. It felt like a huge responsibility. I hugged Luci as she washed down the tablet with some coffee.

For the next three months, in between my work, her rehearsals and our commuting, we shagged like rabbits. Nothing happened. I became a little despondent, but Luci said it could take up to a year. If it's so hard to get pregnant, how had the human population grown to such an unmanageably colossal number around the planet?

On the 4th of October, I caught the 8 pm train back to St Alban's. The magazine company of which I'd now been promoted to deputy editor had recently won the contract to provide an online magazine for all NHS staff. It had started to grow arms and legs to include pensions advice, how best to plan healthy meals whilst working shifts, how to get quality sleep following a night shift and dozens of other bite-size pieces that just seemed to take forever to write and edit. I rarely left the office before six.

Luci had been rehearsing all day but had still made it home before me. I opened the door and tossed the car keys on the kitchen counter. We now shared custody of a three-year-old red Volkswagen Golf. Today I drove it to the station and back. Tomorrow would be Luci's turn.

I heard the shower running and felt tempted to join my gorgeous, talented and sexy fiancée for a soapy rub-down when I spotted an envelope propped up against the toaster. It had my name scrawled on it in Luci's untidy handwriting.

I opened it, tipped it up, and a small plastic strip fell into my hand. Two faint pink lines showed through the little plastic window. I wasn't sure what this meant, but Luci had included a small note with the stick that said, *Hello, Daddy.*

Chapter 22
Baby I Love Your Way

Luci's first four months went like clockwork. Then she started being sick. A lot. She had many tests and checks, but she and the baby seemed fine. 'Nothing to worry about,' the midwife said. 'It happens.'

As first-time potential parents, we were nervous and suspicious of every potential disaster and stopped reading about pregnancy on the internet as most of it seemed to be doom, gloom, death and destruction.

I loved the blossoming body of my wife, though she wasn't too happy with her baby bump as it meant all her theatre costumes had to be let out.

She came home one Friday evening at the end of her seventh month and said, 'That's it, I'm done. I can't waddle about up there any longer. I look ridiculous.' She flopped down on the couch. I shuffled closer and put my arm around her.

She tried to pull away. 'Sam, I stink. I've been on stage, under lights for three hours and the showers are broken.'

I refused to let her go. I didn't care about her sweat. It kind of turned me on. I started to unbutton her top. 'I like it when you're dirty.'

She laughed. 'You're a perv.'

'I am, and you love it.'

We kissed and slipped through to the bedroom for a quickie before she ran a hot bubble bath.

I sat on the toilet seat while she wallowed in the suds. 'So that's it then?'

She nodded. 'Yep, Bridget, my understudy, takes over from tomorrow's matinee. I'm officially unemployed.'

'On maternity, you mean?'

'Unemployed, I'm an actor, remember? Just as well you're working, and we've saved a bit.'

Our bank balance remained reasonably healthy, but my salary wasn't generous. I had about £25,000 worth of shares left, and some were beginning to spiral upwards. I didn't want to touch them unless we had to.

We hadn't thought much beyond this point, Luci had planned to get a nanny and go back full-time as soon as possible, but her opinion had begun to change as her mum had said it might. Beth had been making the trip down from Wigan regularly since her daughter announced her pregnancy. Before then, she'd only spent the occasional weekend in our old flat, mainly to come and see her daughter on stage. We got on OK. I fully understood Luci's need to have her mum around, especially as her due date neared and I continued to work silly hours.

Luci went into early labour on the 3rd of July, an oppressively hot day. I sweated buckets on the early evening train back from work, partly due to the heat and partly out of nervous fear.

This was it. When I made it home, her contractions were about five minutes apart, and we headed to the hospital in Watford. Eventually, after sitting in triage for an hour, we were escorted into a room and introduced to Kelly, who said she'd be our midwife for the next twelve hours. I blinked at her. Twelve hours? Would it take that long?

The next *ten* hours passed in a blur, and the most shocking thing apart from the blood and the baby emerging from such a stupidly tight space turned out to be Luci's language and the general hate directed towards me for getting her pregnant in the first place. I never realised she knew such foul words. I had to go a look some of them up later! Working in theatreland had certainly broadened her vocabulary. The Spanish swear words I didn't even try to figure out.

The midwife assured me this kind of reaction happened all the time and mainly came down to there being nobody else to blame. All was forgiven and forgotten when a baby girl emerged on 4th July at 5.16 am. From the moment I held her and looked into her pale brown eyes, I was smitten.

It genuinely was the most momentous event in my lifetime or any of my lifetimes so far.

Chloe Beth Harris, as we agreed to call her, became the focal point of our lives for the next two years. Luci didn't go back to performing in any capacity during that time. On Chloe's first birthday, we flew out to Portugal, and with a few friends and Beth, we got married in a lovely little pagoda on the beach with drinks and food afterwards in a nearby taverna. Simple, unfussy and beautiful, the perfect day for affirming our relationship and providing that little bit of extra security for Chloe.

I took a break from reminiscing with my newly formed memories and stood up from the bed in Perry Flowers for a toilet break. So far, so good, regarding my recollections, but I knew that whatever had rendered me socially inept, huge and incapable had yet to drop in.

I made some tea, sat back on the bed and awaited the inevitable. I hadn't dared check my phone yet. I didn't want to pre-empt anything. I needed to feel everything, not prejudge myself, as if that made any sense to anyone else in the universe but me.

After returning from Portugal, we settled into domestic bliss. Luci tentatively started looking for more minor roles that didn't involve lengthy contracts, and her agent started to get her some advertising jobs. Radio initially, then she landed a job on TV. The day it happened, she came home all excited.

'I've landed the role of Alicia in the latest YTG travel ad.'

'Brilliant,' I said, sharing her enthusiasm but not knowing what she was on about.

She punched me on the arm. 'YTG?' she said, louder as if that would make me understand better.

'YTG. Right,' I said, 'great.'

'Sam, you're hopeless. YTG stands for Yellow Travel Group.'

The penny dropped. 'WOW, that's who we booked to go to Portugal with.'

'Exactly, huge. I get to go to all sorts of exotic locations, and best of all, you and Chloe get to come with me. They even want to meet Chloe to see if they might also feature her in a few ads. They want to create the perfect family for the ads, and I'm hoping Chloe can be part of it.'

'Really?' I beamed. 'How did you pull that off? What about me?'

'You are now officially my dresser and outfit coordinator.'

'I'm usually your un-dresser and outfit messer-upper.'

She grinned. 'True, but now you'll have to learn to stop that.'

'I don't think I can.'

'Is Chloe asleep?' I nodded. 'Good, I'm horny. Come on.'

She dragged me through to the bedroom for a costume change. Later I asked, 'So who will be playing your husband in these ads?'

'Tony Carioss, you know from the Freak Cop franchise.'

I knew him all right, dark, swathe, devilishly handsome and renowned as a womaniser.

'Oh,' I said quietly.

Chapter 23
Tears In Heaven

The following morning, I left for work as usual. Luci had the car most days now, running Chloe to various classes and activities. I'd observed more than once that Chloe had just enjoyed her second birthday and didn't know the difference between gym nippers and *gym tots*. (Neither did I, come to that, and I'd been to both twice!) My daughter made my point for me by calling them both *nitpickers*, much to my amusement.

She also went to many other activities, which I suspected were more for the benefit of the stay-at-home mums and, given the part of the world we lived in, the stay-at-home nannies and au pairs.

I arrived late to the office, cow on the line at Hendon, and settled behind my desk. I immediately became swamped with work. It wasn't until 11 am that I checked my phone and discovered a text from Luci enclosing a photo, sent at 9.09 am. At first, I couldn't work out what the picture meant. I tapped on it to save and opened it in my photos. I almost dropped the phone excitedly, another little plastic strip with two pink lines. I was going to be a daddy again.

I glanced around the office, but everyone remained engrossed in their work. I didn't want to share anyway. I headed to the coffee room, shut the door and phoned my wife. It went to voicemail. I tried to remember from the planner on the fridge which activity she'd be at and who she might be having lunch with, but I couldn't. I knew she had a meeting with YTG in the afternoon. I tried to phone three times before lunch but then had to attend back-to-back meetings with no phones allowed.

I'd texted Luci and left voice messages, but she'd not responded. I called again at three after escaping from the large glass box that doubled as a meeting venue, but still no answer. Perhaps she'd got into a bad mood because I hadn't responded immediately, or the YTG thing had been complicated and drawn out. I'd take her home something nice from M&S, Pink Prosecco... oops no, perhaps not. The little pink truffles she liked and some cheesy breadstick things she'd had a craving for them with Chloe. Were cravings different for different babies? I had no idea. At least I knew what to expect this time, and Chloe would get a little brother or sister. How cool would that be?

I pretended to be unwell to escape from the office. Leaving early had become an issue since I'd told anyone who needed to go early for whatever reason that *I'd still be there until the work was finished.*

In any event, I had more important priorities right then. On the journey home, I phoned her five times, every time voicemail. Maybe her phone had broken, or Chloe had dropped it.

I felt confident that's what had happened. When I arrived home, the car wasn't in the driveway. Still, there were a million places she could be. I tried the phone again, but nothing.

I sighed, popped the lid off a beer, flopped down on the couch, and watched the news for a while until it got stuck on repeat about the financial crisis, which had seriously dented my share values. But I knew it struck deeper than that, and we'd all end up paying for the greedy bankers somewhere down the line.

Six pm rolled around, came and went, and as seven o'clock drew near, I began to worry. Her phone still went to voicemail. I tried Beth, but she'd not heard from her since breakfast. That phone call to Beth, more than anything else, set me on the road to panic. Luci phoned her mum at least three times a day, every day.

I paced up and down and grabbed my coat. I needed to get out. Where I would have gone, I don't know, but before I had a chance, the doorbell rang.

I hurried to open the door, expecting/hoping it would be my wife and daughter, but instead, two police officers stood there. A man in his late forties, and a younger blonde woman, her hair tied back in a ponytail. For some reason, I noticed she had freckles and a small dab of chocolate at the side of her mouth from whatever she'd been eating on the way over.

When they asked, 'Are you Samuel Harris?' My legs went weak, and I could feel my life going into freefall.

I nodded and grasped the door frame to prevent myself from toppling backwards. The police only ever came to your door for two reasons, to arrest you or to deliver bad news. I'd not committed any crime; therefore, by easy elimination, it must be bad news. The male policeman confirmed this by asking, 'Can we come in? There's been an accident?'

Chapter 24
I Changed the Rules

Back in the clinic, I went outside for some air, walked around to the grassy area behind the buildings, leaned against an old oak tree, and let the pain wash over me—pain like nothing I had ever experienced. I can't describe it adequately. Nothing I'd ever read, experienced or imagined even came close. As a fat loser, I'd had nearly sixteen years to come to terms with it, or not, given the state I'd got myself into.

But a huge part of me felt it for the first time, in glorious technicolour, recalling the first few days of complete numbness that had overwhelmed me. The hours spent with Beth as we both cried ourselves dry, grieving over the death of the two most gorgeous girls in the universe and then the fresh pain when I told Beth that her daughter had been pregnant. Three lives had been taken that day.

The funeral, inquest, and criminal investigation that followed only lengthened the pain and the grieving process, not that I'd ever get over grieving for my lost family.

The feeling of complete emptiness and the lack of joy in everything. The times I'd turn to say something to Luci and suddenly remember she wasn't there. Waking up in the morning, the first fifteen seconds of each day, where everything felt normal before reality came crashing down on me again. Not hearing Chloe giggle and, probably worst of all, the stark reminder of all their things everywhere. In Chloe's room, the plastic bricks that she'd spend hours building into tall towers before knocking them down with a gleeful giggle. The toy garage with the little plastic cars she loved sliding down the plastic chute on the side and her collection of little books and crayons. None of which she would ever play with again.

In our room, all I saw were Luci's clothes, make-up and shoes. How she'd loved her shoes.

Luci had been working on a ballad called *I Changed the Rules* the week she died. I played the recording over and over just to hear her voice. It became my anthem of sadness.

It took me years to part with everything; even then, I kept Chloe's garage and my wife's shoes.

The truck driver, that had completely missed the red light due to texting his girlfriend on his mobile, pled guilty to dangerous driving and a host of other charges and received a five-year prison sentence. If he'd taken a gun and shot them, he'd be looking at life with a twenty-year minimum. As it was, he'd be out in three probably and free to get on with his life. I didn't see the difference between using a fully loaded gun or a fully loaded forty-ton truck. The tragic result is the same.

The police tried to soften the blow by saying Luci and Chloe died quickly with minimum time to feel any pain. I'd seen the photographs of our completely flattened Volkswagen Golf. Even the engine had been reduced to a jumble of spare parts strewn across the crossing where the accident occurred.

That morning they'd gone to their regular slot at a soft toy-themed kids club, then on to the meeting with the Yellow Travel Group to screen-test Chloe.

On her way home afterwards, Luci would have been driving, with her mind no doubt full of thoughts of what had happened at the meeting. She'd also have been pondering on the tiny embryo nestling in her womb and what she or he might become. She'd set off through the junction, trusting the green light, but within seconds the truck smashed into the driver-side door propelling the little car sideways into a tree on the other side of the junction, where it had been squashed, concertinaed into folded metal. During the court case, I'd watched the CCTV footage from the junction camera only once. Once was enough.

They'd found Chloe's little grey teddy she called *tabby* and had returned it to me how I'd wept over tabby. We put it in Chloe's tiny coffin and buried it with her. I visited their grave regularly and lamented over the futility of it all, my emptiness, and the waste. Nothing mattered anymore.

The weeks and months following their deaths were a blur; I have little recollection of the events. It might be down to the fact that all the memories hadn't dropped in, but as the later ones are present, I suspect I had a breakdown of sorts. Beth certainly did. She disappeared into her own little cloud of pain back home in Wigan.

We spoke a few times, but we just served to remind each other of what we'd lost, and eventually, all contact ceased.

The loss of my mother didn't prepare me for the shock of this grief. While I shouldn't compare the two events, as a ten-year-old, I'd had two rabbits, Nibbles and Daisy. How I'd loved those rabbits. Then one day, when they were about four, a fox got into their pen and killed them both. I found them when I came home from school. I cried for weeks every time I looked at their empty pen, the little box they used to sit on and wash each other, and the food bowls they'd never use again.

When my dad returned from the rigs, he disassembled the pen and told me to grow up. Mr Sensitive, my dad.

The point, if I even had a point, was that I'd had time to prepare for my mum dying. Trust me, it didn't make it easier, but I'd mentally steeled myself and knew it would happen. Plus, perversely, it had been a relief as I knew how much she'd been suffering. Nobody should have to go through that. I had no time to prepare when the rabbits and Luci and Chloe died. It felt like being hit by a shockwave.

It occurred to me then, that Luci had died in a car crash years before. Now, once more, she'd succumbed to the same fate. This time along with our daughter. Was this the universe or whatever trying to realign things, or was it just dumb luck? A question I'd probably never be able to answer.

I never went back to work. I just wasn't capable. CS Lewis's words came to mind when he said *no one ever told me that grief felt so like fear.* I had been too scared to do anything. Everything reminded me of my loss, the smell when walking past Greggs. Luci had loved Greggs' sausage rolls during the early part of her pregnancy with Chloe. The sound of rain on the conservatory roof of our cottage, Chloe and I used to rush through during downpours as she loved to watch the rain hammer onto the plexiglass, or whatever the roof structure consisted of, sluice down the grooves and cascade onto the paving stones below.

Even travelling on a bus felt fraught with danger as Chloe always wanted to sit upstairs at the back and wave to anyone behind us.

Everything and anything could set me off and send me scurrying back home to shut out the world and bask in my grief and self-pity.

I discovered that grief evolves. It morphed from the incalculable reminders of what we'd done together and enjoyed, such as the rain, the bus, and sausage rolls, to what they *hadn't* been able to do and missed.

For example, the day when Chloe was due to start school left me unable to function for a week as I dwelled and contemplated what she would have loved and maybe not loved about it.

Silly things like the newest mobile phone incarnation – Luci always got the latest model – once she could afford to. Even the snow that came and went each winter affected me as I thought about the snowmen we'd never build as a family. I always tried to avoid walking on the grass during such times. The snow had to be kept pristine. Snow wasn't for me. It was for Chloe.

On bonfire night, I built a small fire in the back garden for my daughter. I let off a few cheap fireworks, wondering if she could see or hear them or know they were for her. Then I realised she'd gone for good. I wasn't a spiritual person, never had been, never would be. I got angry and kicked the pile of burning wood, managing to set my silly trousers on fire.

I doused them with minimal damage to my skin and wondered why I hadn't just let myself burn and be done with it. How would I get through all the Christmases,

Easters, anniversaries and the B-words? I realised it had taken me nearly a decade to acknowledge Chloe's and Luci's birthdays. I spent them inebriated and blacked out in more ways than one.

I tried to move on, but everything seemed so pointless. I lost my job at the magazine, which didn't surprise me, given the commitment required to maintain the damn thing.

I sold the cottage eventually. Ultimately, it bothered me less than I imagined it would.

Too many precious but painful memories were wrapped up in those walls. It had promised to protect and nourish us. It hadn't. I thought moving away might be good for me.

Over the next decade, I drifted from town to town, squandering money on rent, junk food, and general crap, until by the time I reached my thirty-fifth birthday, I realised I'd not had a steady job since leaving the magazine and my funds had dwindled.

At that point, I tried to get some counselling but the mental health services being as stretched as they were, meant I wasn't on top of anyone's priority list.

Events conspired to take me to Birmingham, working for a company called ZX Energy, phoning customers trying to get them to switch their gas and electricity. I might have done that before. In any event, I'd found myself on a written warning after three weeks and sacked two months later. I found it impossible to give a toss whether someone switched their gas or electricity, which didn't seem to go down particularly well with the supervisors.

Katy, the manager responsible for my performance or lack thereof, decided to try some role plays with me to try and improve my sales technique. 'OK, Sam, you be the customer, and I'll be you, OK?'

'OK.'

We both had phones in the training room. She rang my number, and I answered it. She began her spiel. 'Hello, this is Katy.' At which point I hung up.

'Why did you do that?' She glared at me.

'That's what most customers do when I call them.'

'This is a training session. You don't do that in a training session.' She breathed deeply, 'Let's try again, shall we?'

I nodded.

'Hello,' she said brightly. 'This is Katy, and I'm from ZX Energy.'

Despite her happy tone, I could see her seething inside her black work suit.

'Hello,' I replied quietly.

She paused, staring at me, waiting for me to hang up. I didn't.

A fake smile on her fake face, 'I'm not here to sell you anything, Mr Harris, but I may be able to save you hundreds of pounds on your energy bills.'

'OK.'

'Now, do you currently pay your bills by direct debit?'

'I do.'

'Splendid, that means we may be able to save you even more. Who is your current energy supplier?'

'I don't know.'

'That's OK. Do you have a recent bill from them?' She whispered, 'Just pretend you do, OK?'

I nodded.

'OK, I've got it here.'

'Who's your supplier, Mr Harris?'

'ZX Energy.'

I didn't last long after that, which is how I'd ended up in the same flat waiting for the Rottweilers again on the eve of my fortieth birthday. The symmetry of my earlier experience, occupying the same time and space, albeit via a much different route, made me wonder about the element of fate in everything. At least I hadn't troubled poor Lisa this time around.

I returned to my room and lay on the bed as tears pooled in my eyes. The only thing that consoled me was that I could do something about it so long as the Doc allowed me to continue on the programme. How many second chances does one man need or deserve?

I didn't know.

I needed to pull myself together before dinner. I knew the grief that had overwhelmed me would dissipate slightly as the shock subsided and, in any event, things were not hopeless. I had to remember that. At the time, this version of me had no concept of the future or multiple futures and had yielded to despair with no hope of redemption.

The timeline I'd spent with Hannah had begun to fade, and I updated my notebook with all that I hadn't written down before and added my most recent tragic life in as much detail as I could bear.

At least with Hannah, I'd been able to function and had a reasonably successful life. No. I didn't have the depth of feelings I had for Luci, but I could probably have made a happy life with her, but Luci and Chloe would not have been part of my life. Even though my life with Chloe had been so brief, it had been the worst of times and the best of times. I wouldn't have changed it, despite the desolation I felt.

I stripped off my clothes, manoeuvred my bulk into the tiny shower and cleaned off the sweat. It also felt like I'd been cleaning some of the grief from my mind, too, as I felt a little better when I emerged and tried to dry myself with the inadequately small towel.

I tried not to look at myself in the mirror. It wasn't a pleasant view. I also had a long scar along the bottom of my abdomen. The memory plopped into my head when I examined the angry red line. They'd had to operate and remove a section of blocked and twisted bowel three years ago. I could still remember the pain and stench of the section of my bowel as it had been removed. They'd completed the operation with a spinal anaesthetic. I'd been conscious throughout.

I dressed in clean clothes, grey joggers and a baggy tee shirt and went downstairs to dinner with a heavy heart and heavy everything else.

As I ate, I contemplated the circumstances that had led me once more to the Perry Flowers project. If I got another chance, what would that chance look like?

Would I be transported back to that fateful evening in the nightclub again? Would I be better off sleeping with Gina and simply letting Luci go? Would that be easier for everyone?

Of course, that would mean Chloe would never exist. I couldn't countenance that. Perhaps, given the considerable dent or whatever their deaths had imprinted onto my genome, it seemed almost inevitable that I'd end up back at the point where they died.

After dinner, Dr Jaeger asked me to come to her office, and when I opened the door, she and Sally Henderson looked up as I lumbered through the door.

Sally's hair had been cut into a stylish bob. From my notes, she used to wear it long. The style suited her.

I sat down, and Dr Jaeger beamed me a smile. 'Sam, Sally's got some news for you.'

I nodded. My social worker handed me an A4 envelope. I opened it and scanned the documents inside.

I read it twice before looking up. 'What does this mean?'

Sally answered, 'It means you no longer need to be here. I have made a provisional offer on a flat for you, just a temporary rental. Once you're settled in, you can start looking for somewhere more permanent.'

She smiled. 'I know it will never replace what you lost, but it might help you move on, and that's something we'll aim to help with. As you know, the state's mental health facilities are, well stretched doesn't begin to describe it, especially since the fall out from the Covid crisis.'

She nodded to the papers in my hands, hands that had begun to shake as the enormity of what this might mean began to settle on me. 'But now, well, you don't need any help from the health service. You can afford the best private mental health treatments money can buy.'

I glanced again at the papers. I had no recollection of ever instructing solicitors to sue the lorry company's insurance company for compensation. No recollection at all. I also had no idea why Sally had the paperwork and not me. I didn't care at that point. I couldn't take it all in.

'I'll come and pick you up in the morning, Sam,' Sally said. 'The flat is fully furnished; all you have to do is move in. It's even got Sky.'

'Isn't that great news, Sam?' Dr Jaeger beamed. 'You don't need us anymore, and we can allocate your place to someone more in need. How wonderful.'

I suddenly started sweating, and the room began to spin. I glanced at the smiling faces staring back at me and promptly passed out.

Chapter 25
Reach

When I came around, I still lay where I'd fallen, probably because I'd been too huge to move. The concerned faces of the Doc, Sally and Nurse Paton were bent over me, checking my vital signs, I guess. They got me to sit up slowly.

Nurse Paton said, 'You seem to be fine, but I reckon we should get you to A&E just to make sure.'

I stared at Nurse Paton. 'You're a nurse.' I nodded to the Doc. 'She's a doctor; if you think I'm OK, that's enough for me, probably just shock.'

Sally agreed. 'I perhaps should have introduced the news to you differently.'

She didn't know I didn't give a damn about the money. It was the prospect of being removed from the project that freaked me out. 'I'd still like to continue the treatment,' I told the Doc.

She wouldn't meet my eyes and squirmed in the seat she'd just parked herself in. 'Well, to be honest, Sam, I have already sourced and offered your place to someone else. You can afford a more conventional course of treatment now.'

'You said conventional treatments take too long.'

She sighed. 'Well, yes, usually that's true, but in your case, you can fast-track treatment, you can afford to employ a psychiatrist full time, or even a whole team of specialists. I'll give you the names of some of my colleagues working in private practice.' She stood up. 'Sam, I think a night's sleep will do you a world of good and in the meantime, I need to get back to my office and work on some treatment plans.'

She disappeared, followed by Nurse Paton. Sally asked, 'Are you OK, Sam?'

I shook my head. 'Not really, but I'll just need to be, won't I?' I headed off to my room.

I lay on the bed for a long time. Now that the opportunity to go back had been taken away, the misery and grieving pain washed over me anew. I had been holding on to the hope that I could undo what happened that day, but the consequences of that event had yielded me money I had no genuine interest in. It wouldn't bring back Luci or Chloe; all the psychiatrists in the world couldn't do that.

Was fate dancing with me again? How on earth had it taken nearly sixteen years to process the claim, and why would the case be settled on the eve of me perhaps being able to go back and fix things? I had the feeling forces were at work beyond my control or understanding, or maybe fate and the universe just threw up random coincidences and karma.

I really needed to talk to someone, but nobody in Perry Flowers would be of any use as they'd never believe me or would have me committed, probably to a very high-class mental institution now that I could afford one. I read through the pages of the legal forms once more. After fees and expenses and their cut, I would receive one million, two hundred and twenty-five thousand pounds—an incredible sum. Most people would be jumping around the room, but it represented compensation for something that could never be compensated.

Plus, I had no memory of instructing solicitors in the first place. I had some vague memories of receiving letters from them over the years, but for it to take so long to settle seemed crazy.

I owned a mobile with no contract or reception, but again once I charged it up and connected to the clinic's internet. I searched for Michael Stanton, the driver of the lorry. It took a while, but it seemed he got out of prison on licence, three years eight months after being incarcerated. The injustice of it all didn't surprise me.

I eventually found his Facebook page. He was married now with two daughters. They all looked very pleased with themselves. The irony wasn't lost on me, nor the unfairness of it all. I shed a few more tears for my dead wife and daughter and closed the app. No good would come from looking at the murderer's happy life.

I read over some of the solicitor's paperwork hoping the dullness of the words might send me off to sleep. However, reading between the lines of the legalise, it appeared the reason it took so long to be settled was due to the enormous amount of compensation being pursued by the solicitor's firm. The question of culpability had never been in doubt or contested. Due to the unreasonably high claim, the insurers refused to settle out of court. This meant it fell into the complex legal system, and after various judgements and appeals (all adding 000's to numerous solicitor's fees, no doubt), the case ended up in the high court.

I had no recollection of any of it. But sixteen years, that must be a record? A quick Google search assured me it wasn't. Not even close. It all felt like a racket spun out between the lawyers of the opposing teams to make money from misery and misfortune. Mine, in this case.

I eventually slipped into an uneasy and troubled sleep and awoke unrefreshed and sweaty.

I quickly showered, packed up my belongings, and waited downstairs for Sally. The Doc wasn't about, intentionally, I think.

An hour later, Sally had departed, leaving me sitting in the pleasant living room of a brightly decorated one-bedroom flat on the outskirts of Birmingham. I had over one point two-five million reasons to be cheerful, but none of that mattered. I'd put on a brave face, mainly so Sally would leave.

I sat in a chair, stared at a wall, and, for the first time in a long time (and quite a few timelines), wondered if my life was worth continuing.

The memory of my last one with Hannah had begun to fade, but I'd at least been semi-contented then. Now I had nothing to look forward to and nothing I wanted to look back on.

I'd wasted the last sixteen years, and nobody knew anything about what I'd been through or how I felt. I wanted to punch the wall, smash the TV, break all the windows, and shout and scream until someone arrested or sectioned me. But what would that achieve?

Grief is a highly personal and intimate thing, like reading a book. It's not a team activity. But I'd also been grieving for something that didn't need to happen. I didn't need to go back and open that poxy Pandora's box. I could have settled. This crazy merry-go-round Dr Jaeger had put me on had messed with my mind and body. It also resembled a drug in many ways. I'd become addicted to fixing everything, and now my supply had been cut off.

I wished I could talk to someone who understood.

Then I remembered Elizabeth Auld. She probably wouldn't remember me in this timeline, but at least she might believe me. She couldn't change anything, but perhaps talking to someone who had shared similar experiences might make me feel better or at least provide some perspective. I had her address in my notebook. I didn't have her phone number.

I found her Facebook page but didn't want to message her in case she refused to speak to me. I might have a better chance if I just turned up. I'd head down to her flat in Dartford and knock on her door or at least press the buzzer.

If I set off after lunch, I should be able to get there by dinnertime, by which time she should be home from work. I no longer owned a car, so I'd have to travel by public transport.

Sally had said the solicitor's firm had generously deposited some funds into my bank account to tide me over while they waited on the entire settlement to come through. Very generous of them, considering they were making the best part of eight hundred thousand pounds from my tragedy. Plus, chances were, my creditors would seize the funds as soon as they got wind of any money hitting my account. I quickly withdrew £500 from a cash machine before that happened.

I had to get the number fifteen bus to Birmingham New Street, then a train at two-fifteen, which after a couple of changes, would get me into Dartford station at five-fifteen, followed by a ten-minute taxi journey to her flat.

I had another shower and tried to smarten myself up the best I could. I didn't want to scare the poor girl.

I walked down to the nearest supermarket, bought some basic provisions, put the food away and ate a pot noodle. I brewed some coffee and watched the clock. When it ticked around towards 1 pm, I headed out.

I bought a car magazine at the train station but felt too nervous and distracted to read much of it on the journey to Dartford.

I arrived outside her flat at 5.20 pm and hesitated. She wouldn't remember anything about me, but I hoped the mention of Dr Jaeger might at least get me in the door. I pressed her buzzer and waited. No answer. I pushed again and had been ready to give up when an elderly lady opened the door and stared at me standing, blocking the doorway.

'What do you want?' she said suspiciously, taking in my less-than-pristine appearance.

'I'm supposed to be meeting Elizabeth Auld.' I half lied.

'She's not in.'

'Yeah, I had begun to think that. She's not answering her buzzer.'

'Go away then,' she said, slamming the door and squeezing past me.

'I've come all the way down from Birmingham.'

The old lady squinted at me and said, 'Is this a face that looks like it gives a shit?'

I had to smile at her bolshie attitude. 'No, it doesn't.'

'Good,' she grumped. 'Lizzie works in the City. Won't be back until at least seven.'

She marched away, back straight and head held high. Quite a character, I reckoned. I didn't mind her rudeness. I supposed I'd grown used to it over the years. When you pile on weight, people often feel they're within their rights to tell you stuff they wouldn't usually say. Things like, 'You could do without that, cake/pie/sweet/fizzy drink' or anything they believe would make me fatter. They fuss and mutter when sitting next to me on a train or a bus, complain that I'm being too slow, taking up too much room or whatever—things they wouldn't ever say to a disabled person.

I'm not saying being fat is a disability per se, but they don't take time to think about what might have caused me to get fat. They assume I'm lazy, and I suppose to a point, they are right, but not all fat people are fat due to being lazy.

I'm fat because comfort-eating and drinking helped me cope with losing my wife and child. Other people will no doubt have many other valid reasons. From mental health issues to physical disabilities to faulty genes, people I've encountered make instant judgements. Society, in general, I've found, is fat-ist—one of the few remaining 'ists' left to them.

Thinking about food *had* made me a little peckish, and as there seemed little point in hanging around outside Elizabeth's flat for two hours, I pottered down the road towards a branch of Morrisons. I walked down a few of the aisles and came to the cafe. I ordered two cheese omelettes, a coffee and a small cake. As usual, I got a few looks but did my best to ignore them. My problem is that I've been fat, thin, gym bunny fit and then fat again. I'd forgotten what it had been like to be big and the unwelcome attention that brought. I'd also grown conscious of being out of breath, and I'd only walked about three hundred yards.

I considered going home. Meeting with Elizabeth likely wouldn't help me in any way. I'd have to do the whole Groundhog Day thing again. Eventually, she'd probably believe me, given her experiences, but then what? What could she do? Nothing.

I ate my dinner and read through the car magazine I'd bought. Eventually, I would get myself a car, and it occupied me while I hoovered up the food.

I hung around in the cafe until a few minutes past seven. The waitress/table cleaner/cashier/cook had been over to clear my table three times. I eventually took the hint and noticed a suggestion box near the exit. For a moment, I contemplated leaving a note suggesting they employed more staff in the cafe, but in the end, I waddled out the doors and headed back along the street towards Elizabeth's block. The evening had worsened, and a light rain had started to fall, but it being November and cold, I suspected the heavens would open shortly.

I hurried along the busy road. Headlights blinded me every few yards, and the slosh of tyres on the pot-hole-strewn road blocked out most other sounds.

I arrived back at the flat entrance and pressed the buzzer. The tinny voice of Elizabeth Auld said, 'Who is it?'

For some unknown reason, I had the overwhelming urge to say *The Bogey Man* and laugh fiendishly. I didn't. 'My name is Sam Harris, we met once before, but you won't remember. I've been on a—'

Her tinny voice interrupted me. 'Sorry, I can't hear a word you're saying.' The buzzer buzzed, and the door opened, admitting me into the warm, dry hallway. The silence that greeted me after the noisy main road felt most welcome.

I climbed the flight of stairs, and as before, her landing door opened, and she peered out at me. 'Did you say your name was Sam?'

I nodded, out of breath and wheezing. After one flight of stairs, not a good sign. I eventually gasped, 'I'm under, I was under the care of Dr Jaeger, a programme you also took part in, down in Kent, I think.'

She nodded slowly and leaned over to get a closer look at me. 'Weird. Have you got any ID?'

I fished about in my wallet. I had my driving licence and handed it to her. The picture bore a passable likeness, maybe five stones ago. She studied it briefly, then squinted at me and handed it back. 'Come in.'

She stood aside as I squeezed past her, trying not to touch her, but due to the narrowness of the hallway, my considerable bulk almost flattened her against the wall. To my utmost surprise, she started giggling.

'Come and sit in the lounge.'

I was surprised by her willingness to let me into her home. I had been expecting, at the very least, a protracted conversation on the stairs where I tried to convince her I wasn't certifiable.

Tea, coffee?' she offered.

'No thanks, I've just come from Morrison's Cafe. I came by earlier, but you weren't in.'

'I work in the City.'

'Your neighbour told me.'

Elizabeth smiled. 'The terrorist. Mrs Langley.'

'The feisty old lady?'

Elizabeth laughed. 'Yeah, don't ever let her hear you call her old, however. You'll be in trouble then.'

'Why do you call her the terrorist?'

'She terrorises me in a good way, but still, she can get a bit wearing. Lecturing me about my work-life balance, my love life….'

'Does she know you're gay?'

Elizabeth stared at me for a moment. 'She does, yes. How did you know?'

'We've met before. You won't remember I….'

'I don't directly remember no, but I made notes.' She bent down and pulled a notebook from the bottom shelf of a shelving unit near the chair she'd perched on.

'The notes survived?' I asked, amazed again by the note conundrum. 'What about the selfie?'

'Selfie? I don't remember that. I have no direct memory of you ever being here. I'm assuming that got erased when you made your last trip. Now, just to be sure, what happened to me whilst in the care of Dr Jaeger?'

'She kicked you out because you thought you were a time-traveller.'

'Yeah, OK, not that bit; she could have told you that. What did I do when I went back?'

'Saved your sister?'

'How?'

I smiled. 'By becoming psychotic and smashing a canoe.'

She laughed. 'OK, I believe you now. I had wondered if you'd come and look me up again.'

'I needed someone to talk to who wouldn't think I'd become certifiable.'

'Just to double check – where is my sister now?'

'France, I think, and your relationship with….' I glanced around the wall, but now only the photograph with her sister remained.

'What is it?' Elizabeth asked.

'Did you take the picture of, I'm sorry, I don't remember her name, off the wall?'

'Who?'

'I can't recall. There used to be a photo of you and a dark-haired girl. Your relationship had recently ended.'

Elizabeth frowned. 'I'm seeing a girl called Fay, red hair, a bit like me; people think we're sisters, which has its uses. We've been together for about a year on and off. Having said that, I've no reason to doubt you. It's weird, don't you think?'

I did think. 'Can I ask, do you work for an investment bank?'

'I do, so that's not changed then.'

I took a deep breath. 'Actually, the last time I saw you, or maybe the last timeline I saw you, might be a better description. You were just about to start that job.'

'I've been in this current job for nearly three years. This is enough to make your head hurt.'

We both sat silently for a minute, trying to understand what it all meant. We weren't physicists or geniuses, so we could have sat there until our sun went supernova and not worked it out. I, altering my timeline, had inadvertently changed hers as well. For all I knew, perhaps everyone in the world's timeline. Mind boggling didn't do it justice.

Eventually, Elizabeth said, 'This means that everyone on the programme has the power to change our lives completely, and we wouldn't know a thing about it.'

More boggling of minds.

Could this explain fate? A handful of strangers changing their personal tragedies with unforeseen and unknown consequences for everyone else. I couldn't ponder on it right then; something for later.

I took a moment and then outlined to Elizabeth what had happened to me in the last session.

After I'd finished, she had tears in her eyes, 'Oh, Sam, that is truly heartbreaking. The universe seems to have it in for you and yours. It's like a ripple effect, like dropping a pebble in a pond. The ripples spread out, eventually crossing the whole pond and reducing in size as they go. For some reason, you, getting married, having a child, and doing all those other things caused ripples that crossed over into my life and probably many other lives too. It's a paradox.'

'How?'

Elizabeth mustered a tired smile. 'I don't know exactly, but perhaps you winning that magazine job in the City meant someone else didn't. Then they took another job that perhaps someone else would have taken until perhaps my boss got her job because of you, way back down the chain and then hired me as a result.'

'Wow.'

'I've been doing a bit of reading; there's a thing called the *Grand-father-paradox*. Imagine if you were to go back in time and kill your mum's father in his childhood. It would result in your mum and, thus, you not being born. But, if you weren't born, you wouldn't have been able to go back in time and kill him in the first place. Therefore, he wouldn't be dead, and your mum would be born, and so would you, thus freeing you up to go and kill him again.'

'I'm not killing anyone's grandfather.'

'No, I know you're not, but it explains why time travel isn't as dangerous as you think.'

'I hadn't considered the danger of it. I just wanted my wife back.'

'Not at first, you didn't. You just wanted to change your crappy childhood.'

'I did that, and then I wanted my wife.'

'Yes, you managed to change your past and then wanted to change your future past.'

I stared at Elizabeth, 'Is that even a thing?'

She giggled. 'I don't know, let me look it up.' She tapped away at her phone for a moment. 'It's a film.'

'About time travel?'

'I don't know. I've not seen it.'

'That's not much help.'

She smiled. 'I'm just guessing here, Sam. Maybe it's a kind of temporal Butterfly Effect in action. At least you've got another chance to go back again. It's not the end.'

I shook my head. 'I'm off the programme.'

'How?'

I explained about the compensation and my conversation with Dr Jaeger. We were both silent for a while afterwards.

'God, you'd have been better not taking that last trip,' Elizabeth said eventually.

'I don't know, then I'd never have met Chloe, but I'd never have lost her. Oh, it's so complicated.'

'Why not pay her?'

'Pay who?' I asked.

'Dr Jaeger.'

'What, like a bribe?'

Elizabeth scoffed. 'Not exactly, but in a round-about way. I'm sure they would welcome extra funding for this project. Why not offer them money on the condition that you get one more treatment?'

'Do you think that'd work?'

'What have you got to lose besides money, which you don't seem to want or need anyway? Just promise me one thing?'

'What?'

'Come back and tell me how you get on.'

'I will.'

It was nearly midnight when I made it back to my flat. It didn't feel like home, but then nothing had felt like home since the death of Luci and Chloe. Home had nothing to do with location.

Chapter 26
Everybody Hurts

Morning arrived, grey and overcast. I ate some more toast, with jam this time, showered and changed into my best grey joggers and tee shirt. They call them sweatpants in America, and that description suited me much better, given the amount of perspiration dripping from my body.

The flat didn't feel particularly warm, but I switched the heating off anyway. I pulled on my large dark overcoat and headed out into the chill November air, still sweating.

I could have got a taxi, but I felt like walking. It might make me feel less sluggish. Perry Flowers lay approximately three miles from my new flat. I would walk the whole way. I needed the exercise, and if I ended up stuck in this life, I needed to shed some of the bulk.

I passed two Greggs within two hundred yards of each other and resisted the strong urge to buy cakes. I approached a police station and paused as a blue-lighted van screamed out of the yard, siren blaring and tyres skidding. What kind of emergency required that sort of response on a school-day morning, I wondered.

I decided a rest was in order. I leaned against the wall of the police station and took a look around me. The sun peeked its bright, cheery face between ominous black clouds and gently bathed the urban scene in an ethereal glow. I smiled, took a deep breath and slowly slid down the wall to the ground. Everything seemed to be bathed in amber light, reminiscent of my long-dead wife's intoxicating irises, including the passing cars, the rooftops of the terraced houses, the cat sitting on the wall opposite and the middle-aged couple who bent down to speak to me. I don't know what they said. I didn't know what anyone said. I felt saliva dribbling from the side of my mouth. I couldn't stop it. I felt embarrassed, a big lumbering pile of blubber who couldn't even swallow properly. What must they think of me?

****

I awoke. No, that's not true; I slowly became aware of my surroundings—a dark room with things beeping and gurgling. A hospital, I assumed, from the smell; nothing smells like a hospital.

My mouth felt parched and disgusting as if a hamster had crawled in and died on my tongue. I tried to speak, but my lips were cracked, sore, and dry.

A sharp pain alerted me to the fact I had a cannula inserted on the back of my right hand and another tube bit into my willy, a catheter perhaps. It made me wince. The cannula led to an IV line connected to a bag somewhere northeast of my head, but moving my bonce even an inch to try and see, hurt like hell.

I tried to raise my left arm to scratch my nose, but it didn't respond. I couldn't move my left leg, either. An alarm flashed across my brain. I wanted to panic but wasn't in a fit state to do anything other than moan a little. Nobody appeared. I tried to moan a little louder and pull out the catheter. I failed miserably at both tasks and promptly fell asleep again.

The next time I woke, daylight streamed through the window. A crowd of doctors surrounded my bed. I knew crowd was the correct collective noun. Well, I assumed they were doctors. They all wore white coats. I suppose they could have been butchers, but only one of them had blood on their coat, maybe a crowd of doctors and one butcher then, or lab technicians; they all wore white coats too. I couldn't think who else might.

I mumbled something unintelligible even to me, and it had formed in my brain. One of the physicians leaned over and shone a torch in my eyes.

I mumbled again. Another doctor leaned in, saying, 'We are reviewing your prognosis with some final-year medical students. Just in case you are wondering what we are all doing here.'

I blinked, the only response I could muster. He turned and addressed his entourage. 'Mr Harris has suffered a cerebrovascular accident, and early indications from cutaneous pinprick response indicate a hemiplegic weakness on the left side of the body.'

I kind of got the word accident. The rest washed over me. I don't remember anything about an accident. I remember leaning on a wall and amber halos, then nothing. 'Where's Dr Jaeger?' I managed to mutter.

The doctor seemed puzzled. 'I'll get a nurse to come and get you some water.'

I didn't want water; I wanted Dr Jaeger, but I inexplicably fell asleep again.

The waking/sleeping episodes continued for a while. It might have been days, might have been weeks. I had no idea. Then, one morning I woke up and stayed awake for more than ten minutes. I now seemed to be in a room on my own rather than a general ward, but I had no recollection of being moved. Everything felt hazy and dull.

I tried to sit up but failed miserably. It didn't help that I couldn't feel anything on my left side. I could just about raise my left hand off the bed but below that, nothing moved. My brain sent the signal, but it didn't get there. My right side worked OK, but trying to sit up when pushing twenty stones is hard enough with a fully functioning body, with only half working. It proved to be beyond me.

I guessed I'd suffered a stroke. The vague memories of some doctor mentioning an accident must be a mistake. The symptoms I could vaguely remember outside the police station hinted at a stroke though the experience hadn't been entirely unpleasant. I wouldn't say I liked the dribbling or the sliding down the wall bit, but the amber glow and general feeling of weightlessness had been quite pleasant.

The source of the stroke I had no trouble identifying. Pulling around a fat, unhealthy body, eating junk food twenty-four-seven, combined with the stress of remembering that I'd lost my wife and child, would be enough on its own. If you then add in multiple trips across or through time and being dropped from the programme, then it almost became inevitable.

I groaned at the realisation that I'd probably lost all chance of being accepted back on the Doc's project, regardless of the size of contribution offered. I had no idea how long I'd been in the hospital, how long it might take me to recover, or if I ever *would* recover. I promptly fell asleep again.

The next time consciousness reappeared, I found an attractive nurse bent over me, adjusting my cannula. She smelt lovely. I mumbled something and passed out again.

A day, or maybe a century later, I awoke again, this time feeling much more alert. I didn't try and sit up this time. I just lay listening to the general background noise of a busy hospital. Eventually, a nurse, not the one that smelled lovely, appeared. This one smelled OK, just not as pleasant as the last one. I asked. 'What happened?'

'You had a stroke, a serious one. We've been keeping you sedated to allow the body time to heal. We stopped the striplllinnednrtdzer (that's what it sounded like to me) drip this morning, so you should begin to feel much more alert.'

'How long have I been....' I didn't get to finish.

'Six weeks, almost to the day. You've got a long hard road ahead of you, Mr Harris.'

She perched on the edge of the bed and took my pulse. I read her name badge, Jill Gordon. She then checked my eyes and sat back. 'We've been unable to contact your next of kin or anyone. We had your wallet, but your driver's licence address wasn't current, and nobody reported you missing.'

It didn't surprise me that I hadn't been missed. I might have expected Sally, my social worker, to check up on me, but she more than likely had more worthy cases to worry about now. Since I'd come into money, I no longer fitted the profile of a lost cause.

'I don't have any family.'

'You were wearing a wedding ring when you first came in, so we….' She shrugged her shoulders.

'Yeah, my wife and daughter, they died. A long time ago.'

'I'm sorry,' said Jill.

I nodded. 'Yeah, me too.'

'So, there's nobody?'

I shook my head. I thought about mentioning Dr Jaeger and Sally, but there wasn't much they could do or offer. I thought about telling her about Elizabeth Auld but decided against it. We weren't friends, more acquaintances and why burden her with my problems?

'You've developed some bed sores on your lower extremities.'

I assumed she meant my bum, as I could feel something smarting down there.

'As soon as we get the physio booked in, we'll try and get you up and about, which will help, but your muscles will have atrophied after all this time, so we'll take it slow.'

'How bad is it? The stroke, not the sores.'

She winced. 'We never really know for sure. In your favour, you're relatively young, so with time, we would hope you'd develop some feeling back on your left side, but to be honest with you, Mr Harris, you are likely to have a weakness for the rest of your life.'

It appeared as if she was about to say something else; about losing weight if I had to guess, but she paused and smiled instead. Baby steps.

Later, Dr Paul Cosby, whom I estimated to be in early puberty, explained in more detail. 'You had an ischemic stroke, Sam, a blood clot that caused a blockage in your brain. The good news is that the ambulance brought you here quickly enough to allow us to treat you with alteplase which saved your life. The bad news is that considerable damage had been done by then, you'll be on anti-stroke medication for the rest of your life, and you need to lose weight.'

The next ten weeks were perhaps the most frustrating, physically painful and uplifting of my life, except for my time with Luci and Chloe.

Some days I sank into a dark place where life without my family seemed pointless, and why should I bother? Whilst physically, it had been nearly two decades since they'd passed, it had only been weeks for a part of me. I had one goal, one aim in life, to get out of the hospital and back onto the Perry Flowers programme, my motivation, my sole purpose, my reason for living.

Maria, my designated physiotherapist, would have been right at home as part of a KGB torture team. She cajoled, bribed, threatened, humiliated and pushed me to a point where I hated, loved, feared and respected her. After three and a half months of her ministering, I'd made it out of my wheelchair and could stagger around with sticks. I was stable enough to be allowed home, which brought about another issue. I didn't have one. My flat had long since been re-let. That seemed fair, considering I hadn't paid any rent nor lived there.

I needed a ground-floor flat that would be easy for me to negotiate with my sticks and wheelchair. I ordered an iPad online and Apple delivered it to the hospital ward. Amazing.

I spent a few hours searching local property websites and emailed a few letting agents outlining what I needed in the short term. More money had dropped into my account from the solicitors, but the full payment had yet to come through. Still, I had more than enough for the time being.

Later, after a particularly brutal physio session, I returned to my rehab room. (I'd been moved out of the acute ward to a special unit that specialised in stroke and paralysis victims). I opened Facebook and smiled as my account showed my old Filipino friends looking for a husband. A few dozen Nigerian hopefuls had also joined them, some offering *private photos* if I responded. I resisted. Even if I'd been tempted, as I'm sure many men are, I doubted they would want to take me on in my current state.

After a few minutes, I found Hannah. In this timeline, she'd married a policeman and had a three-year-old son. She beamed from the screen, and a warmth filled my heart. I'm glad she'd found happiness, something I doubt I'd have provided for her if I'd stayed in her life.

I found Lisa too, married to her trucker and, as before, with twin girls. I smiled and wondered about that. Every time, no matter what happened to me, or us, she ended up in the same place with the same result. Maybe fate, maybe blind luck, possibly forces I knew nothing about and shouldn't be meddling with.

I searched and found Elizabeth looking very pretty in a black dress at some formal event. A merchant bank night out, maybe. I imagined merchant bank events were a cut above any I'd ever been to. I sent her a quick hello message. She messaged back almost immediately, which surprised me.

She asked how I'd been, so I told her, I kept it brief, but she dug for more detail than I wanted to give. She said she'd come and see me the next day.

I said, *Elizabeth, don't go out of your way. I'm fine, really, I am.* I wasn't fine, I'd not been fine for a long time, but I didn't want her sympathy, or maybe I did. I had no idea. I felt lonely, lost and in pain, both literally and figuratively. Perhaps I did need her sympathy. I needed more than the single focused goal that dominated my thoughts. I needed a friend.

Chapter 27
I Will Survive

'I got away at lunchtime,' Elizabeth explained as she appeared in my room and plonked herself on the chair opposite mine. A few nurses and Maria appeared and stared in surprise at the pretty girl. I'd told them all I had no friends, yet here they saw a lovely red-haired girl leaning over and kissing my stubbly cheek.

They were all too busy to stand and stare for long, but I'd no doubt get the third degree later.

Elizabeth pulled her diary-sized notebook from her bag. 'I've been adding notes to my logbook. I'd wondered what had happened to you as nothing had changed for me. I guessed either you hadn't persuaded Dr Jaeger to let you back onto the programme or you'd gone back and fixed your life, but it hadn't affected mine. I didn't know you'd ended up in here.'

'Yeah. Things aren't going to plan.'

'What happened? I know you said you had a stroke, but what, when, and where?'

I gave her a condensed version of events, culminating in my move to the unit and my impending discharge later next week.

She considered all this for a moment. 'Well, first of all, you're looking better.'

'I'm partially paralysed.'

She smiled. 'Yeah, well, apart from that. You've lost weight.'

I'd dropped at least a dress size, maybe two, if I wore dresses which I didn't, but that's what Maria told me. I still pushed the scales over eighteen stone, but the weight had begun to drop slowly.

'Where are you living?'

'Here, at the moment. I've leased a flat near Edgbaston, disabled-friendly. I get the keys on Monday, in theory.'

'That's near the cricket ground. That's handy if you like cricket.'

'I suppose, I don't really. They made me play it at school, bloody hard ball.'

'Yeah, same as hockey for me, brutal.'

We chatted away like old friends, which surprised me. I'm not the world's best conversationalist, well hadn't been for a long time, but I supposed we had something in common nobody else had. Either that or we were both stark-staring bonkers, which remained a distinct possibility.

'Listen,' she said, 'Fay and I have a few days off next week. We could help you move in and get settled.'

'Don't be silly. You don't want to spend your free time helping a lump like me. You should go away for a few days or something.'

'We can do that anytime; you, however, need sorting out.'

The rest of my protests went unheeded, and half an hour later, she left, promising to meet me at the hospital entrance on Monday afternoon at two.

The minute she left, the nurses who had been treating me and who, to be honest, I'd grown very fond of descended on me like locusts.

'Who was that?'

'Elizabeth.'

'Ooo, Elizabeth, very posh.'

'You said you had no friends.'

'Well, maybe one.'

'Just a friend?' asked Dawn in her lovely Irish accent.

'I'm afraid so; she'd be more interested in getting into your knickers than mine.' A bit crude, I know, but that's how Dawn talked, so I felt OK saying it like that.

'Ahh, so, like that is it?' she grinned.

'It is,' I confirmed, and the questions eventually dried up.

By Monday, I'd been in the hospital for nearly five months. Christmas, New Year, all of January, February and a chunk of March had already slipped past.

Christmas in the hospital had been my best one for years, which is sad, I suppose and summed up how my life had panned out. Everyone had been cheerful, well, those of us who were no longer in danger of dying, at any rate. Dawn had even smuggled in some Irish Whiskey, and she got her grown-up daughter Cheila to slip me a small glass under cover of darkness at the end of her shift. She repeated this on New Year's Eve, and whilst I didn't particularly like whiskey, I very much appreciated the gesture and drinking it certainly helped me slip off to sleep. I'm pretty sure it wouldn't become hospital policy.

This morning, Maria had personally got me ready and had me waiting at the front door in my wheelchair. No tears were shed as I was far from being released from her care. Three follow-up physio sessions for the next six weeks were already in the diary on my iPad. She'd warned me they'd be some of the worst as she upped the game.

I couldn't wait for the little sadist to get a hold of me again. She'd become a motivator and torturer all rolled into one micro-package. Five feet one inch tall with muscles like Dwayne Johnson, all of which she used on me, or at least that's how it felt. She had brown hair in bangs, which always seemed to get caught on something when she worked on me. Blue eyes and a cheeky smile. Maria: pretty with a lovely soul, despite her sadistic streak at work. Her husband had left her for a French girl he'd met at his office. She'd become, and remained for the moment, a single mother, trying her best to get by.

I suppose that's what most of us are trying to do, get by. She'd done a better job than me, that's for sure.

I'd miss the staff, I'm not sure they'd miss me, but when you spend more time with people than you see your own family, a certain bond forms, and I'd never forget their kindness and dedication, that's for sure.

A five series BMW pulled up to the kerb, and Elizabeth jumped out of the passenger seat. She smiled at Maria, bent down, and kissed me on the cheek. They manoeuvred me into the back seat. My wheelchair folded easily into the cavernous boot. I said hi to Fay, who sat in the driver's seat, not looking particularly happy.

Maria disappeared inside to torture some other poor bugger, and we drove off to the letting agency to pick up the keys to my new flat.

Fay seemed to cheer up when we arrived at my apartment. Perhaps I'd misjudged her, and her gloomy expression was her default face, unlike the perpetually cheerful and trusting Elizabeth.

My new home had a ramp fitted to the steps outside, and they trundled me into a tastefully furnished living room with expensive wooden floors. Grey seemed to be the recurring theme, grey-painted walls, grey kitchen units, worktops, grey and white bathroom tiles, and grey duvets and pillowcases.

I wasn't complaining. Compared to my old place that the Rottweilers invaded, it felt like a palace. I'd become proficient, thanks to Maria, at walking with my sticks now, and I'd regained quite a bit of feeling on my left side. I'd never run the hundred metres, but walking normally again might be within my grasp.

Elizabeth wouldn't let me help, they parked me in front of the massive wall-mounted TV, and she and Fay went about sorting the heating timers and rearranging the kitchen so I didn't have to reach into the upper cupboards. They did a food shop and stocked the fridge.

I watched them reorganise things; I believe that it takes a woman to make a home, and they did an excellent job. They departed around six for dinner and a movie. They left me with a casserole bubbling in the oven. Elizabeth promised to come around in a day or two to talk strategy, whatever that meant.

After they left, the flat felt empty. I distracted myself from negative thoughts by heaping some casserole on a plate, took a bottle of sparkling water from the fridge and settled down to watch a Netflix boxset.

I went to bed at ten and slept.

When I opened my eyes the next day, I reached across the bed, searching for the warm body of Luci, as I'd done for many years and for not very long at all. The memories came flooding back, and the knowledge that my wife's body was long dead and very cold.

No wonder I'd been/was depressed. Moving is much more complicated when half of your body doesn't work correctly. Eventually, I scrambled out of bed and scrambled some eggs for breakfast. The flat felt toasty thanks to Elizabeth setting the heating timer. I sat at the small grey (what other colour would it *be*?) table in the kitchen, ate my eggs and checked my iPad and phone.

I got a text from Elizabeth, hoping I'd slept well, a notification from O2 that my new contract had been activated, and an email from the power company confirming my tariff and that the first bill would be due next week, payable quarterly in advance.

That puzzled me. How could they know how much power I'd use? I might be a power junkie with every conceivable electrical appliance running twenty-four-seven or a hermit wrapped in multiple duvets sitting in candlelight.

Anyway, I had more important considerations. Somehow, I had to work out how to convince the Doc to give me another chance. I searched online for Perry Flowers's number, dialled and waited.

A woman answered, and I asked if Dr Jaeger was available. She asked me to hold. A minute or so later, the woman returned to the phone. 'Can I ask what this is about?'

I wasn't sure why she couldn't have asked that initially. 'Yes, I'm a patient of hers and wanted a quick word.'

'Oh, I see. Well, I'm afraid Dr Jaeger no longer works here. She and her project team have concluded the programme. I'm sorry.'

The words thudded home. *Concluded the programme.* That wasn't right; they were supposed to run it for another few months. Maybe they'd started again somewhere else. 'Do you know where she's based?'

'I'm sorry, I don't. Goodbye.' She hung up.

Now what?

The stark reality hit home. The programme had closed. Did that mean forever, or had they packed up their stall and moved on to another venue? They'd done it before, hadn't they? Elizabeth had been a participant down in Kent. Perry Flowers had been situated in Birmingham, so maybe they'd headed north to Manchester, Hull or Scotland. They could be in Shetland for all I cared, so long as I could get back on the programme.

I dropped my dirty dishes into the sink and hobbled through the bathroom to shower.

Everything seemed to take three times longer than it used to due to my infirmity, apart from watching TV – that hadn't changed.

I was lucky to be alive, but the dark thoughts that were never far away posed the question: what was the point? I had to find the Doc for one more turn of the cards, one more roll of the dice, one more spin of the wheel – I couldn't think of any more gambling analogies.

In any event, I couldn't end up much worse than I'd become now. Yes, I had money, blood money, is how I thought of it. But money can't buy your wife and child back, nor your health, as I'd recently realised.

Chapter 28
Move on Up

Regardless of where she'd gone, I decided to track the Doc down. I'd beg if I had to. Somehow, I'd get some of her magic potion, even if it took every penny I had.

Bolstered by my plan, which had no structure yet, I spent the rest of the day stumbling around the flat. I realised I only had two sets of clothes: joggers, hoodies and pyjamas, plus three pairs of boxer shorts.

I discovered the joy of online shopping, and soon my flat became the home of boxes and parcels galore. Mostly clothes and shoes, plus a few household items and a present for Elizabeth and Fay for helping me move. I spent considerable time searching online for a suitable gift, and various rude things assaulted my senses, together with inappropriate Mrs & Mrs monogrammed stuff. I decided that a huge luxury food and pamper hamper would be more welcome. I ordered it at three pm, and it arrived at Elizabeth's just after eight that evening. She texted me to say thanks. This online same-day delivery lark was all right.

By the time Elizabeth came to see me on Thursday evening, I'd managed to tidy most of the purchases away, except for the giant furry cat-shaped slippers that had appeared earlier in the day. I didn't recall ordering them. I must have added them to my Amazon basket on a whim after two glasses of Chardonnay, then forgot they were there when I ordered something else. Still, they were warm and comfy but not very conducive to walking when one is semi-paralyzed.

Elizabeth laughed so much that tears trickled down her cheeks when she saw me dressed in my claret dressing gown/housecoat that I'd ordered from Ted Baker's outlet website—a bargain at only £29.99.

'I'll just call you Noel from now on,' she squeaked.

She could laugh, but the Noel Coward air of sophistication had been my aim; maybe eighty years too late, but everything comes back around. Besides, that's what happens when you're married to an actress, well, when you were *once* married to an actress.

She made us both tea and placed my mug on the grey (just in case you were wondering) coffee table and sat opposite, smiling at me over her drink.

'All you need is a cigarillo, and you're all set.'

'I might just do that,' I said, pretending to be in a huff.

Elizabeth shook her head. 'Have you contacted Dr Jaeger yet?'

'She's gone, moved on, but I can't find out where to. There's virtually nothing about the project online, and I can't find her profile anywhere. No Facebook, Instagram, not even a LinkedIn entry; weird, don't you think?'

Elizabeth frowned. 'Maybe, maybe not. She's probably trying to keep her work low key, it is very experimental after all, plus she's probably trying to avoid cranks, weirdos and would be Noel Coward's phoning her.' She cracked up and laughed so hard that tears formed in her eyes again. I started to defend myself, but her laughter became infectious, and a few seconds later, I shook, too, as I joined in.

It took a moment or two before we stopped. I felt much better. Laughter is a tonic. Plus, Elizabeth was funny, kind, caring and gay. I reminded myself before my musings went down a path they shouldn't. That might be why I liked her and felt comfortable in her company, there was no pressure to try and impress her or be anything else, plus we shared a secret, a big one, a crazy one.

'I'm assuming you haven't shared your adventures with Fay?'

She smiled. 'What, and have her think I'm crazy? No thanks. Did you tell Luci on any of your trips?'

'No, I'd been tempted, but as you say, it's not something you can prove so....'

'Exactly.'

She finished her tea. 'Well, as much as I don't mind helping you, Sam, I know this isn't where you want to be, living a life of solitude with a broken body, so we need to find Dr Jaeger and convince her to help you again.'

'How, though?'

'Check her GMC registration. Here, pass me your iPad.'

Elizabeth tapped away for a few minutes, then said, 'OK, she seems to be based at Birmingham University, in the Department of Education, which is nowhere near Birmingham University. It's on the outskirts of Wolverhampton. Here.' She passed the tablet back to me. 'She might have moved on. I'm not sure how up-to-date these things are.'

I felt miffed that she'd found the Doc in less than five minutes, and I'd spent hours searching. I tapped on the link, and a picture of a depressing-looking sixties block appeared, displaying signage of BU Dept. Of Ed. I tried the phone number, but it went to her voicemail. I assumed that meant she worked there. I didn't leave a message. I should see her face to face like I'd planned last time, before my stroke got in the way.

'Is your plan still to offer her money?' Elizabeth asked.

'Yeah.'

'How much?'

'All of it if I have to.'

Elizabeth scoffed. 'Maybe not. If she thinks you're bankrupting yourself to get back on the programme, that'll do two things: make her very suspicious and make her doubt your motive or sanity or both. How much are you due to get from the settlement?'

'One and a quarter million.'

'OK, offer her say, a hundred and fifty thousand towards costs and stuff on the condition that you are accepted back into the programme, make up some bullshit about how much good it had been doing you and, plus, now you're partially disabled your mental health has slumped again, which it probably has and certainly will if she disagrees. Plus, as you can now contribute, you feel it would only be fair that others get the benefits you did. Make it sound altruistic. She's more likely to buy that.'

'Sounds like a plan.'

Elizabeth got up. 'Great, let me know how you get on. Text me.'

She hugged me. 'Don't get up. I'll see myself out. Good luck, Sam.'

*

The following day, I awoke with a sense of purpose. I phoned the Department of Education and asked, 'Is Dr Jaeger available?'

The receptionist wouldn't tell me; she said, 'If you leave your name and number, I'll make sure the doctor gets your message.'

I hung up and phoned back ten minutes later, hoping they didn't log caller numbers, but as I received an identical greeting from the same voice, I assumed not.

'This is Dennis.' *Dennis? Where the hell had I pulled that from?* 'From Amazon and have a delivery due for….' I paused for effect as I pretended to read something, 'For a Dr Jaeger, he needs to sign for it personally. Will he be in today?'

'She,' corrected the receptionist. 'Dr Jaeger is a woman, and yes, *she'll* be in from eleven am.'

'OK, thanks.' I hung up—the power of Amazon.

I aimed to arrive just before noon in case she turned up late. I ordered an Uber for 11.15 am.

I fizzed with nervous excitement, trepidation and worry. What if I failed today? What then? I shuddered; it didn't bear thinking about.

The Uber driver, a goth girl with more tattoos than Justin Bieber, wasn't the talkative type which suited me fine. She dropped me outside the hulking public building and even waited without tutting as I clambered awkwardly out the back of the car. I'd brought both my sticks today to ensure I stayed upright.

I paid her, gave a healthy tip and waddled slowly towards the main entrance. The receptionist (the one I'd spoken to earlier, I assumed) waved a finger at me as she tried to end a phone call. She hung up, smiled and said, 'Can I help you?'

'I'd like to speak to Dr Jaeger, please.'

'Do you have an appointment?'

I knew that she knew I didn't. She had to ask; I suppose. 'I haven't, but I'm a former patient of hers, and I'm sure if you mention my name, she'll give me some time.' I shut up and waited. I wobbled on my sticks for effect. After a short hesitation, she picked up the phone and spoke to the Doc.

'I have a gentleman in reception asking to see you. No, I know you don't have any appointments today. No, yes, well, he said you'd want to speak to him.' She nodded into the phone, leaned forward and asked, 'What's your name?'

'Sam Harris.'

She relayed that information to the Doc and then hung up. 'You've got ten minutes.' She pointed towards the lifts and said, 'Third floor, room 12.'

I thanked her and stumbled my way towards the lifts. I could feel my nerves on the way up, making me shake even more.

The lift lurched to a stop, and I stumbled out onto a carpeted, hushed corridor, much plusher than the waiting area downstairs. It was apparent where the money got spent here. I made my way along the corridor and found room 12. I knocked and waited.

'Come in.' I recognised the voice.

I pushed the handle down, opened the door and entered a large room flooded with light from ceiling-to-floor windows overlooking the Wolverhampton skyline. Not exactly New York, but impressive enough.

Dr Jaeger sat behind a paper-strewn desk, typing into a MacBook. She took in my demeanour.

'What happened, Sam?'

I plonked myself down into one of the two chairs in front of her desk, laid my sticks on the floor and said, 'I had a stroke.'

Chapter 29
Changes

My dramatic news had probably bought me an extra fifteen minutes, but not much more. I relayed the whole sorry drama to the Doc in as few words as possible. When I'd finished, she said, 'I'm sorry, Sam, we thought… your social worker and I thought that you'd maybe just taken off somewhere hot and sunny with your windfall.'

'That would have been preferable to lying in a hospital bed for months, but I'm OK now, well OK's, maybe pushing it, but I'm on the mend.'

Dr Jaeger nodded. 'We didn't know, or we would have….'

She didn't finish her sentence. I didn't need her to. What would she have done, visited me and brought grapes and flowers? I doubted it. Sally might have made an appearance, but I'd managed with Elizabeth's help.

Instead, she said, 'I'm sure the money will help your recuperation and pay for the psychotherapy we discussed.'

'Maybe, but I've got a proposition for you.'

The Doc looked slightly alarmed. 'No, nothing like that,' I assured her without knowing what she'd been picturing. 'I'd like to make a generous donation to the research work you've been doing with the….' I'd forgotten the name of the amber concoction.'

'Genome Plasma Compound. GPC for short.'

'Yeah, that. I have to say the treatment and your care made me feel, well, probably the best I've felt in years, and I'm prepared to invest one hundred and fifty thousand pounds towards your ongoing research.'

The Doc's eyes boggled wide. 'That's very generous, but—'

I cut across her. 'It's not quite out of the goodness of my heart, I want to undergo at least one more treatment with you, possibly more, but I'll see how I feel after one. I can afford to contribute now, and it feels right that others should be able to benefit from the project.'

The Doc smiled. 'I had been about to say the project is winding down, and we have moved onto another field of study.'

I tried to remember the Doc's original enthusiasm for the project, which I didn't, only fragments from the notes, but I'm pretty sure she'd claimed it would be revolutionary, breaking new ground, all sorts of stuff, not including time travel of course but even so. 'You said it would revolutionise the field of mental health treatment?'

She smiled. 'I don't quite remember claiming that, but I had high hopes.'

'What happened?'

'I don't think I can discuss that with you, Sam.'

'Not even for a hundred and fifty grand?'

She sighed. 'We have run out of the key treatment.'

'What, the Amber fluid?

'No, we have plenty of that; there's nothing extraordinary about that. It's just a chemically enhanced blood plasma mixed with a sedative that shows where the genome is damaged. We've run out of the second injection we give you, which you won't remember as you are generally asleep by then. It's a special protein-based compound. We called it SPC for short.

'Can't you just make some more?'

'We tried. I gave some to two commercial laboratories, but neither could synthesise it correctly.'

'Why not?'

Dr Jaeger paused, wondering if she should reveal any more. 'It's a natural substance that I can't access.'

'Why?'

She paused and stared at me, internally debating something, if I had to guess, as she didn't enlighten me. She did, however, continue. 'Originally, I had a sample brought to me by a post-grad student here in Birmingham.' I didn't point out that we were in Wolverhampton. 'She originally hailed from the Solomon Islands.'

I didn't know where they were. I did an English Lit degree, not geography.

As if reading my mind, she said, 'A group of islands in the South Pacific about two thousand miles from Australia.' I nodded, none the wiser.

'Anyway, we lab tested it for dangerous impurities, then received a provisional licence to proceed with animal and eventually human tests, using a group of paid volunteers. The results were, well, unusual. The grad student, by then a fully-fledged practising psychiatrist, travelled home for Christmas. She returned in January with much more of the compound, and that's when we launched the project you took part in, as did she.

The Doc sat back in her chair and ran a hand through her hair. 'The student used to be part of our team. You'll remember her as Dr Ramos.'

Little Miss Gorgeous. 'She's very er…memorable.'

A sad smile drifted across her face. 'She died.'

It felt like she'd reached out across the desk and slapped me. 'Died?'

The Doc sighed. 'She'd gone home for a few months, back to Honiara, where her parents lived. Whilst there, on January 15th, a cyclone made landfall, wiped out a huge part of the town, hundreds died, and thousands were made homeless. Dr Ramos was killed. Her father died too. Her mother survived. Contacting me hadn't been top of her priority list. It took her some time to let me know what had happened.'

I could imagine. I also couldn't help thinking about Luci and Chloe's deaths and wondered if somehow anyone who knew me was cursed. I tried not to dwell on that for now.

'I can see that this has shocked you, Sam. I perhaps shouldn't have told you in your current condition.'

I waved her concerns away. 'No, it's such a waste, that's all.'

The Doc nodded, she knew I'd be thinking about my wife and daughter, but that brought me back to the point of my visit. 'So, you can't get more protein thingmajig?'

'What do you know about the Solomon Islands?'

'Not a lot.'

'They are a group of around six hundred islands. Janice hailed from the Guadalcanal Province, which formed a crucial role in stopping the Japanese advance in World War Two. Nowadays, it's something of a tourist hub. It's very beautiful, so Janice... Dr Ramos used to tell me, with lush forests, long sandy beaches and volcanic mountains. Many relics from the war remain and are, in some part, retained by the locals for the tourists. Anyway, it's an island that has a modern society with a more traditional element living side by side. The traditional, mainly tribal groups, retain many primitive beliefs and practices going back hundreds if not thousands of years. Dr Ramos grew up cut off but not isolated from the traditional ways. Her parents were teachers at the university, and she had a very modern upbringing in many ways, but as I say, it's a diverse culture.'

This all sounded fascinating, but something I could have read on Wikipedia. I wondered why she had decided to tell me all this, but I didn't want to interrupt as I assumed it must be important.

'In her final year at university, she'd been studying medicine, already specialising in psychiatry, and spent another two years refining her skills and knowledge at Kings College Hospital London. We were introduced at a seminar we both attended. She knew that I'd been looking into alternative mental health procedures, and we put our heads together, and she let me into her little secret about the SPC.'

She paused and said, 'Do you want a coffee?'

'Yes, please.'

'What do you take in it?'

'Just a little milk, please.'

The Doc disappeared. I took the time to try and collect my thoughts. The news of Janice's death had shaken me. Despite this, I needed to focus on my primary objective. Dr Jaeger reappeared and handed me a steaming mug. She took a sip from her own cup and said, 'Where had I got to?'

'You and Janice had put your heads together.'

'Ah, yes, right. Well, I didn't take her seriously at first. Still, I like to think I have an open mind on such things and undertook some personal research. I discovered that despite the troubles and strife the Solomon Islands have suffered and continue to experience, they enjoy one of the lowest levels of mental illness in the world.'

She waited for me to comment. I didn't know what to say but nodded and said, 'Interesting.'

I must have struck the right note as she said, '*Very* interesting. That's when Janice explained how the SPC is used by the primitive tribes across the islands as a kind of cure-all, brewed into teas and poultices. It is mainly administered when someone is feeling a little down in the dumps. It originates from a small village just along the coast from her home. Unfortunately, the original samples that Janice brought back were quite contaminated and caused some severe side effects, vomiting, diarrhoea, raised heart rates, and extreme headaches. We were in danger of losing our licence, but Janice refused to give up. She returned home and brought back a new batch which she claimed would be much purer, having been made up by a very old tribal elder.'

I must have looked surprised as the Doc smiled.

'I reacted similarly, but we tested it. We found it to be more refined, and it produced much better results. It still took nearly eighteen months and extensive tests to get a licence to begin proper trials. Some people still suffer an upset tummy now and then, as you know, but overall, the side effects were much milder.'

'What's it made of?' I asked.

'Well, that's the thing; I don't know. The labs I sent it to couldn't give me a specific answer, a mixture of cellulose fibre, phloem, animal protein, bone fragments and a little local alcohol, made from fermented pineapples, and something else. A curious and unknown protein. The best way to describe it is as something like a mixture of animal and plant. If you like, a cross between a peanut and an insect. Weird.'

I hadn't understood much of the last few sentences, but the look on the Doc's face told me she was out of her depth almost as much as me. She continued, 'The principal application of the SPC in combination with the Amber liquid allowed us to target and repair the damaged genes, as we discussed when you started the programme.'

I sat back in my chair. I had been leaning forward, listening intently to the Doc without realising it. I'd learned much more than I'd expected when I turned up here this morning, and my allotted ten minutes had come and gone some time ago.

'However, with Janice's death, the programme ended. Only she had access to the SPC; without it, there's no treatment.'

Her pronouncement sounded final to me. A dark cloud drifted across my soul.

She paused, finished her coffee and continued. 'It is a big loss. As we had begun to make real progress with patients, you experienced how helpful even a short course could be; the long-term positive prognosis for severely debilitated patients would have been enormous.' She finished speaking with a sigh.

I couldn't give up hope. 'I could help you go there to try and seek out her source. Her mother might know.'

The Doc smiled. 'I appreciate the offer, Sam, but I can't go trekking into the Solomon Islands jungle. I've got commitments, patients, and programmes to run.'

'Can you not get some of your students to go on a fully funded field trip?'

'A fully funded wild-goose chase.'

'They might get lucky.'

'It would take so long to organise.'

I could see she might be warming to the idea. At least her resistance was wavering. 'I'd fund it all and get people to organise everything. You won't need to do anything except oversee it.'

She smiled at my enthusiasm. 'It would be a shame to give up completely, and I'm sure the university would be open to the idea.'

I returned the smile. 'That's the spirit. Even if it takes years to get any return on my investment, I'll wait.'

'All so you can have one more treatment?'

I nodded.

She thought for a moment. 'OK, Sam. Let's give it a go.' She started at me for a moment. 'Also, you might not need to wait that long for a treatment.

'Why's that?'

She opened her desk drawer and pulled out a small, sealed jar. 'There is a little left. I had been hoping, as I explained, to synthesise it commercially, but that hasn't worked. There's more than enough here for one treatment, perhaps two, but I'd need some time to prepare as all the equipment is still at Perry Flowers, plus I'd need to make sure it's still all functioning properly.'

I stared intently at the golden elixir, slowly sloshing about in her hand. More valuable than all the money in my bank and yet to come from the lawyers. I'd even willingly sell my soul for it. Perhaps I already had.

Chapter 30
Up Where We Belong

I texted Elizabeth on the way home. *Game on.*

She texted back, *Cool, phone me.*

I did and gave her an update on the happenings, focusing primarily on Dr Ramos's death and the strange substance she'd brought to Dr Jaeger.

Elizabeth had never met Janice, so I don't think it resonated with her the way it had with me.

On the way home, it felt like a weight had been lifted from my shoulders. Of course, I had no idea if it would work and if I could fix what went wrong, but as long as I could get back to the point before Luci and Chloe got into that car, it couldn't be any worse. Even if she ran off with Tony Carioss, she and Chloe would be alive at least.

My friendly goth Uber driver dropped me outside the Perry Flowers unit on Friday morning. I pushed open the door, and an enclosed reception greeted me. This looked new, but I couldn't be sure, of course. The man behind the desk glanced up from typing when I hobbled in and said, 'I have an appointment with Dr Jaeger.'

He said, 'Orchid room.' and waved me through. I lumbered along the carpeted corridor. Instead of Cholis labs, the rooms had the names of flowers, which seemed more appropriate considering the facility's name. Daisy, Rose, Tulip, Lily and eventually Orchid. I opened the door and entered a room with a desk, three padded chairs, a hospital-style bed, and a clinical trolley loaded with varying-sized syringes and bottles. It all felt strangely familiar. Dr Jaeger sat in an office chair behind the desk. Two padded chairs were vacant, and the other supported the weight of a large woman wearing nurse attire. Her badge said, Claire Ingles. She smiled at me as I hobbled into the room and sat down. 'I transferred the funds this morning, Doctor, so the money should turn up later.'

'Thank you, Sam.'

We chatted for a while, exchanging pleasantries. The Doc's attitude towards me had changed now that I'd become a benefactor rather than simply a patient. Eventually, she said, 'Now, let's begin with what happened to your wife and daughter.'

I sighed but knew I'd have to do this. I relived the events from what happened nearly twenty years ago but which I'd only known about for months with the Doc. I hoped this had left a massive dent in my genome, which she could target with her magic potion. By the time we'd finished, I'd been blubbering and unable to control it.

Dr Jaeger said, 'I can see how painful this is for you, Sam, and whilst we cannot take those memories away, I'm hoping today we can target that area and perhaps help you gain some closure.'

I nodded, lay on the bed and waited while the Doc fetched the nurse back into the room.

The first injection slipped into my vein. I felt my eyes closing, then nothing.

The next thing I knew was of a quiet, warm darkness and the fact that I could move my body, all of it and the tingling that had infested my left hand had gone.

I became aware of the regular breathing at my back. I turned in the bed, and there sleeping beside me, I found the gorgeous, wonderful, beautiful, very much dead to the world but at the same time very much alive, Luci.

Adrenalin flooded into my system. I didn't want to wake her, but I desperately wanted to touch, hold, and love her. I leaned over, put my arm around her sleeping form, and snuggled beside her. I thanked the universe, God, Dr Jaeger, Elizabeth, the Solomon Islands and Dr Ramos. Anyone and everyone that had helped me get back here. Probably for the last time. I realised that if I changed the timeline, I'd never get the money, and neither would Dr Jaeger and the project would grind to a halt. Maybe that would be for the best. I didn't know.

I leaned over and pressed the home button of Luci's latest iPhone 4s, which was by now probably nestled in a museum somewhere, 5.45 am. I wouldn't be able to sleep, but lying here in the dark hugging my wife, I didn't care.

Her phone alarm went off forty-five minutes later, and she struggled to get free of my arms to flip it silent. 'Sam,' she complained, giggling. 'What's got into you?'

'I love you so much.'

'I love you too, but you've got to go to work, and I've got that meeting with YTG later to see if they want to use Chloe too.'

My blood ran cold. It was *that* morning, I hadn't been given much warning, but enough I hoped. 'Can I come too?'

She stared at me with sleepy eyes and bed hair. I didn't care. She looked just so sweetly gorgeous. I loved her so much. My heart was packed so full of emotion that it might burst.

'Why?'

I shrugged. 'I just can't bear being parted from you today.'

'What about work? You can't just not go.'

'I'll phone in sick. God knows they owe me enough hours.'

She stared at me, trying to work out what had gotten into me, and then her face broke into a huge grin. 'It's Tony bloody Carioss, isn't it. The green-eyed monster again. What are you like?'

I smiled. I'd take that.

'Come if you want, it might be handy having you there to entertain Chloe anyway, but you'll have to suffer Hardy Harker's first.'

I couldn't wait. I went for a shower while Luci dressed and fussed over our daughter. How lovely that sounded, *our daughter*. Alive and well, not buried with her teddy in a cold dark grave. I shuddered even though the water felt hot on my thin, healthy body. Given what I'd been through recently, I felt thankful and appreciative. I would never take anything for granted again, ever.

Chapter 31
Perfect Day

Hardy Harker's turned out to be bedlam. I watched as somewhere between twenty and thirty toddlers dashed madly about a room half the size of a tennis court, chasing balls, toys and each other while the group of mums, child-minders and au pairs sat together in small groups drinking coffee and chatting. I felt like an outsider, eyed suspiciously by a few of the yummy mummies, but I didn't care.

Later, in the head office of YTG in London's West End, I felt about as welcome as Donald Trump at a Climate Change debate as I watched the advertising and TV executives poke, prod and consider Chloe's suitability to play her mother's daughter in the series of ads.

They left me sitting in a small glass-walled room while they pondered and pontificated about my darling daughter. Luci's eyes shone when they confirmed she'd be ideal. However, my highlight was when Chloe started to scream the place down after Tony Carioss picked her up. Luci quickly grabbed her and thrust her into my arms while she, Tony and the rest of the entourage disappeared to talk tactics or whatever they needed to discuss.

Chloe and I found a canteen, and soon she had smeared chocolate cake all over her face and me.

I just laughed. I couldn't believe I was there, with my daughter fussing about cake. I tried to cuddle her, but she squeezed and wriggled and complained. Chloe was never a huge hugger. Still, compared to the last time I'd seen her… I banished the thought. I didn't need that darkness today.

I cleaned her up the best I could, and even a sticky chocolatey daughter couldn't dampen my wife's mood as we left the building. It had been the perfect day, she said.

My heart ached at the thought of her being so happy and filled with the thoughts of the future and never getting to share it with me last time, this time, or whatever.

Taking a car into central London is not anyone's idea of fun, but today with everything happening, I could see why it had made sense.

'Let's celebrate,' I suggested.

Luci beamed, 'We'll need to go home first, get changed and….'

We were going nowhere in that bloody car for the rest of today. 'We're up West already. Let's leave the car. I'll collect it tomorrow. It's in a multi-storey, I'll pay the ticket for twenty-four hours, and we'll go from there. If we go home, Chloe will want to be fed, you'll faff about, and we'll end up not going anywhere.'

'I don't faff.'

'Luci, you are the world champion at faffing. You're an artiste, I get that, but today, you're just Luci Harris, wife and mother who deserves a damn good pampering.'

She smiled. 'I thought you were about to say something rude and suggestive there, Mr Harris.'

I laughed, 'That comes later.'

'OK, so where are we going?'

I remembered Chloe's fussy knickers, who didn't like anything that wasn't drizzled in breadcrumbs and fried. 'Wizzles – Chloe likes it there.'

A cheer from Chloe and a shrug from my wife. 'They serve that Merlot you like?' Wizzles were part of a chain of Mexican/Swedish fusion restaurants, the interior intentionally designed to resemble a school dinner hall circa 1969, but they did spicy meatballs in breadcrumbs and Tacos that Chloe, for some reason, couldn't get enough of, plus they didn't mind kids making a mess, in fact, at times they seemed to actively encourage it.

'Yes, OK, let's go, but I'm not in the mood for wine?'

I raised my eyebrows. 'Since when?'

She fished about in her handbag and handed me the plastic stick she'd sent me a picture of all those years ago and not yet at all. I'd forgotten in all the excitement. I pretended to be puzzled, examined it closely, then grabbed hold of Luci and swung her around, bumping into a bunch of young girls dressed to kill or thrill, depending on your point of view.

One said, 'Hey, watch it, you prick.' Such a lovely turn of phrase. I was too happy to respond likewise and said, 'We're pregnant.'

The foul-mouthed teen looked down her nose at us and spat, 'Glad it's not me.' She strutted off as fast as her silly heels would let her.

'She's a credit to her parents,' Luci remarked, grabbing my hand. We walked slowly, mainly because the crowded streets made pushing Chloe in her buggy like an obstacle course.

'I hope Chloe doesn't turn out like that,' I said, gleefully remembering that this conversation should never have happened. What an incredible life or lives I was leading.

'No chance,' said my wife, 'not with me as her mother.'

Very true, I thought.

Wizzles was fun, not the sort of place we'd ever have ever gone to before Chloe came along, but having kids changes everything in so many ways, most of which you'll never appreciate unless you get to lose them and come back to find them like I had.

I'd never tire of looking at her beautiful little face, even when it eventually becomes a slightly spotty, scrunched-up grumpy teenage face. I'm sure over the years, she'll give me a reason to complain, worry, fear and laugh but at some point, in my fortieth year, with any luck, I'll once again appreciate just what a lucky man I've been. Unless, of course, some other disaster awaited me. I recalled Elizabeth's words; *the universe seems to have it in for you and yours*.

What if she turned out to be right? What if, no matter what I did, Luci ended up dead? After all, she wasn't supposed to make it much beyond her twenty-first birthday. What could I do about that? No manual existed for this. Nobody had written any rules, guidance notes, or anything. Then I remembered that she hadn't died on all the trips. The one where I'd been with Hannah, she'd been with that rugby guy. So, maybe the catalyst of death only applied to me. Did that make me a jinx? A harbinger of doom? Surely not. I noticed Luci peering at me and my frowning face.

I forced a smile back onto my lips and tried to banish those thoughts to the back of my mind. Tonight was a night for rejoicing. Luci would think we were doing it to celebrate her new job and pregnancy, and it would be, but for me, it was about so much more than that, so much more.

After dinner, we walked the streets of London for a while, unconsciously heading towards the bright lights of Leicester Square, Piccadilly and, of course, Shaftsbury Avenue, where at least three of the theatres once displayed my wife's name in giant letters.

I glanced over at her as we passed by. Her face remained serene and peaceful, but inside, I'm sure part of her missed the glamour, the curtain calls, the applause and the sheer guts it takes to get out onto a stage night after night. I could never do anything like that, but it felt to me that Luci had been born to entertain.

She has this inner glow that lights up the world. Yes, I'm biased because I'm in love with her, I've always been in love with her, I always will be, yet I'm not wrong. She's not unique. Extraordinary, but not singular. I've met others like her. In the theatres where she worked and in the bars and restaurants after shows, they stand out, a special quality that draws others in, like moths to flames. When she was playing Izabella in the too-short run of When the Wall Came Down, roughly based around the fall of the Berlin Wall, her co-star Sharon Axle, a weird name I know, shone with the same intensity as Luci. The two of them together captivated audiences and fellow actors alike. Alas, neither the script nor the score was good enough to fuel anything but a brief run in London, but the two of them, on and off stage, were captivating.

She missed this life, I'm sure, but she had another life just now, being a mother, becoming a mother again, all things being willing. Was it as fulfilling as an audience cheering you every night? Only she could answer that. I may ask her one day. I may not.

Somewhere inside me, I knew her potential had hardly been tapped, she had a deep well of ability that may never be completely fulfilled, but perhaps that's true of all of us. How many people truly achieve what they *could* achieve, and by that, I'm not referring to the bankers and those who con and sleaze their way to riches and fame but genuinely those who could give back so much in kindness, achievement from hard work and practice, or from a pure talent that is nurtured and developed.

I'm not sure where this philosophical bent stemmed from. I suspect it might have been born from my recent experiences and the pain suffered following the stroke, the physical, mental and emotional distress. The memories of which would soon begin to dim and darken. I needed to write them all down, or they'd vanish altogether. There were valuable lessons in all that pain, and I didn't want to forget them.

Chloe fell asleep, tucked up in her buggy, rug wrapped around her legs, keeping the chill night air at bay.

We stopped for a drink at a bar with some tables outside, something that will become much more commonplace following the pandemic, but all that is yet to come in this timeline and not something I can prevent.

As I sat sipping on a beer, watching Luci fuss over Chloe, I thought of all the pain and strife yet to come between now, and when I would wake up again, none of which I could do anything to prevent; the Manchester Bombing, the London Bridge Stabbings, the Russian invasion of Ukraine and God knows how many others, I don't remember. Of those I do remember, I don't know the dates.

I took a pad from the back of the buggy, which Luci had used to make notes during the meeting earlier. I wrote down as many significant events that lay ahead as I could remember. I also made a note to myself to buy as many shares as possible at the beginning of the pandemic as they will mostly recover by the following summer. I scribbled down a few other things I could quickly recall, Donald Trump becoming president in 2017, Leicester City winning the Premier League in 2016, and a young lady named Emma Raducanu winning the US Open tennis in 2021. Our funds needed replenishing after cashing in most of the shares to buy our house.

I hoped the version of me that returned to this body would take the scribblings seriously. I made a little note at the end, which I hoped would help, then another as an afterthought.

We finished our drinks and headed home. We talked about everything and nothing, both on a high. Luci because of her wonderful day and me because of the wonderful life I'd never truly appreciated until now. Frank Capra and Jimmy Stewart, eat your heart out.

Chloe woke up as we tried to lift her from her buggy into her bed. She moaned and got grumpy, but Luci soon soothed her off to sleep again. She'd been a terrible baby for sleeping but a great toddler, and once she fell asleep, she rarely woke up.

Luci ran a bath with bubbles, and I joined her in the tub, something we used to do a lot until Chloe came along, lots of bubbles, soapy sex and usually Prosecco, but tonight, two mugs of tea rested on the shelf at the end of the bath, a sign of how things had changed and would change further with the new life growing inside my wife. I remember a colleague at work, Tony Warden, had offered some advice shortly before Chloe had been born, 'Your first kid, Sam, is a great leap into the unknown, you worry about everything, cholic, cot death, child abduction, child abusers, carbon dioxide poisoning, childhood cancers, child cardiac problems, colds, chills, carcinogens, clean-air, contamination of their food and loads of others, all beginning with C, as you'll have noticed, it's not a coincidence that children and childhood both begin with the letter C.'

He'd missed one – car crashes, but he did give me some insight. Tony had four daughters aged between four and twelve. 'What you'll find is the first child will get cossetted and fussed and worried over, the second slightly less so, by the time the third comes along, you're a dab hand at it and by the time the fourth one pops out, you just toss it into soft-play and head for the pub.'

I'd laughed, knowing he'd been joking, hoping he'd been joking, but he had a point. Chloe had been so precious, and we'd been so scared of her getting hurt or harmed. Still, babies, as we discovered, are tough little buggers and not easily damaged by the occasional fall or deterred from trying to give their parents heart attacks by drinking out of the toilet, sticking their fingers in plug sockets and deciding the TV would look better smashed on the floor than sitting on the drawers in our bedroom. That particular incident remained fresh in my mind for some reason. We'd both rushed into the bedroom. Chloe had looked up, pointed to the TV and said, 'Bwoken.'

It certainly was, but she'd been unhurt more to the point.

I stared across at my beautiful wife. She'd got slightly distracted by a ragged nail on her finger and nibbled at it, somewhat cross-eyed, trying to fix it. It allowed me to stare at her without her knowing.

'Why are you staring at me, Sam?'

'Because you are so beautiful.'

'It's not like you to fire me compliments, not that I'm complaining.'

'We have a great life, don't we?'

Nail now fixed; she focused her full attention on me. 'I suppose we do, I've always thought that, but I'm not sure you always did.'

'I do now. I can't imagine being anywhere else than with you, Chloe and whoever that turns out to be.' I poked my toe gently into her tummy.

She giggled.

Of course, I didn't have to imagine what my life or various lives would be like without her in it, but I couldn't tell her that. Would I ever be able to? Maybe one day I'd have to.

Later, we made love in our cosy bed, the rain and wind hammering off the window. It seemed to do that a lot when I returned, but then we lived on a tiny windswept island in the North Atlantic.

We lay entwined. Luci, warm, sensuous and scented with bath oils and sex, slipped into a quiet deep sleep. I lay awake for a while, listening to the weather raging hard outside and wondered what the next few years would bring. I hoped I'd now live them without further disasters, but even if I did, I wouldn't remember them completely when I returned. The memories would drop in, and the current ones would fade, but I'd never be completely whole. Maybe as much as ten per cent would be missing, but ninety per cent of the memories with my wife and family is better than zero per cent, which I'd left behind or had left in front. I still found it incredibly confusing, but then who wouldn't?

Eventually, I slipped into a contented sleep, my first for months, perhaps years.

Chapter 32
The Language Of Love

I awoke, confused and concerned as usual, from my trip down the rabbit hole. The memory of being snuggled and warm beside Luci's lovely body and listening to the rain still lingered. It took me a moment to realise the smiling face of Nurse Paton meant I'd returned to my time, or perhaps knowing what I knew now, a personal determiner like *my* time, is/was wholly inaccurate. I felt more confused than usual because I'm sure Nurse Paton hadn't been there when I'd drifted off.

I could hear the nurse and Dr Jaeger talking to me, but I wasn't taking anything in yet. The warm fuzziness following a day with my family hadn't completely dissipated. I also needed to know what had changed for me. For a start, I could move my left arm and leg. No stiffness remained from the stroke. That meant I'd either made a miraculous recovery, or it had never happened. I glanced down at my slim body. I'd come in here wearing sweatpants and a hoodie. I now wore jeans, leather boots and a fitted shirt. The blimp had vanished again. My body felt in good shape, not gym bunny like I'd been once, but decent, which meant I might see my fiftieth birthday, which been in serious doubt before.

I tuned into the Doc. She looked tired, with bags under her eyes, and her makeup had been applied in a rush.

'Sam, are you feeling OK?'

I smiled and took a moment to consider her question. If I tried to answer it honestly, considering all that had happened to me, we might we there a while. Instead, I said, 'I feel pretty good. How long have I been out?'

'Nearly three hours, we'd started to get concerned, but your vitals all seem fine.'

'Better than when I came in anyway.'

Dr Jaeger raised her eyebrows. 'You look the same to me.'

'I know,' I replied. 'I feel a little confuddled still. Can I take a few minutes?'

Dr Jaeger said, 'Of course, we can debrief later. Dinner is at six tonight.'

'OK,' I said, a little uncertain. 'Where's my room again?'

They both stared at me for a minute. 'Really, you don't remember?'

I shrugged. 'Befuddled.'

Dr Jaeger said, 'Confuddled.'

I laughed. 'Yeah, that too.' I stood up and rubbed my face.

The Doc said, 'Room seven.' I patted my pocket and touched what felt like a credit card. I pulled out a key card. 'OK, I'll see you later. Thanks.'

I left the room. The door still said Orchid on it; that felt familiar, but I knew I hadn't been a resident earlier. I'd walked or rather stumbled in here as a stroke patient and had planned to stumble back out again if it hadn't worked. A few minutes later I found room seven, opened the door and flopped down onto the bed. On the night table sat my mobile, blinking away with unread text messages. I didn't want to read anything yet. I needed to wait for the memories to drop in. So far, everything remained blank—disconcerting but not unexpected.

I did pick up the letter beside my mobile, printed on Birmingham University notepaper.

Sam Harris
23 Bletchworth Drive
St Albans
Hertfordshire
AL5 3SX

15ᵗʰ August

Dear Mr Harris

Following our recent meeting and discussion, I am pleased to be able to inform you that we have managed to secure a place for you on the upcoming Epigenetic Research and Testing programme.

We have attached the joining details on the attached sheet, and we very much look forward to welcoming you to Perry Flowers. The programme, as we discussed, will be on a residential basis for one week beginning 15ᵗʰ November. A room has been reserved for your convenience.

Should you have any questions or need clarification, please contact our chief administrator Ms Ursula Goodall.

Yours sincerely

Dr Lynda Jaeger

There were a bunch of telephone numbers and email addresses underneath that I didn't bother to read. I sat back and tried to understand what had happened. I remembered my note at the bottom of the list I'd left myself and wondered if, over the years, I'd bet on Trump, Leicester City and Emma Raducanu.

The most significant change seemed to be that when I'd waddled into Perry Flowers, having handed over a load of cash, it had been early May, and now I was back in November. I suppose as I hadn't lost my family in the crash, and I hadn't got fat and unhealthy, the stroke and the months of rehabilitation hadn't occurred. Confusing or what?

I scribbled down my thoughts and memories into the notebook I found lying at the top of my travel bag. Then I lay down on the bed and waited.

The pennies slowly began to drop into my brain like those arcade games from which the afternoon game show *Tipping Point* is derived. As the memories plinked in, they pushed the existing ones out. I glanced over at the notebook. My only anchor to a world or worlds that no longer existed, proof that I'm not mad, or perhaps a journal that confirmed my insanity beyond any reasonable doubt; time, as they say, would tell. My journal of craziness.

As before, the earlier memories came first, and I relaxed back onto my pillow and hitched on for the ride, which would no doubt be bumpy.

The first significant worry occurred when Luci reached her eighth month of pregnancy. She'd been filming her latest instalment of the YTG adverts with Tony Carioss.

They'd become a huge hit, and viewers waited eagerly for the next instalment. The first series had seen Luci and Tony young free and single, dancing the night away in an open-air nightclub in Ibiza, on a cruise for young couples and on a short break in Rome. The second instalment showed them on a family holiday in Sicily with Chloe. I hadn't been able to go on that one due to work, but it rained a lot, so Luci had said. They also drove Route 66 with Chloe in an open-topped Cadillac. (The travel company hadn't funded a trip to the States and instead found a dusty road in southern France that resembled a portion of the iconic route.)

The one they filmed most recently showed them sitting in a golf buggy, Chloe in the back and Tony in the front, driving with his hand on Luci's bump. I remember not liking that at all, but she got well paid for it, plus her profile had gone sky high, and the offers for TV and theatre roles had poured in, most for after she'd given birth. However, a famous branded clothing company had engaged her for a poster campaign for their pregnancy jeans.

On the day in question, she'd gone into the Pinewood Studios for some editing shots (I'm not sure what that entailed precisely), but she'd been up and away by the time I got up. I got the call at 11 am that she'd started bleeding, and Chloe and I rushed to the Hillingdon Maternity Unit.

Lots of tears and lots of tests, always lots of tests, agonising then relief when we got the news that all seemed to be fine – but Luci had been warned to rest at home.

It took less than three hours for her to become bored. She started hoovering the floor and picking up toys. I'd arranged to work from home for a few days and on hearing the vacuum cleaner I galloped down the stairs and ushered her back to the couch.

'The house is a disgrace, Sam. It needs cleaning, painting and....'

'It's fine,' I said, which was entirely the wrong thing to say.

'You're fine living in a dump; it's like that student flat in Edinburgh, you know what? It's worse.'

I surveyed the room, the lovely stone floor with rugs and quality furniture, a huge flatscreen TV on the wall, various solid oak trunks where Chloe's toys lived when she wasn't scattering them around the house, large bi-fold doors leading to an immaculate lawn and apple and plum trees with Chloe's playhouse and swing set. Yep, just like my old flat, with the bathroom that even rats wouldn't live in, stinking from the last six months of curry take-outs.

'Yep, it's a dump, OK? Maybe I'll get some students to move in to tidy up the place?'

She punched me on the arm but managed a weak smile. 'I wanted to get the place sorted before Mia arrives.'

We'd discovered ages ago that our next precious little parcel of love and chaos would be a girl, and Luci had the name ready. I liked the name Mia, but even if I hadn't, I wouldn't have said anything initially. There had been plenty of time for my wife to change her mind, I almost expected her to, but Mia had stuck.

I didn't know women wanted to do the nesting thing for the second child, but I suppose it made sense.

'Why don't I get a decorating firm in to do it? You need to take it easy.'

'How do we know they'll be any good?'

'Ask your Uncle Jeremy.'

'Good idea, Sam, you're on the ball today.' She reached for her phone, took it from her bag and dropped it on the floor as she curled up, well as curled up as a heavily pregnant woman can, and groaned in agony. Chloe came skidding through on her trike and said, 'What's wrong, Mummy?'

A puddle of viscous liquid soaked the couch and dripped onto the floor.

'That's not good,' I said aloud but didn't mean to.

'No shit, Sherlock.' Luci groaned.

It took nearly forty minutes to drive to the hospital, it might have been better waiting for an ambulance, but we probably did it quicker on balance.

They took Luci to the labour ward, but I had to wait for Luci's friend Caroline Hunter to show up. They'd met at one of the playgroups or maybe at all the playgroups. She often came back to our house with Luci and occasionally stayed over. I liked her, and she was a single BY CHOICE yummy mummy to Beatrice, a dark-haired elfin toddler whom Chloe adored. Caroline said, BY CHOICE, so often I now called her Caroline BY CHOICE Hunter, though not to her face.

She appeared, removed Chloe from the chaos and left me to go in search of my wife. I found her sitting up in a bed eating toast. Not what I'd expected.

The midwife, a small pretty bundle of Welsh happiness called Fiona, assured me all was fine. Luci had gone into premature labour, but being only four weeks from her due date, nobody needed to panic. Everything would be fine. Fiona liked the word fine. She used it a lot. Over the next eight hours, she must have said fine, maybe two hundred times.

Near the end of Fiona's shift, Mia emerged. She came kicking and screaming into the world, a little ball of dark-haired fury who wouldn't settle unless attached to Luci's boob.

The next day, we took her home to meet her big sister, and so began the complex and unique relationship that sisters have. Chloe's birthday was in July and Mia's in November. If you plan to have children, you should ensure they are all either born in the summer or the winter. One in each will cause issues. Chloe's birthday parties were usually outside in the sunshine, Mia's in some dark warm hall or venue protected from the elements. Mia hated it; as she grew older, she said to her mum every year near her birthday, 'Why couldn't I have been born in the summer?'

Luci never came up with an answer that satisfied her. Mia turned out to be hard to satisfy at the best of times. Chloe's nature had always been easy going and relaxed, Mia's hyper and easily bored.

The memories were dropping in quickly now, the night Caroline BY CHOICE Hunter cornered me in the toilets at a wedding and insisted that I take her home and shag her. She'd been drunk, but I told Luci anyway, who confronted her outside the hotel near the tennis courts.

Caroline BY CHOICE Hunter didn't come to our house again, though Luci did see her occasionally, mainly because Chloe and Beatrice's relationship hadn't been affected by Caroline's proposition.

The anxieties of the girls being ill over the intervening years breezed through my brain like hail in a storm, but they'd been OK. The wonder of Christmas mornings, Chloe's first day at school, what an emotional rollercoaster that had been, her first teacher Mrs Lawson, pudgy and lovely. Her last day at junior school and all the tears shed for teachers she wouldn't see any more and a class of kids scattered to the four winds.

We'd considered private schooling for high school, especially as I had heeded my advice and bet on Trump, Leicester City and a particular young tennis player. I'd also invested what I could during the market downturn of 2020. Financially we were secure, but the local high school had an outstanding reputation, and we'd need money for the girls later, so state schooling it would be.

Chloe's first broken leg, there were three in all, competition gymnastics took its toll on her bones, meant she missed a month of year five, a month of year six and six weeks in her first year of high school.

Her first proper boyfriend, Harry from her year, who took her virginity on her sixteenth birthday and broke her heart simultaneously, drifted in and out of our lives. She never told me, but Luci did, making me swear I'd never mention it. It had happened to her, too, I remembered.

What resonated through all of this was the love I felt for Luci. It had never wavered nor lessened and, if anything, had grown. Different from when we first got together. We had kids, so our lives were sprinkled with occasional arguments and spats, but I'd always been truthful with her, even in the Caroline BY CHOICE Hunter episode. She'd been very attentive towards me for a while after that, the green-eyed monster again; shame nobody else took such an apparent fancy to me over the years.

I remembered all this and yet didn't remember any of it in the way I'd recorded my trips in my notebook. Luci's breath erotically washing over me on the wall outside school that afternoon, the day and night together in my student dump in Edinburgh, standing in the rain outside the theatre waiting for her to emerge and my most recent trip, falling asleep snuggled up naked with her, listening to the weather raging outside.

The rest will never be wholly mine; bits of me will always exist out of or between time, but that's OK; I have my girls and my health, both priceless.

The memories will all settle on me and, eventually, in me, and I'll know everything I need to know with the occasional gap, as I've learned that not everything always slots back in. Some fragments remain in the cloud – whether that's a physical or metaphorical thing, I don't know, and I probably never will.

The next piece to drop in was when I approached my fortieth birthday. I'd driven something of a wedge between us. I suspected I knew the reason, but my memories hadn't yet arrived. Despite that, I felt elated, we were all alive and well. We'd not had any more children, not for a lack of trying, but we had two beautiful, healthy daughters, more than enough for us. We knew we were lucky, blessed in ways neither of us knew at that point. Bearing in mind that the younger versions of me had no idea what the older me had been up to. He just proceeded as if life was this effortless, wonderful journey.

A few years ago, I bought my wife a MacBook, digital audio software, and an expensive keyboard. She'd not been playing the piano much over the years, and now with the girls at high school, it seemed like an ideal time to indulge herself. I often came home and listened to her latest masterpiece. Her early efforts were a bit shit, if I'm honest, as she got used to the software.

Although she'd starred in seven big stage musicals, she found that belting out a number on a stage and singing in a studio mic were completely different things, plus she'd be her own worst critic. What sounded perfect to me, she pulled apart and agonised over.

Luci's normal speaking voice also had a trace of a Spanish accent – which had always puzzled me as we'd grown up in Wigan, but perhaps it was a hangover from rabbiting away in Spanish with her mother. They still did that when they didn't want me to know what they were talking about.

On stage, she was adept at taking on various accents, American Mid-West for Oklahoma and Cockney for Eliza Doolittle for example. However, she discovered her own singing voice had that Spanish hangover that made words like "leaving" sound like "living." I liked it as it gave her words an exotic twist.

However, Luci disagreed and tried to banish it in her compositions. As her frustration increased, I began to wish I'd never bought the stuff for her. Then, one Friday, when I rolled in from work early, she sat me on the sofa, put headphones over my ears and played one of the most beautiful songs I'd ever heard. I didn't know she'd written it at first. I thought she'd downloaded a track from somewhere.

But it was her composition, a piano-based melody with some upbeat synth elements called The Language of Love. She wrote a few more, then sent them off to some of her show-business contacts who passed them on to other music business people.

Eventually, one day, three months after she'd plonked the headphones on my head, she got a call from the manager of Milas Minto. Milas, a Danish/British girl, had been headlining festivals across Europe most of the summer and she wanted to record one of Luci's songs.

It became a top ten UK download, and Luci's life as a songwriter began, something I'd always believed she should have done earlier. Unlike me, however, she hadn't been able to go back in time. She wanted to release her songs under her own name, but then the world went into lockdown, and everything stopped.

Luci caught Covid in the spring of 2020, and we had a few anxious days where she coughed and spluttered but recovered quickly. I tested positive but had no symptoms. Mia and Chloe tested positive, too, but apart from Mia being more moody than usual, we got off lightly.

Then, a few months ago, the shit hit the fan.

My fault, of course, well, the future me. It all revolved around that note I'd written to myself all those years ago and only a few hours ago.

As well as the advice around the shares and Trump et al. I'd told my younger self something I'd heeded. I didn't know if I'd believe the note when I'd written it, but it felt like an insurance policy I had to have on balance. Despite the risk of alienating and possibly losing my wife's trust. It felt like something I had to do.

Chapter 33
About Damn Time

Luci found the letter from Dr Jaeger confirming the large donation to her research programme. Perhaps I wanted her to see it. Maybe that had been easier than trying to explain it.

I'm not sure what angered her the most, the fact I'd squandered, in her eyes, a lot of money on a medical study or that I'd not discussed it with her. Probably the latter.

The row had been blazing, hurtful and probably the worst we'd had in the fifteen years we'd been married. Luci resorted to a litany of Spanish expletives, a trait she displayed when furious. Off the scale, in other words, and made worse by the fact I didn't have a good explanation or defence. Following the instructions of a note I'd made more than a decade ago made no sense even to me, which of course, at that point, knew nothing of the future and what would/had – pick your tense – happen/ed.

The fact that the programme was a mental health one, in and of itself, made a kind of sense given the completely crazy irrational actions that had preceded my attending. In the end, Luci left me to go and stay with her mother, whose health had declined recently. It gave her an excuse to leave without admitting she needed some space from me. It fell on the week of Mia's birthday. Luci had planned to take the girls out of school and for the four of us to fly off somewhere hot and humid for a week. Partly to appease Mia's complaints about being born in November, which had never diminished and partly because we needed a break. St Lucia had been the plan, but they went to Wigan without me instead. Neither Chloe nor Mia would speak to me. Mainly because Wigan in November is not as pleasant as St Lucia in November, or in any other month come to that.

I felt terrible. I'd apologised and tried to explain more than once, but nothing I'd said made sense, and why would it? The fact I'd made a few very profitable bets and predicted a substantial stock-market fall and rise didn't seem enough to override the irrational decision to gift a considerable chunk of money to a bunch of strangers nor sign up for the said programme, run by the same bunch of strangers.

Only now that my two selves had melded together did everything make some sense. Still, even with my newly acquired knowledge, I'm not sure I'd be able to persuade Luci that anything about what had happened had any logic attached to it.

The worst-case scenario would be that Luci left me, but at least she, Chloe, and Mia would be alive, which would be a huge step forward from last time. We also had money and a decent life, so it seemed.

I had progressed to the editor-in-chief role of a conglomerate of online and published magazines covering various subjects. Lifestyle, including cars, boats, trains and more obscure topics, to widely distributed puzzle weeklies, computer reviews and tips, and in-house magazines for large corporations and even small governments. We even had a magazine that reviewed all our other magazines, which sounded almost as bonkers as time travel.

I earned a generous salary with bonuses stacked on top depending on the distribution. Luci had returned to her first love, theatre, now producing and directing in addition to acting, depending on the contracts available. Covid had hit theatre land hard, and appetites had changed. Shorter, less lavish (for that read, less expensive) productions were in vogue with smaller budgets. Having someone like Luci who could produce, direct and star delighted the backers, one salary instead of three. Cast sizes had also been scaled back to ensure a run could recoup the initial outlay much quicker.

Her song writing had tapered off as she came home most evenings exhausted. There's nothing like being creative for twelve hours straight to stop you from being creative the rest of the time.

A knock on my room door pulled me from my thoughts and back to the present, whatever that was. I padded across the room to answer it, revelling in the fact that I wasn't partially paralysed, and I weighed less than twelve stones compared to earlier that same day, which boggled my mind. It felt like walking on air.

Angus greeted me. 'Hey man, dinner's nearly ready; you hungry?'

Angus! It felt like an age since I'd spoken to him. It had been months in my reality, probably hours in his. I resisted the urge to hug him. 'Sure.' I'd also been amazed he'd managed to utter a sentence without the word shit in it. I still hadn't grasped that I'd been transported back onto the programme in November.

I slipped on my shoes, closed the door and walked beside him. 'Italian tonight; I bet the lasagne is shit,' he complained.

I smiled; regular service had been resumed.

He sat beside me at dinner. The other residents were mostly familiar. Molly remained Angus's main focus over dinner. I noticed another attractive woman had joined us, early thirties with blonde hair pulled back into a ponytail and blue eyes that nervously scanned the room. Her name badge said, Karen. Angus occasionally glanced in her direction, but she didn't notice.

I wore a wedding ring, as did Amanda. Everyone else, including the newcomer, who may have been here for weeks, for all I knew, didn't. I wonder what ripple effect I'd caused to bring Karen into our little group. I don't suppose it mattered much.

Dr Jaeger intercepted me after my evening snooker match with Angus. I beat him comfortably again. I still didn't remember how or when I'd learned to play. A fragment that will be forever lost in the cloud, I guess.

We headed to her office, now situated a few doors from the Orchid lab. Maybe it had always been there. She sat at her desk and fired up her PC. It bleeped and beeped, and eventually, the Doc started typing.

'You are quite remarkable, you know,' she told me.

I didn't know how to respond, so I just nodded.

'Your genome profile showed extensive damage.'

'I'm sorry about that.'

She flashed me a smile. 'By rights, you should be sitting in a padded cell, or at the very least be projecting a socially awkward personality. Instead, you have a successful career, a gifted wife and lovely children. Goes against all my training.'

She paused and frowned. 'Have we had a similar conversation before? This feels very familiar?'

I nodded. 'Possibly.'

'Anyway, I'm not sorry to be proven wrong in your case. When we collected your DNA sample, we had to re-test it a few times to ensure we hadn't made an error. Have we discussed this before as well?'

'Maybe. Déjà vu?'

She smiled. 'It's something. Anyway, I'd like to thank you for your generous contribution to the project now that we've finished your course of treatment.'

'Thank you for the opportunity.'

I felt so grateful for the gift the Doc had bestowed upon me, even though she had no idea. It had allowed me to fix what once went wrong, I'd been truly blessed. In this timeline, in her timeline, all the episodes of my treatment had been seamless. In my world, not so much.

'I'm assuming you'll be going home tomorrow as planned?' Dr Jaeger asked, gathering up her paperwork.

'I might leave this evening. The roads will be quieter than tomorrow morning, and I'm anxious to get home.'

'To your wife and daughters.'

'They're staying with Luci's mother in Wigan, so I'll get some alone time.'

'Ah, we all need that,' she said, a throwaway remark, but I knew better. I'd had years of alone time across multiple lifetimes.

She stood up, and we shook hands. 'It's been quite a journey,' I said.

Dr Jaeger cocked her head to one side. 'You don't seem much changed from when you arrived?'

'That's what you think.' I laughed. 'Thank you, Doctor. I'll be forever in your debt.'

I turned and left a bemused psychiatrist standing behind her desk staring at me. I hadn't asked, but the fact Dr Janice Ramos's name remained on the whiteboard at reception told me she hadn't died yet. I went back to my room and composed a letter. It took me a while to work out how to word it properly, but in the end, I just wrote what I felt.

Dear Dr Ramos,

First, thank you for listening to me while I was on the programme. I found our time together helpful, positive and sometimes life-affirming. (I wasn't sure how much she would remember, so I kept it vague.)

I know that the main ingredient of the compound (SPC) used to fix the faulty genome comes from your home island and that the main constituents cannot be replicated in a laboratory. I know this because Dr Jaeger told me this in an alternative timeline. She will not remember any of our conversations because, at that point, there was hardly any compound left, and there was no way of obtaining any more. (Please bear with me.)

I'm also aware that you are the main driving force behind the programme, as you brought the idea to Dr Jaeger a few years ago and obtained the SPC from a tribal elder near your home. I also know that the islanders have used it for generations. I also realise that on its own, it would not cause the effects on me that it has, but in combination with the plasma stuff that Dr

Jaeger injects into me, it effectively seems to repair the affected genome, not chemically, as Dr Jaeger appears to believe, but by transporting the patient back in time to the actual event that caused the problem to occur. This allows the patient to prevent the event from happening in the first place.

Listen, I completely understand how crazy this sounds, and whilst I get that you are a psychiatrist and probably believe (quite rightly) that I'm a delusional nutcase, I hope that just a tiny fragment of your psyche has retained that mystical outlook shared by your people. In any event, whether you believe me or not, what have you got to lose? I know you plan to go home to the Solomon Islands for a visit soon. (I don't remember the exact dates because Dr Jaeger never told me, and I didn't ask), but you will be there on January 15th when a devastating cyclone will hit the island, and you and your father will die. Your mother will survive.

Here's a thought, regardless of whether you believe a word of this or not, why not invite your parents over to the UK for Christmas and beyond? Let them have an extended stay until the end of January, to be on the safe side. What have you got to lose? Nothing. And if it turns out that I'm a delusional freak, the worst that has happened is that you've spent some quality time with your parents.

Please, don't disregard this letter, even if you don't believe me, don't take the risk...

Kindest regards

Sam Harris.

I didn't know how she'd react. She might discuss it with Dr Jaeger and move to have me assessed and sectioned, toss it in the bin, or hang on to it and consider my words. Anyway, I'd done what I could. Given her background and upbringing, I suspected Dr Ramos might be more open-minded than Dr Jaeger, but who knows?

I stuffed my clothes and belongings into my bag, picked up my journal, checked I'd not left anything and walked to reception. I handed the letter to the receptionist, who assured me that Dr Ramos would get it in the morning. I watched as he put it in with a pile of other mail in her pigeonhole behind him.

I walked out to the car park, beeped the black Mercedes, which I knew by osmosis to be mine, dropped my bag into the boot, started the engine and headed for the gates.

I glanced back once at the low-rise buildings. I'd spent the last few weeks/years/hours, depending on your point of view, inside those plain looking structures. My experiences inside, had changed my life, the lives of my nearest and dearest and the lives of people I'd never met before. I shook my head in bewilderment and pointed the car towards home. I still had work to do.

Chapter 34
Messy In Heaven

Our house in St Albans was just as I remembered it, and yet, nothing like I remembered it. I'd been here physically a few hours ago, but, at the same time, it had been thirteen years ago. A lot can change in thirteen years. All the baby and toddler paraphernalia had gone, some to friends, some in the bin, most to charity. The décor had been updated, and an extension added to the back to accommodate another two bedrooms and extend the kitchen diner. We'd lost some of the garden, but that meant less grass to cut, which was fine by me.

A grand piano now took pride of place beside a huge picture window that overlooked the apple and plum trees. I had no memory of that coming. Maybe it would appear later in my brain, maybe it wouldn't. I wandered from room to room, marvelling at Luci's cosy little recording studio, which had once been our bedroom, the mess that indicated Mia's room and the unnatural tidiness that signified I stood in Chloe's private space.

I walked into our large bedroom, now tucked away in the quietest corner of the house, with an en-suite shower room and doors that opened onto the side of the garden, where the sun only shone on summer mornings.

Our personal, intimate space felt both strange and familiar. Luci and I had spent some nights apart in recent years, but not many. In this bed we talked about the future, worried about our kids, made love, and resolved our problems.

The memories of my life without my family had begun to fade, but that didn't worry me. I had it all written down. I knew how lucky and charmed my life was, and I'd never let myself forget that.

Tonight, I'd be without my wife and daughters. Tomorrow they'd come home, and Luci and I needed to talk. I had to decide what to say and knew that would be a challenge.

I phoned Luci, but it went to voicemail like it had every time I'd phoned her recently. I checked the call log; eleven calls had been directed to her voicemail. I didn't leave a message. I didn't know what to say.

There were numerous text messages from Andy and Graham. They were my best friends. Andy dated back to my university days, and Graham I'd met in the local pub one evening when Luci and I had been out for a meal. He introduced me to the joys of St Albans FC, the local football team. I now went to most home games with him. Male friends were a welcome new addition to my social circle, something sadly lacking in my previous timelines. Quite how that had happened eluded me, but they added balance and perspective to my life.

I texted them back confirming to Graham I'd make the match next weekend and headed off to bed.

I slept OK, considering and woke early. I knew I was supposed to return to work on Monday, so that gave me two days with Luci, assuming she came home today.

I showered, dressed, picked at some food, paced the house, watched some old films, and pottered about in the garden.

At half-past one, I heard her key in the door. I didn't get up from the couch; I just waited.

I knew what she looked like in her fortieth year, but part of me still remembered her as twenty-seven when we'd walked through the door that evening thirteen years ago or yesterday afternoon. Her face still looked fresh, but her eyes were tired. The amber glow had lost some of its sparkle. Her eyes looked their age, but the rest of her didn't. She flashed me a weak smile and asked, 'How did it go?'

'Good,' I replied. 'Where are…'

'In town, I dropped them off and gave them money to buy clothes. We need some time alone.'

Her tone sounded ominous. I wanted to grab her, pull her into bed, and tear her clothes off, but I decided that might not be terribly well received today. Today was for business, a day for fixing what needed fixing if it could be fixed.

'Tea?' I offered.

She puffed out her cheeks. 'Bugger tea, white wine, please.'

I poured us both a glass, and we took them into the lounge and sat on the couch together, a metre apart.

'How's your mum? I tried to phone but….'

'I know. I'm sorry I didn't want to talk to you.'

'Thanks.'

She shrugged. 'Mum's not good; the doctors reckon her heart's failing. Her angina's been getting worse, and she's not a good candidate for a transplant assuming she even got on the list, which she won't due to her age. She needs proper care.'

'Bring her here?'

'What?'

'We'll clear out our bedroom. She can have that with its own bathroom. We can move into the spare room and do it up. It'll be fine.'

Luci stared at me. 'Why?'

'Why what?'

'Why now? We've had this conversation before, and you weren't keen.'

'I've had some thinking time. I'll always be in debt to your mum for what she did for my mum, the girls, and you.'

'But we both work and....'

'We'll pay for help. We can afford it.'

Luci didn't speak for a moment, then said, 'That will ease my mind a lot, Sam, thank you.'

'Don't be silly. It's what we should have done ages ago.'

Luci smiled. 'She'd never have come ages ago. She likes her independence.'

'She might not come now?'

Luci nodded. 'I think she will. She's scared.' She got up and refilled our glasses. 'Right, let's get to the heart of things. What is going on with *you*?'

I'd spent most of the previous evening and this morning trying to find a way to explain to my wife what had been going on with me. It had been a struggle because I couldn't really explain it to myself.

'I don't know where to start.'

'At the beginning is usually best.'

'Perhaps not in this case.' I sipped some wine. 'Do you remember all those years ago, that time in Edinburgh when you stayed over after our... our separation?'

'Vaguely.'

I remembered it like it had been a few months ago, which in my life it had. 'I made you write down many things, some of it about shares?'

'I've still got that somewhere. That finance student gave you tips or something?'

'Something like that, and they all came good, didn't they?'

Luci frowned. 'Most of them, except Scoppex.'

'Scoppex? I thought they were one of the best. The South African mining company that went global?'

'South African mining company that went tits up, you mean.'

'When?'

'What do you mean when? Years ago, you...we didn't have much with them. Why do you think they went global?'

Good question. In my previous timelines, Scoppex were one of the best-known mining companies on the planet. My notebook said so. Their founder, Edward Sliss, became famous as an ambassador for climate change and a leading investor in environmental technologies. That had made him even more money. He and his wife, American pop-singer turned fashion designer Caley Regis, had become global icons.

'Edward Sliss, the owner, entrepreneur, and ambassador for climate change, what happened to him?'

Luci looked at me, 'He got eaten by ants.'

'Eaten by ants?'

'It was on the news. Don't you remember? He got lost looking for Inca gold in the Ecuadorian mountains.

'And got eaten by ants?'

'So, they said.'

I had no memory of him not being what he'd been. I wondered how someone went from marrying a pop star to being eaten by ants. I didn't even know ants ate people. I didn't say anything to Luci. The conversation had become surreal enough already—another fragment lost in the cloud. I wondered what had changed to make that happen. I'd probably never know.

Luci searched my face. 'What were they doing to you in that place? Electric shock therapy or something?'

'No nothing like that, just trying to sort out some stuff in my head.'

'There's been nothing wrong with your head for the last forty years; why now?'

'I'm trying to explain.' I took a deep breath. 'Anyway, Scoppex aside, the rest of the shares did well, giving us the money to buy this house with the help of a humongous mortgage?'

She nodded. 'The tips were good, in the main.'

'Ok, well, I also wrote myself a letter when you were pregnant with Mia.'

'A letter?'

'Kind of, yeah. I didn't tell you about it. The weird thing is that whilst it was in my handwriting and everything, at the time, I had no memory of writing it. I know that sounds crazy.'

'Is that why you didn't tell me? In case I thought you were losing it?'

'Maybe? I'm not sure. It seemed easier as time passed not to discuss it, just in case.' 'What was in it?'

'Things about the future mainly. Like the market fall in January 2020, I used that to make a small fortune and payoff said humungous mortgage.'

'You did. You said it was luck.'

'I did. Then I also had the bets on Donald Trump, Leicester City and Emma Raducanu.'

'You got lucky, very lucky.'

I sighed. 'I didn't, though. I knew.'

'Knew what? That the shares would bounce back within eight months? You knew that Donald Trump would run and become president before he knew himself. You also knew that Leicester City would become premier league champions and that a virtually unknown teenage qualifier would win the US Open? You always said you were just lucky.'

'Think back on what you've just said. I know we've talked about this in the past and how lucky we were, but rationally does that feel like luck to you?'

Luci sat silent for a minute. 'So, what, you're clairvoyant? Are you going to buy a crystal ball and set yourself up in a circus?'

'I'm not clairvoyant, and until recently, I had no idea how I'd been able to predict all those things from the notes I'd made all those years ago. I mean, think about it, Luci, Emma Raducanu was probably in nursery school when I wrote that letter.'.

'The letter you have no memory of writing?'

'Yeah, another thing I'd written in the note was never to let your children attend an Ariana Grande concert, which didn't become an issue as neither became huge fans.'

Luci went pale. 'You mean you guessed about the bombing? I find that hard to believe.'

I held my hands up. 'I didn't guess about the bombing; all I had scribbled down was '*Never let your kids go to an Ariana Grande concert.*' That's it. I didn't know why. It made no sense until, well, eventually, it did.'

'Why should I believe you, Sam? For the last few weeks, it's been like living with a stranger, like the man I've known all my life had been kidnapped and replaced with a Doppelganger.'

In my head, I'd been aware that my behaviour had been out of character. The letter I'd left myself all those years ago and yesterday afternoon remained fresh in my brain, plus I'd written it all up in my notebook.

Note to self – SAM, all this future knowledge/good luck you will have is not what you think it is. I won't put down here what it is as you won't believe yourself. All the things I've written above will come to pass. Trust them and make some money – but you must do one thing, or all the good might be undone. In the lead-up to your 40th birthday, you must seek out a mental health programme being run by Dr Lynda Jaeger. You MUST get yourself on that programme, even if you need to make a large donation to the project to do so – once they test your genome, they'll agree, trust me, trust yourself. You MUST do this regardless of what Luci or anyone else thinks – if you don't, everything could turn to shit. All the above will come true, but it could all unravel unless you take the final step and meet with Dr Jaeger. Luci could die, and so could your children. You **have to** *do it – don't take that risk.*

When I'd written that all down, I didn't know if it had been/would be true. Would the whole thing unravel if I didn't go to Perry Flowers? Would I find myself back in my flat waiting for the Rottweilers? I honestly didn't know.

It made sense in my head. But nothing was clear, so I'd never shared it with Luci. 'Luci, I know that I've not been myself. I've been trying to deal with some things.'

'What things? Are you having an affair?'

I blinked at her, 'What? No, of course not. I'd never; how could you think that? I love you more than anything. I couldn't, wouldn't ever do that.'

'Sorry, it's just that when we talked about you going onto the course and spending all that money, you were evasive, secretive and downright weird about it. I had no idea what you were up to, so I thought the worst.'

'I don't blame you, Luci, I really don't. It sounds crazy even to me, but what I'm about to tell you is real. Either that or I'm certifiable, which is possible, but I'll let you decide after I've told you. I need you to believe me, but if you don't and want me to leave and live somewhere else, I will because that will be a better outcome than any of the others so far.'

'Any other what, Sam? You're starting to scare me.'

'I'm scaring myself.' I took a glug of wine, pulled out my notebook and began.

Luci stared at me open-mouthed for good portions of my recital. I detected a few tears when I told my wife about her and Chloe dying in a car crash and the stroke I'd suffered years later. I brought it all up to date and stopped talking. We stared at each other for what felt like forever.

Chapter 35
Easy on Me

Eventually, she said, 'That's quite a story, Sam. You should have been a writer.'

'It's true, Luci, either that or I need a straight jacket.'

Luci shook her head. 'I don't think you're crazy, Sam, but for some reason, I can tell by the look on your face that you believe what you've just told me. To you, it's all real, but surely you must realise that it can't be true.'

I had a choice now. I could concede this point to Luci and agree that I'd suffered some kind of breakdown. Then, eventually, life would return to a semblance of normality, or I could continue down the road I was on and ultimately risk losing Luci and my girls.

I'd made poor choices in the past, in several pasts, and my obstinance had gotten in the way of everything. Declining Luci's help outside the high school that day, refusing to go travelling with her after university, blaming her success for me becoming unhappy and cheating on her. All down to me. All my fault. I had to learn from my mistakes. What did it matter now anyway? I'd made it back to my fortieth year and had my family with me, maybe they had always been with me, and everything else had been an illusion.

I flipped back to the earliest pages of my notebook. 'Dr Jaeger called it FMS, False Memory Syndrome. A patient can have factually incorrect recollections, but it feels like the truth to them. As you said, the person having them believes it to be reality. The trigger for it can be as unique as the individual.'

'So, is that why you went there, to get help?'

I nodded. It was the truth. I went to get help, and who the hell knows, all the other stuff that had happened might all be symptomatic of the FMS. I might have been daydreaming, suffering psychotic episodes, and being delusional. All of it, to be fair, would be preferable to believing I'd been time travelling.

'Yes, and I needed to get onto that study. It's experimental and unconventional. They call it Epigenetic Regression targeting and fixing faulty genes on my genome.'

'Epi, what?'

'I'll explain later, but anyway, I seem to be better.' I smiled.

'For that amount of money, I'd hope so. Are you sure you've not been scammed?'

'I hope not.'

'You said everyone has a trigger. I'm assuming yours turned out to be the luck you've had; you know, the shares, the bets, thinking you'd become a time-traveller because you thought you knew in advance what would happen?'

I nodded. 'It's as good an explanation as any.'

'And you're sure you're OK now?'

'Yeah, I'll probably get some regular counselling on top, just to make sure, but I reckon I'm right when and where I'm supposed to be now.'

I closed the gap on the couch between us and snuggled up to my wife. She kissed me, and we pushed our foreheads together like we had so many times over the years, our wine breath mingling this time. 'I love you, Luci. I'm so lucky to be here with you.'

'What, because you lost me in your previous lifetimes or whatever was happening in your head?'

I sighed. 'It felt real to me, so yes, it feels like I know what life is like without you.'

'Plus, you always get fat.'

'Nearly always. I make bad choices.'

Luci flipped her tongue out and licked my top lip. 'Let's go to bed.'

'I'm not tired.'

'Neither am I.'

Chapter 36
Better Days

And that would probably have been it. The version of events that I'd told Luci would, in time, have become the truth for me. I'm sure the counselling sessions I genuinely meant to arrange would have reinforced that truth in as much as time travel wasn't real, didn't exist, and therefore must have been made up by my sick brain.

For a few months, that's exactly what happened. I told Chloe and Mia that I'd not been well and that work and worrying had brought about a minor breakdown, which explained my strange behaviour. However, now that I'd received appropriate treatment, everything should be fine.

In February, I checked on the GMC register, and Dr Janice Ramos remained registered, despite the cyclone devastating the Solomon Islands. Her Facebook page had a link to a Just Giving page for disaster victims. I assumed she'd taken my warning seriously, and I hope she'd told her parents too. I made an anonymous and generous donation and wished I could have done more. It didn't sit with the version of reality I'd told Luci but choosing to ignore the evidence made my life easier.

One sunny Friday afternoon in early April, I was working from home—something I did most Fridays if I could get away with it. Luci was in the West End, beavering away on a future production, and the girls were in school. Luci's mother, Beth, had settled into life in our house, and her health had improved.

Apart from her and Luci occasionally babbling away in Spanish, we all got on well, all things considered.

Beth had thrown herself into life in St Albans to the point where she now had a better social life than we did. Being a Friday, she had been picked up by one of her new friends from the film club, and they'd gone to the cinema.

I'd just taken a break from editing the copy for a new electric car magazine when I heard a loud knocking on the door. I opened it to a familiar face. A face that had shown me kindness and grace when nobody else had. Elizabeth recognised me too and invited herself inside before I could speak.

'You promised to let me know what happened.'

'How did you find me?'

'I didn't. I found your wife first. She's a celebrity.'

Of course, I'd forgotten telling Elizabeth all about Luci's talent, or perhaps I'd never remembered in the first place.

I sighed. 'I know, I'm sorry, but that was when I believed what I believed, but now I'm no longer sure *what* I believe. It might all just be false memory syndrome.'

Elizabeth wrinkled up her nose. 'What, both of us having it at the same time about the same stuff?'

'I'm in permanent denial then.'

Elizabeth appraised the house nodding. 'Done all right for yourself this time around, eh?'

I smiled. 'Yeah, it all came together in the end.'

She plonked herself down on the couch. I made us coffee, and we sat silently for a minute or so.

Eventually, she spoke. 'I don't remember last time, but I made detailed notes.'

'How's Fay?'

'Fay never happened.' I frowned. She smiled. 'Weird, huh? I know about her because I put her in my notebook, but somehow you changed that. Crazy or what?'

'I'm sorry, you seemed well suited.'

'It's fine. I went looking for her. She moved to Seattle and is living with a nurse in a lovely old stone apartment building. She looked happy. I reckon it wouldn't have changed that much if we'd been destined to be together.'

I admired her philosophical outlook.

'I'm with Georgia just now, she's lovely, but I don't think she's the one, if you know what I mean?'

'I do. When you know, you know.'

'What's with you now, then?' She waved her mug for a refill. I obliged.

I told her the story, including the awkward last month or two when I'd bought my way onto Dr Jaeger's programme.

Elizabeth raised her eyebrows. 'Cheaper than the one and a quarter million you were going to give her last time.'

I blinked at her. 'That much?'

She nodded. I'd not written *that* in *my* notebook. No wonder.

'I convinced you to reduce it to one fifty; otherwise, it would have looked desperate. Fifty grand seems like a bargain in comparison.'

'I had been desperate, and it *was* a bargain.'

Elizabeth cast her eye around the room, alighting on the framed pictures of Luci, Chloe and Mia. 'Worth every penny, I'd say.'

I didn't disagree.

She stared at me for a moment, and her expression softened. 'Sam, I'm so glad that it worked out for you in the end. I don't remember how I felt when I saw you in the hospital, but from what I wrote, it moved me. You'd had such a rough ride that, well, let's say you weren't long for this world if you hadn't been able to change things. How'd you got through the previous years to that point, I don't know.'

'Eating mainly.' I smiled.

She nodded. 'I suppose we both got what we wanted, but I think it's time to leave well alone now, yeah?'

'Absolutely, there's no way I'm gambling on this.' I indicated the room. 'No matter what.'

'What if another disaster happens?'

The thought hadn't occurred to me. 'Like what?'

'Like your wife being killed or one or both of your daughters.'

'That's a cheery thought.'

Elizabeth smiled. 'Sorry; I know, the harbinger of doom.'

That rang a bell. I didn't know how to respond. I said, 'Oh, I don't know, I think I've used up all my goodwill with Dr Jaeger, plus they only have a limited supply of the stuff left.'

'Oh right, the other doctor's dead, isn't she?'

I bit my lip.

Elizabeth said, 'What?'

'I wrote her a letter just before I left, telling her what her fate might be.'

Elizabeth blinked at me and swallowed. 'And?

'Well, as far as I can see, she's alive and well. Her Facebook page has a Just Giving link for disaster victims, so I assume she heeded my warning.'

'Did you do that so there'd be more chance of another trip back in the future?'

That hadn't been my motivation. I just thought I could help, so I did. 'No, it wasn't.'

Elizabeth didn't seem to believe me, but I don't suppose it mattered much.

The atmosphere between us had cooled. I couldn't quite understand why. As far as I could see, all I'd done had been to save a lovely person from dying.

Elizabeth stood to leave. 'I just wanted to see if you got your happy ending, and it looks like you did.'

I smiled, tears pricked the corners of my eyes, and I sniffed. 'I know I owe you a huge vote of gratitude. I'm not really sure how much, to be honest. Even with my notes, it's hazy, but I probably wouldn't be here without you.'

She stared at me momentarily, then the coldness left her eyes, and tears slid down her cheeks. She pulled me into a huge hug. 'I'd like to stay in touch but realise that might be awkward, so let's just leave it and see what happens. You know what fate's like, huh?' She kissed me, took one last look around the room and at the photos of my girls and left.

I closed the door behind me and let the tears flow. Tears of joy and hurt all mixed in a little salty cocktail that trailed down my face.

I washed up the mugs and opened the doors to the garden to clear the lingering scent of Elizabeth's perfume. I didn't want to explain to Luci why a strange woman had visited me during the day.

I wished I could think of a way to introduce Elizabeth to everyone without the whole time-travelling saga opening up again. Luci never mentioned it anymore, and I kept my silence though today had banished any thoughts about pretending it didn't happen. Elizabeth and I could be delusional, but when I'd spoken to her, she'd been so rational and lucid that I couldn't believe that.

Later, with my brood all safe and sleeping under my roof, I snuggled up to Luci and decided that I'd forever keep my silence on the matter. A small price to pay, considering everything.

Chapter 37
What's Going On?

Eighteen months had drifted past since the day Elizabeth visited me. I thought about her every so often and occasionally checked out her social media profiles. She had a Facebook account that she sporadically updated. Georgia had come and gone, and she seemed to be single for now. I did feel a pang of guilt, having erased Fay from her life with some sort of twist in time, but she understood that, or perhaps didn't understand that as much as I didn't, but at least she knew it had been beyond my control.

In a week, Chloe would leave home. Bristol University beckoned; her chosen subject, Theatre and Film. Not quite following in her mother's footsteps, but near enough. Chloe's fascination centred on the production and organisational side of the performing arts. She had little desire to be on stage.

Luci had been moody for weeks now, as had I; we'd been snapping at each other, which hardly happened. The strain and worry of losing one of our children weighed heavily on our shoulders, especially Luci's. I had the consolation of knowing that this should never have happened and could look at it philosophically. My wife didn't have that insight.

On a gloomy September Saturday morning, we all drove down to the Bristol. We'd bought a flat on Gloucester Road for her to live in during her tenure at the university. The apartment was situated above a line of shops; a hairdressing salon, a seven-to-eleven grocery, a kebab shop, a gourmet coffee place and a nail bar. What else would a bunch of female students need?

We knew the upside to this. Our daughter going to university should have been an occasion for joy and sorrow, a real bitter-sweet moment. It should have been even more joyous for me, given the fate that had befallen her in my past, future, or whatever the hell it was. But the effect of her moving on affected Luci and me deeply. It felt natural, normal and healthy but, at the same time, challenging. We would all adjust, but it would take time.

The car overflowed with her stuff. The money being demanded for student halls we'd decided had been extortionate. At least this way, we'd not be forking out dead money. Plus, if Chloe decided to make her home in Bristol after her course ended, she'd have somewhere to live. Two other first-year girls, Isla and Millie, would share with her, which would cover the mortgage. Happy days.

It took me back to my flat share in Edinburgh, but so far, this apartment's bathroom was immaculate. I doubted three girls would make a mess of things, well Chloe wouldn't, with her fastidious personality. When it became Mia's turn, that would be a different kettle of fish altogether.

We got her settled, and with many tears all around, we drove home with a much emptier car, spiritually and physically. Although they fought like cats and dogs, Mia would miss her sister, her best friend and constant companion since birth. We both knew the separation would be as hard, if not harder, for her. Luci had set up a few activities for them, a weekend spa break in

Edinburgh and a trip to Paris in October. I wasn't invited, but I was cool with that. This would be mother-daughter time, and they both needed it.

I knew we'd see Chloe regularly, but it would be different, she now got to make up and live by her own set of rules, not ours, and whilst being an essential part of growing up, it would be a tricky transition for all of us.

Apart from the incident with Harry when she'd been sixteen, Chloe had been no trouble. She'd studied hard and kept herself away from being hurt again. Now she'd probably make up for lost time, but she had to live her life. A life she was lucky to have, I reminded myself constantly. Whatever she did with it now would be up to her. I wouldn't, couldn't intervene from the future. Things were now how they should be.

Luci seemed calmer when we got home. Chloe phoned every evening for the first week. Then as her course started and fresher's week took over, the calls became more sporadic as she settled into her new life. They texted each other, even I received one now and then as we settled into our new world, one daughter down.

Chloe came home for the October half-term week and flew to Paris with Luci and Mia; she also came home for Christmas with a friend Alesha who had nowhere to go for the festive season. Her parents had died of cancer in the last few years, and she didn't see eye to eye with her grandparents.

Alesha seemed like a nice girl, with auburn hair, bright green eyes and slim though she mostly wore baggy outfits. Initially, she came across as a little quiet, but we put it down to the fact that she'd be spending Christmas with strangers, and her parents were gone. Enough to make anyone quiet. Alesha and Mia didn't seem to get on, but again, I put that down to her, stealing Chloe's attention. We did our best to make Alesha feel welcome.

We drove them all back to Bristol on the 8th of January. Alesha had grown in confidence during her time with us and now felt like one of the family. Alesha and Luci's mum Beth had really hit it off and one day had even gone off to London together for an impromptu shopping trip.

We were late setting off. Then, heavy traffic and heavy snow delayed us getting to Bristol.

We dropped Alesha off at her residence. She'd agreed to move into Chloe's flat for the summer term when one of the current occupants, Isla, had arranged to go and live with her boyfriend. As neither Isla nor Millie had returned, we decided to stay the night and leave in the morning.

The flat would be cold and devoid of food, so rather than unload Chloe's bags now, we parked the car, and all four of us walked through the blizzard to an Italian restaurant less than three hundred yards away. Despite the short distance we were still cold and wet when we pushed open the door. The warm garlic infused air made our mouths water.

The food turned out to be as tasty as the aroma had promised and the plate sizes generously portioned and not expensive. This being student land, the restaurant owner knew his target market. We'd just paid the bill and were getting ready to leave when a text pinged into my phone.

Where R U? unknown number.

Luci noticed my puzzled face, I assumed, and asked, 'What is it?'

'Someone wants to know where I am.'

'Who?'

'I don't know.'

'Ask.'

I texted back, *Who RU?*

Tell u in a minute – where RU?

I was intrigued and replied, *Italian restaurant, Bristol.*

Nr the flat?

Yes, Gloucester Rd.

Don't move.

I smiled up at Luci. 'I've not to move, apparently.'

'Who is it?'

I shrugged. 'No idea.'

We'd just finished gathering our things together when the door burst open, and a familiar and very beautiful face appeared and stared around the restaurant with a concerned expression.

She spotted me and visibly relaxed, then rushed over and enveloped me in a huge hug; tears streaming down her face. She sobbed. 'Sam, I'm so glad to see you. You have no idea.'

Then her tear-stained face stared into mine, and she gave me a big kiss on the mouth before falling onto me again, sobbing uncontrollably.

I slowly became aware of the three other females at the table staring at me with open mouths. One of them had a very dark expression to accompany the open mouth. I noted that the green-eyed monster was ready to go nuclear. Not without provocation.

Chapter 38
Bruises

'Who is *this*?' Luci asked, not an unreasonable query, all things considered.

'Dr Janice Ramos, one of the psychiatrists from the clinic I attended, remember?'

'Your psychiatrist? Why is your psychiatrist kissing you?'

'A very good question,' I responded.

My wife took a deep breath. 'I know it's a good question, which is why I asked it.'

'Janice, why are you kissing me?' I asked.

She gazed around at the four of us. 'You're still alive.'

Luci took this one. 'We are, thank you very much. Did you kiss my husband every day at the clinic simply for being alive? If so, it might go some way to explain why he'd been so keen to go and also why he paid a lot of money to do so?'

Janice turned her beam onto my wife, who, to be fair, was immune. 'You're Luci, and this must be Chloe and Mia?'

'Correct,' Luci said, frowning. 'Why are you here, kissing aside?'

Tears slipped from Janice's eyes. 'To save your lives, which I think I now have.'

Luci ran her hand through her hair. 'You've saved our lives by coming here and kissing my husband?'

'If that's what it takes, then yes,' she replied.

Luci turned her eyes to me. 'Are you sure this is a psychiatrist, not a fellow patient?'

This made Janice giggle, I tried not to smile, but I may have smirked, which didn't help.

Luci decided she'd had enough. She picked up her bag and said, 'C'mon girls, let's get out of here.'

She stormed out of the restaurant, surprisingly pursued by Janice. I didn't rate her chances of calming Luci down. My wife didn't go ballistic often, but when Vesuvius erupted, it usually took a few hours for the lava to cease flowing.

Chloe, Mia and I eventually caught up with them barely thirty yards from the flat. Janice was physically restraining my wife from moving, not an easy task given Luci's recent gym and fitness kick. She'd decided that as her fortieth birthday loomed, she needed to get fit and had been pursuing a vigorous regime with a personal trainer/sadist/staff sergeant called Kate five mornings a week.

As we closed the gap on them through the still heavy snowfall, Luci yelled, 'Get your girlfriend off me, Sam. Otherwise, I *will* punch her in the face.'

I had mentioned the Vesuvius thing earlier but hadn't mentioned it to Janice, who shouted very loudly toward me, belying her small stature, 'What time is it?'

I checked my watch. 'Nearly eight.'

'OK, please, Luci, just wait a few more minutes, then I'll stop all this,' Janice pleaded.

Luci decided a few minutes were a few minutes too many and promptly punched my psychiatrist girlfriend (according to Luci) square on the nose. It erupted in a fountain of blood. I watched in shock initially as Janice crumpled and the snow turned crimson. Temporarily frozen in place at witnessing the violence, I didn't know what to do next. I flipped my gaze between Janice on her knees squealing and Luci storming along the pavement towards the flat.

Janice lifted her blood-covered face to me and squeaked, 'Stop her, Sam, or she'll die.'

I suppose it might be the different life experiences or perhaps experiencing different lives that made me react. Had I not lived through the various versions of my reality, I would have questioned Janice on her sanity or reasoning and fatally delayed.

Instead, I sprinted after my wife sliding and slipping on the treacherous snow-laden pavement and caught up with her just outside the deserted kebab shop. Deserted mainly due to the weather and the hour. Too late for the dinner crowd, too early for the stagger home from the pub crowd.

The proprietor, Usman, and his brother Asif, who were no doubt enjoying some well-earned leisure time, were then treated to a physical wrestling match, which would undoubtedly never rival any WWF tussles, between myself and my wife, which subsequently became a four-way tag-team bout when Chloe and Mia joined in, trying to wrench us apart.

I was trying to hold onto Luci and had locked my arms around her waist and ducked my head under her armpit to avoid the blows she'd been reduced to raining down onto my back. Painful but bearable. Janice eventually hobbled up with her face still bloodied, and at this point I noticed Asif reach for his mobile, no doubt to summon the police. The sight of blood usually spurred action.

Then suddenly, all five of us were on our backs. In an untidy heap. On the pavement. In the snow. I'd also gone deaf. Or rather I had a ringing in my ears that muffled everything else.

I lay and watched debris rain down on the pavement a few metres in front of us. Most of it seemed to be pieces of wood, chunks of glass and soft-furnishing detritus. I recognised only one thing as it plopped into the snow near my feet. Tabby. Chloe's teddy.

I remember the trauma on her fourth birthday when she'd inadvertently left him in the soft-play centre where she'd had her birthday party. The soft-play centre had closed by the time we'd realised he was missing (bedtime). We luckily managed to retrieve him the following morning (standing outside before it opened) to ensure no grubby-fingered toddler claimed him for themselves, following a largely sleepless night due to Tabby's absence.

I also remembered from my notes the poignancy of having placed him in her little coffin during the bleakest episode of my many bleak trips back to fix my broken genome and, ultimately, broken lives.

Chloe crawled across me in the snow to grab and pull him close to her chest. Chloe had an ample bosom, and Tabby all but vanished from view. From what I could glimpse of him, his foot seemed a little singed, but apart from that, he appeared relatively intact. More than could be said for the flat he'd been blasted from or the downstairs hairdressers now blazing away merrily, casting an incongruous warm glow on an otherwise freezing night.

I glanced across at Janice, lying on her side, staring at me. An impish grin appeared on her blood-streaked face, which made her seem a bit scary, if I'm honest, like some grinning apparition from an old Hammer horror film.

I guess this is what she'd meant by saving our lives.

We wisely shifted away from the detritus, and Usman and Asif warmly welcomed us into their deserted shop. Asif made another call to the fire brigade this time.

Luci was first to speak though her voice still sounded muffled and distant. I caught what she said. 'What just happened?'

Probably the question we all wanted to know the answer to. The one person who might be able to answer it, Janice, promptly fainted. Well, I hoped that's what she'd done.

Asif made it a full house and called for an ambulance too.

Chapter 39
Sweet But Psycho

One of the paramedics slipped and dropped the stretcher my kissing psychiatrist had been placed on. I'd never considered that this could happen. You took on trust that professional caregivers like paramedics wouldn't do something like that, but I surmised they were human, and it was treacherous underfoot. Fortunately, the paramedic, also called Janice coincidentally, who'd slipped, had been carrying the bottom of the stretcher. Janice probably got a fright, and the impact would have jarred her body with the ground. Both Janice's perhaps were shocked, but neither seemed any worse for the slip. Plus, it did wake Janice, the psychiatrist, up.

We all piled into the ambulance. The paramedics had suggested we should all get checked out. Luci had a series of minor cuts on her forehead, and Janice (the paramedic, not the fainting psychiatrist) had removed a chunk of glass that had embedded itself into Chloe's shoulder shortly after she'd reached across and gathered up Tabby.

Mia and I seemed to have got off lightly with just a lump on the head (for me) and a twisted ankle for her.

Luci's cuts slowly dripped blood down the left side of her face. I could almost see her brain whirring behind her eyes, but she didn't get a chance to say much or perhaps didn't want to say much to Janice, with Janice sitting there listening to what would only be described as a surreal conversation.

At the hospital, Janice and Janice went to a different part of A&E, and we were made to wait with the other casualties. The slippery snowy weather that night had filled the Southmead Hospital waiting room to bursting. Three hours later, we'd been assessed, treated where necessary and discharged to go home. Given that our only remaining refuge was one hundred and fifty miles away. We found a hotel with rooms and collapsed into bed with exhaustion. We'd sort the mess out tomorrow.

Breakfast the following day turned out to be a quiet affair. Shock probably played a part, but so did the mystery of Janice, apparently knowing our flat had been about to explode. I had some ideas, but Luci didn't want to entertain what I'd agreed to put in the past, especially not with the girls sitting and listening. Luci offered an alternative explanation. 'She might have planted a bomb.'

'She's a psychiatrist, not a terrorist; besides, why plant a bomb, then come and warn us about it and risk a broken nose from you in the process?' I didn't know for sure that her nose had been broken, but given its flattened nature, the last time I'd seen it, I felt it to be a safe assumption.

Luci didn't have an answer to that, so she dropped the subject.

I wanted to return to the hospital to see Janice and listen to her explanation which I hoped would counter Luci's of her being a rubbish terrorist, but we had some practicalities to deal with.

The police wanted to interview us concerning the explosion, and we needed to find alternative accommodation for Chloe, whose winter term started in three days. We also felt responsible for the other two girls who had been rendered homeless for the duration of the next term.

Student lets were understandably scarce at that time of year, and we forked out a small fortune for a penthouse flat on Bristol Waterfront overlooking the SS *Great Britain*. I'm sure the boat's presence added at least three hundred a month to the rent. We had little choice until the insurance company decided what to do about our flat and possibly the hairdressers.

The girls wouldn't be able to move in until the following Saturday, so we also put up the funds for hotel rooms until then, plus they'd all need new stuff. A small bonus, if it could be described as such, Chloe hadn't moved her clothes from the boot of our car, so they were fine. Our eldest daughter phoned her two flatmates with the news. Isla decided to move in with her boyfriend early, which only left Millie needing help. Plus, it meant Alesha could take her place once we sorted everything.

We spent the afternoon with the Bristol police, a sarcastic detective sergeant called DS Brodie, in his early forties with thinning hair and Detective Constable Karen Goldie, in her late twenties with red hair pulled back in a tight ponytail. She wasn't quite as cynical or sarcastic as her colleague but, she hadn't got as many years under her belt yet.

He played bad cop, and she played not-quite-so-bad cop.

We all agreed before going in, not to mention the warning by the psychiatrist/terrorist (Luci had still refused to accept that Janice hadn't planted a device).

The main reasons why we'd agreed on this strategy were:

1.   We had no evidence at this stage that any bomb had been planted. The fire brigade's early prognosis had indicated a gas leak.
2.   It might hold up our insurance claim.
3.   It would make us sound crazy.

I'm not sure why crazy had been relegated to number three on the list, but there you are.

'Let me get this straight,' DS Brodie said, checking his notes. 'The reason you were struggling with Ms Janice Ramos in the street, Mrs Harris, was because she'd kissed your husband in the restaurant, and you'd got the wrong idea?'

Luci nodded.

He stared at my wife for a moment. 'OK. What then, was the right idea?'

My wife didn't have a good response. Whilst our story almost certainly sounded very fishy, DC Brodie either couldn't identify the fish or didn't want to venture any further into what he probably put down to a domestic that had no bearing on the explosion except, of course, that her altercation with Luci and then the rest of us in front of the Emir brothers, had almost certainly saved our lives.

By the time we'd got through all that, it had grown too late to return to the hospital to talk to Janice, which my wife now seemed keen to do, having cogitated on it for the last thirty-six hours or so. She wanted answers beyond what I could offer or what she could make up.

The following day only Luci and I ventured to the hospital to discover that Janice had been discharged and, as far as we could tell, had gone home to Birmingham. No explanation would be forthcoming any time soon.

Luci and I both had work commitments and the following day, we left for home with Mia, leaving Chloe and Millie in their hotel room, waiting to move into the penthouse overlooking the ship that had been the longest in the world back in 1845.

The next few days were busy, which meant Luci and I didn't see much of each other, which was probably a blessing. I wouldn't say Janice's intervention into our lives had been disastrous. We were, after all, alive and grateful to be so, but accepting my explanation, the only one I could give her would open the can of worms that would undermine Luci's nice safe and logical view of the world. It would also mean acknowledging everything she'd known to be a lie, to a certain extent. However, I'd had much longer to come to terms with it all, and whilst I didn't begin to understand it, I had accepted it, and for me, that was enough.

At work in central London on the Thursday following our return from Bristol, I received a text from Janice saying she'd be heading down to our house to visit us that afternoon.

I had sent numerous messages asking her to come to London, offering to travel to Birmingham, but I had not received anything back until now. I had half-assumed she'd fled back to the Solomon Islands, where she wouldn't get punched in the face by jealous wives.

I phoned Luci, who was already at home. Given Janice's timescale, she'd likely get there before I arrived home. I didn't want a repeat of the fisticuffs.

I left early and returned before five to find Janice had already arrived. She and Luci seemed to have drawn up an uneasy truce. Both were drinking wine. I hoped Luci hadn't poisoned our guest's drink, nor mine, as she handed me a glass.

Janice had two black eyes and still had a piece of tape across the bridge of her nose. Her nose no longer looked flat, so I assumed I had been reset.

Mia had swimming after school and wouldn't be back until seven, giving us a couple of hours to sort out whatever we could.

We skirted around the previous weekend's events before Luci asked, 'Why were you kissing my husband?'

Of all the things that had happened, this still seemed to irk her more than anything, which I did find weird, but then I'm a man, and my brain is much simpler than a woman's with a lot of empty space.

'To be honest, I'm not sure. I believe I reacted that way because I was pleased to see he was still alive, and I wasn't too late.'

'You knew the flat would explode?'

She nodded.

'How?' my wife asked, frowning. I suspected she wouldn't like the answer.

'Nearly two years ago, Sam left me a letter when he finished the programme.' Luci turned her gaze to me. I shrugged and nodded towards the psychiatrist as if to say, *listen to the rest.*

Janice continued. 'In that letter, he made some wild claims that, as a psychiatrist, let's say, led me to worry about his sanity. However, I grew up in a different part of the world. Here, traditional beliefs and the more spiritual aspects of life often clashed with my parents' Westernised views. I, personally, have tried to keep more of an open mind on things. Things, that perhaps we've lost touch with over the centuries. Anyway, what did I have to lose? Sam wasn't asking me to do anything crazy. He just suggested that I invite my parents over to England for Christmas, rather than me going home, which had been my original plan.

Luci interrupted. 'Sorry, where are you from exactly?'

'Oh, I thought Sam would have told you, the Solomon Islands in the South Pacific. My parents came to stay in mid-December, which felt like a small miracle, as my father hardly ever took time out from his work at the university. On the 15th of January, as predicted in Sam's letter, a cyclone, probably the worst in living memory, devastated our island, and our family home was destroyed along with most of the university campus. Hundreds died, and thousands were made homeless. You probably remember it from the news at the time.'

Luci shook her head. 'No, sorry, but then I don't get to see the news much. You're saying that Sam told you to get your mum and dad out of there before it hit?'

'Not just that, he knew the exact date the storm would make landfall. Whilst I'd been sceptical, I'm so glad that I heeded his warning.' She beamed over at me and appeared like she might want to hug me again but then decided one broken nose was enough.

'How?' Luci asked me.

'I have told you, sweetie, but we agreed that I'd been delusional, remember, and so….'

She waved her hand in the air. 'Yes, I know all that, but how did you know what would be in the future? You told me you could only go *back* in time?'

Smart cookie, my wife, plus it meant that despite our agreement to forget the whole thing, she'd been brooding on it for some time. I explained as best I could about the stroke and how it added roughly six months to my timeline, which I got back when I returned and undid the events that led up to me having a stroke in the first place. This meant I didn't have a stroke and didn't spend all that time in hospital and rehab. I'd also learned that my advice had been heeded, and Janice didn't die.

Luci looked very confused, and I couldn't blame her. She shook her head and asked Janice, 'So how did the other night come about then?'

Janice began, 'This is where it gets confusing.' She smiled at Luci. 'Even more confusing. I know what happened the other night, but it wasn't me in charge; it was an older version of me that had come back from some point in the future.' She took in my wife's expression.

'Look, I know it sounds crazy, totally crazy. I get that, I'm a trained psychiatrist, for God's sake, and I know how this appears, but it is the only explanation I can give you.' She paused and sipped some wine. 'All I'm saying is I'm aware of what happened.' She touched her nose and winced. 'I'm not sure why or how it all played out or my motivation as obviously, I had no idea before the future me arrived what was going to happen to you, well what nearly happened to you.'

Janice put her glass down and continued. 'The only reason I know anything at all is that the older version of me left me a written, well, a typed explanation, and that's what I'm going off, OK? It seems that the SPC, a Special Protein Compound that I acquired from home is the key, had been the key, to this anomaly, for lack of a better word. My parents brought over a little bit when they visited because I'd asked them to, but the region and the people they got it from were wiped out in the storm, so there is no more, and there probably will be no more.'

I had a question. 'What is the compound?'

Janice scoffed. 'Nobody knows for sure. A few tribal elders knew how to make it; they are all gone now. It's locally known as Fell Beta, which means feel better. In case you didn't know, English is the official language in the Solomons, but the locals use a kind of Creole Pidgin English most of the time, some of which is quite clear and some so obscure you haven't a clue what they're on about. Anyway, Fell Beta or feel better is its name.'

'How much is left?' I asked.

'Not much. I keep it in a cool box in my garage, and the future me obviously decided to use it to come back and fix something on my genome that had been damaged. I'm assuming it had something to do with what happened to you all, and the guilt it probably registered somewhere inside me.

She paused. 'I had meant to contact you after the cyclone happened, but there seemed to be so much to do. I went back with my parents to try and help, but the mess… our home had been swept off the hillside as if a huge hand had picked it up and flung it across the peninsula. By the time I got back to the UK… well, I wasn't sure it was a conversation I wanted to have anymore. I felt bad about that for so long, and it seems to have eaten away at me both now and in the future, especially after what happened to you, or rather what now didn't happen to you.'

She paused again and sipped her wine, staring at me. 'I wasn't sure whether to tell you the next bit, but the future me wrote it down, so I suppose I should. In the original version of events, not everyone was killed. Sam, you survived but would have spent the rest of your life in a wheelchair mourning your lost family.'

She let that sink in for a moment and concluded with, 'When I passed out, I'm assuming that's when I left to go back to wherever or rather whenever I came from and, in so doing, erased that particular stain on my genome and for all I know, my soul too.'

We all sat in silence for a minute or two. Janice and I were comfortable with the explanation, now being fellow time travellers. Luci had the difficult bit, deciding to go with it or phone someone to come and section the both of us.

Chapter 40
The Promise

In the end, Luci accepted our explanations to a point. We agreed that we would not share it with our daughters. They had enough on their plates with being teenagers without having their reality tilted.

My wife eventually grudgingly accepted that Janice hadn't planted a bomb. The fire investigation department filed a report with the insurance company that pointed to a boiler problem that led to the leak and the subsequent explosion. Chloe had set the timer to come on at eight pm, igniting the gas that blew up the flat and most of the hairdressers below.

Luci never admitted that she fully believed me, even after I'd introduced her to Elizabeth and she'd added her story into the mix.

Luci and Elizabeth seemed to be on the same wavelength and hit it off. They didn't become 'besties' as such, but they did/do meet up regularly. I'm sure part of the attraction was that Elizabeth could be pumped for information independently from me. Elizabeth certainly benefited as Luci introduced her to a few of her actress buddies. Within a year, Yasmine Britton, a young actress from Brighton, moved in with her, and Elizabeth officially became a West End Widow. She seemed delighted with the arrangement. I liked to think that she could now put a new framed picture on her wall.

Almost a year from the day of the incident, we were back in Bristol, inspecting the newly built flat that the builders had just signed off on. The insurance company had come through and provided Luci and, by default,

Chloe funds to buy new furniture and fittings, which is how we'd spent most of the day.

Luci and Chloe were wandering around the rooms, compiling a snagging list of things that needed fixing. Not a long list but some basic things, like the taps being on the wrong way around and the electric oven not working, annoyed Luci and Chloe. Mia and I were quite happy to potter about an empty flat, marvel at the new smell, and wonder how long it would take Alesha to trash her room. Alesha was a lovely girl but on the Mia scale of tidiness.

Later, Mia went to stay with Chloe in the penthouse flat we were still paying for. Luci and I had checked into the Hilton near the motorway. We had a lovely dinner in a steakhouse restaurant nearby and stopped at a quiet bar on the way back to our hotel.

We talked about our girls, Chloe well into her second year now and Mia being desperate to leave school and join the RAF. She wanted to fly planes. This had been a recent development that had caught us unawares. We'd expected her to follow her sister through the higher education system.

'I'm not sure I'd want to be on a plane Mia was piloting,' I observed dryly.

Luci punched me on the thigh. 'Don't be mean. She's very clever and capable.'

'Agreed, but not very organised.'

'Maybe the discipline in something like the RAF would give her that?'

Luci had a point. 'Maybe, but she's got at least another year before she can even apply; she might change her mind again by then.'

Luci agreed.

We sat in comfortable silence for a moment before Luci shuffled closer and leaned her forehead against mine. Like she had done so many times from the first time sitting on the wall outside my school until now, middle-aged parents, sitting in a bar drinking wine. 'I'm not saying I still completely believe everything you and your girlfriends have told me.' She began and waited for me to react, but I let it go. She kissed my nose and continued. 'Elizabeth said something disturbing the other day. She said that the universe had it in for us.'

'Yeah, she said that to me once, or maybe more than once.'

'Do you think that's true?'

I pondered for a moment and sighed. 'Luci, I honestly don't know. It's been a crazy life or lives. I've lost you so many times, both physically and emotionally, that I am just so thankful we've made it to this point. According to Janice, it happened again, and who knows what the future holds? Nobody does know, and from what I've learned, nobody probably *should* know.'

I kissed my wife's nose, the nose that should have been dead and buried a long, long time ago and said, 'Elizabeth also said to me once that by doing what I was doing, I was trying to future-proof my life. She might have been right, and I've had some success. But don't many people try to do that? Isn't sending your kids to private school a way of trying to future-proof their lives? Or nurturing a gift like music or art is another way of doing that? What's the difference?'

'Most don't have the luxury of time travel,' Luci remarked.

I nodded. 'True, most people don't get to go back and fix what went wrong. I've been privileged enough to have been able to do that. I was also lucky that I decided to meddle and save Janis, or she'd never have been able to come back and save *us*. Therefore, I'd say the opposite regarding the universe having it in for us. The universe, God, whoever or whatever is in control out there, has had my back, our backs. If it all ended tonight, I'd be eternally grateful for what I now have.'

'How did you cope, especially burying little Chloe and me? That would have broken me.'

'It broke me too. I had a stroke remember?'

Luci moved back and sipped her wine. 'If I believe all this, which I'm still struggling to do, I should never have lived this life.'

'No, me neither.'

'No Chloe, no Mia, no us.'

'I know. How much poorer would the world have been without them and you in it?'

Luci smiled. 'What about Lisa and Hannah?'

I smiled. 'Poor Lisa, I made her life hell, but for her, none of that happened. She's happily married with her kids. Hannah, too, she's with someone else and seems, from what I can tell from her Facebook photos, happy enough.'

'I wrote a song for you, for us. You know, my way of dealing with all of this?'

I knew. 'What's it called?'

'*The Promise.*'

'Can I hear it?'

'In a minute, it's on my phone.' She gazed deep into my eyes. 'Do you never wonder what if? You know, with Hannah especially?'

I laughed. 'Not for a second.' I took her hands in mine and pulled her close, our foreheads together again. Once more, our breath mingled. Tears slipped from my eyes and slipped down both our cheeks. I'm sure that had happened once before, or maybe more than once.

'Never, not for one second; there's only ever been you, Luci, there's only ever been you, even when you weren't there.'

She kissed me, pressed play on her music app, and the universe smiled down on us, or at least, I hoped it did.

Author Notes

Thank you for reading this story. There's a lot of choice out there, and every time you, the reader, decide to read a book, it's a commitment of both faith and time. I'm a reader, too, I understand. I hope Future Proof didn't disappoint. If you enjoyed it, I'd be grateful if you could leave a short review, it helps so much. I have no hope of matching the marketing budgets the large publishers have and a good review really does make a difference. I do read them all, I promise. If you want to ask me anything feel free to email me at: collectivecharmbooks@gmail.com

Background to the story: Epigenetics is a complex field of genetics. In early drafts, I went into a lot of detail about the processes and development of the science. However, reading it back later, it didn't add a much to the narrative and acted as a distraction. Plus, this is a fiction yarn, not a science textbook. Therefore, I pared it back. There are many articles are out there on the subject if you want to look. My version of how it is manipulated in the story uses a huge amount of artistic licence and does not bear much resemblance to the work being carried out by gifted scientists in the real world. As far as I know, no currently developed epigenetic treatments have resulted in any time travel. But then, given the way timelines work in my mind, I probably wouldn't notice if they did/had.

I contacted prominent epigenetic specialists to see if they could spare me any time and emailed them an outline of what I hoped to do. I also sent them a list of questions, but they didn't respond. Maybe my questions were too simple, or they were so overwhelmed with work that they didn't have the time to respond. Therefore, any errors or omissions (of which I'm sure there are many) are entirely down to me.

Music: The decision to write music to accompany the book was initially inspired by Luci, her love of songs, and her enthusiasm for the world of theatre and film. Whether it is a success or not, I guess, is down to you, the reader/listener, to decide. I hope the songs will enhance the reading experience. Thank you once again.

I chose to use the name Memerine for the music (an anagram of my daughter's names) and it can be found by searching under this on all of the usual musical streaming sites and the Collective Charm Records YOUTUBE page.

Printed in Great Britain
by Amazon